TERROR MACHINE

A *RIVETT* THRILLER

by

Denison Hatch

THE RIVETT THRILLERS

FLASH CRASH

NEVER GO ALONE

TERROR MACHINE

TERROR MACHINE is a work of fiction. Names, characters, places, and incidents are the products of the author's imagination and/or are used fictitiously. Any resemblance to actual events, locales, or persons, living or dead, is entirely coincidental.

.

CHAPTER ONE

THE MAN IN THE TRUCK knew he was going to die. A part of him wanted to slam on the brakes, jump out, and sprint away. But that section of his brain had no power—not anymore. He knew his mission. He was certainly aware that the scholar, the *alim*, didn't think it was the right time. The right time was later. Always later. That's what the alim had said last night. The plan was bigger than any of them, they'd been told. It was much more elaborate than they could imagine. The stakes were higher and perfect execution was required. But for the man, "later" simply no longer cut it. The alim would be irate. So would the others. Maybe even the doctor. In fact, the man knew that he was probably jeopardizing his group's entire existence. But now that he had access to the truck, he couldn't wait. The second his hands had touched the steering wheel of the vehicle, he simply hadn't been able to stop himself. His life motivation had narrowed into a scope with one target. The man was a Muslim, but this had nothing to do with religion. He used to be devout. But over the last few years, he'd lost all of his convictions. He didn't believe the story about the awaiting virgins, he barely subscribed to the effectiveness of jihad, and he didn't care if any money was delivered to his family back home. Most of the others believed in at least some of the tenets of the struggle. But the man didn't. Not at all, no longer, no way—that was for sure. There was only one resonating fact that had grown from a whisper to an unavoidable bass line and now defined his entire life: Abdel Hayat hated himself with an all-consuming passion.

▪

Bryant Park's Winter Village was buzzing with optimism and capitalism a few days after Thanksgiving. The small square in the center of Midtown Manhattan was packed with hundreds of stalls selling any manner of Christmas and holiday-related wares. Whether it was a customized ornament, socks with embroidered Bernese mountain dogs, or sunglasses carved out of wood—it was available at the Winter Village. The market was overwhelmed with shoppers in the midafternoon hours before the sun dropped for the day. The patrons came from the tall skyscrapers that framed the area. They were bankers and lawyers and entertainment executives on a quick coffee break before a few more hours of end-of-the-year computer time. The shoppers came from Connecticut, and New Jersey, and California. They arrived in family packs and poured out of tour buses. The people also came from everywhere in between, with their strollers and their backpacks and even their ice skates—there was a temporary ice-skating rink set up in the middle of the park.

And it was right in that moment, when no one was expecting anything at all, that the screams began.

▪

Abdel Hayat's truck barreled through the market without prejudice. No one was targeted but no one was spared—except by luck. Abdel's only mission was to reach the center of the ice-skating rink. The truck was big and heavy and it did an immense amount of damage on the way in. He ran directly through the newly painted green stalls of the market, and he impacted squarely with dozens of innocent civilians. Abdel turned from a murderer to a mass murderer within seconds, but he was in a daze by that point. His death was already imminent.

Abdel's windshield cracked into a thousand spider webs. The glass was painted red with blood, but he could just make out the ice-skating rink in front of him. The people ahead were finally figuring out what was happening and fleeing in every direction, creating a path of sorts for Abdel's truck. He easily broke through the small wall separating the rink from the rest of the park, and his truck skidded to a stop in the middle of the ice.

The wailing was the first sound Abdel heard when he exited the truck's cab, and it contributed to his daze. He had a gun in his hands. It was loaded. He lifted the weapon up and into his sight line and stared down the barrel at a little boy who was sitting on the rink ahead of him, watching Abdel with frightened but also curious eyes.

"You're not the mission," Abdel mumbled.

Abdel didn't shoot. He pivoted away from the boy, taking in more stragglers who were attempting to flee from the rink. He lifted his gun into the air and let off a few warning rounds to keep any heroes at bay. Then he calmly walked around to the back of the truck. It had a ladder installed on its rear end, which Abdel climbed.

He soon stood atop the truck and watched as the little boy's mom slid across the ice in front of him and scooped up her son. As she sprinted away, she slipped and collapsed onto the ice. Scrambling, she covered her son while crawling for the side.

Abdel did nothing. Amid the noise, he could make out the ringing of police sirens. It had only been a minute, maybe less, but the NYPD was already there. He heard a bullet whistle past his ear and he ducked down.

He pulled off a backpack and unzipped it. Inside was a red gas canister. He poured the gasoline all over himself and around the roof of the truck. As he stood, holding the fuel can above his head with gas dripping all over him, he heard a few more shots ring out. One rushed past his head. The next impacted him directly in his neck. The third cut through his sweater. But it did more than that—it ignited Abdel completely.

He couldn't even bring himself to scream out the words the alim would have wanted him to say as the flames grew. Not because he couldn't, but because he didn't want to. He didn't care. He'd accomplished everything that had been asked of him. He'd completed his mission. He was on the ice-skating rink in Bryant Park's Winter Village, wasn't he? No one would ever forget about him. They'd all know his name. They'd know his face. Abdel Hayat was no longer anonymous, and, best of all, he'd no longer be unhappy. Of course, he'd be dead. But for him, the absolute nothingness of death was better than the total awareness of the emptiness of life.

Abdel's body burned bright atop the truck, like a macabre Christmas ornament turning the holiday completely on its head. Now the people around the edges of the park just watched him burn—those not attempting to provide first aid to injured and dying civilians who had been in the path of the truck. The blaze was excruciatingly hot, as Abdel had poured a copious volume of gasoline over everything. His supernova of a body soon melted through the top of the truck as the fire spread. The flames ripped down the sides of the truck and began to consume the vehicle. Uniformed police officers, multiplying exponentially as the seconds ticked by, slowly approached the melting mass. Sirens could be heard, ringing from all directions. Help was coming. But no one was quite sure what to do . . .

And no one knew that Abdel had planned a final assault on the optimism of humanity, and this city, and it sat placidly inside the truck for about ten more seconds while the flames worked their way towards it. The load was six keg-sized plastic containers, brimming with combustible liquid chemicals, and daisy-chained to one another. The bombs exploded in a gargantuan and fiery blast of pure evil, and Bryant Park's skating rink fragmented into a million razor-sharp icicles, which pelted all four sides of the block and every person standing in their path like sleet from Hell.

CHAPTER TWO

"WILL YOU MARRY ME?" DETECTIVE Jake Rivett asked on bended knee.

Eighteen months prior, Rivett wouldn't have been able to imagine having a girlfriend, let alone a wife. But Mona Rosas was everything he'd never known he needed and much, much more. Now here they were—staring over a glowing Manhattan out of the diagonally slanted Art Deco windows in the observatory of the Chrysler Building. He had one knee on the floor and was looking up at his future. And she was saying . . .

"Yes!"

Jake Rivett had lived his entire life fighting crime and living in grime. To have known Rivett only a few years ago was to know a man unmoored from the rules of civil society. It's not that he wasn't a good man. He was. He had been a cop for close to a decade, after all. But Rivett had never felt fulfilled by living the way the rest of the cops and detectives on the force did. Whenever Jake had tried to fit in, he'd lost. And when he'd been forced to fit in, he'd also lost. It made him dislike the stable neutral zone of conventional life. That's why he drove a Ducati through the city every night, instead of a pre-owned BMW or minivan in New Jersey. He felt more at home in dive bars filled with rough-and-tumbles than the gentrified local cop pubs. He had stayed undercover for years, refusing to take any promotions to desk jobs and watching as his friend Tony Villalon leapfrogged way past him and up the ladder. Ah, the career ladder. Jake hated the politics of the ladder. He didn't think a man or woman's purpose in life should have anything to do with internal posturing. His purpose in life was to make the world a better place by removing bad guys from it. Ironically, this very mindset had catapulted Jake full circle into a world of publicly celebrated success. He was a known entity. He'd been in the news many times. His success as a detective had gone from brief write-ups on internet crime blotters to local news until he'd finally appeared on CNN. The anchor had even brought up Jake's hobby as the lead singer of a screamo band. Due to the publicity, as well as Mona, Jake had finally taken a more conventional job within the Major Crimes division of the NYPD. And although he didn't crack every single case, he still maintained the lowest ratio of unsolved cases of any detective. Everyone who mattered knew this, and it was one of the reasons that the hardest cases were thrown at him by the chief of police, Susan Herlihy. Jake believed she was secretly just trying to bring him down to size, but nothing had stumped him recently. There was only one issue with Jake's success—life was fantastic and it scared him. He was posting big wins all the way from work to his love life and back again. While this would thrill most people, it made Jake tense. That's because discord was Jake's great motivator. Ever since he was a little kid, conflict had pushed him to keep reaching for his goals. As he stared up at Mona's excited face, Jake wondered what he was going to do if things became too good.

"Yes. I will, Jake! Oh my god!" Mona was ecstatic and also a bit shocked. She stared at the diamond ring that Jake was sliding onto her finger. After he'd placed it on, they embraced.

"Did you tell my sister first?" Mona finally asked.

"Of course I did. Adriana just wanted to know why I'd waited so long . . ."

"She didn't hear that from me. No way . . ."

"Sure." Jake chuckled.

In a way, she was joking. But in another, he knew she wasn't. Mona certainly wasn't a conventional chick in any sense of the word. That's probably why they were so good for each other. They were similar because they both felt more comfortable at the margins of society. After all, they'd met at an illegal rave inside an abandoned warehouse in Red Hook. She hadn't pressured him about marriage. They had barely talked about it. But it was exactly like Jake to take a risk on a proposal without any assurances.

"Did you really get permission for us to be up here?" Mona asked.

"Permission, or, official police business. One or the other," Jake said with a grin. "But that's what you want to know? What about the ring?"

"I love this ring. It's . . . insane. But I don't need it. Don't spend too much money on me, Jake. We might need it later."

"C'mon, I literally have nothing to spend money on. What do you think I'm gonna do? Buy some clothes?" Jake replied.

Rivett specialized in ascetic simplicity. His clothes were old and black. He'd never owned a car. His personal belongings could be packed up into a backpack—at least before he'd met Mona. Remarkably, the whole "not trying" ensemble gave him a uniquely trendy look.

"Well, you actually could consider that . . ." Mona started up before changing gears again. "Holy crap. We're gonna get married!"

Mona jumped for joy. It made Jake incredibly happy to know he'd found her. This was the woman he was going to spend the rest of his life with and that was no joke. To know Jake Rivett was to know that his word was his bond. Yeah, he could be moody. He could be downright impossible. But when he went down on one knee, that meant a choice had been made and he would stubbornly stick with it forever. He was just like his father in that way, as much as he hated the bastard.

"So . . . when?" Mona asked with a smile.

"Whenever you want, babe. I'll hit the courthouse tomorrow."

"Let me think about it," Mona said. "But if we have a wedding, I'm not wearing a white dress."

"And I'm not wearing a suit."

"Wouldn't have it any other way," Mona replied. "So are you thinking what I'm thinking?"

"What's that?"

"We gotta get the heck out of here so we can go home and—"

Ring. Riiing. Riiiiiing.

It was at that very moment that Jake's cell phone started to ring. He took one look at it, and his face dropped.

"Who is it?" Mona asked.

"It was Tony," Jake said. He began to read a text message, also from Tony.

"Tell him to get in line. Just this once. Please?"

"I can't."

"Why?"

Jake's disappointed face had turned to utter horror. He suddenly looked up and raced towards the closest window of the observatory. He gazed down at the city streets below. Bryant Park was only four blocks away from the Chrysler Building. He could make out a wonderland of emergency lights and hear a growing cacophony of sirens. Without pause, he grabbed Mona's hand and sprinted towards the elevator.

"You have to go home. Immediately. Promise me you will?" Jake finally said.

"What happened?"

"Some guy just blew the hell out of Bryant Park."

"I'm coming with you."

"No. Absolutely not."

"When will you be back?" Mona asked.

"Don't know. But with any luck, this is the end, not the beginning."

"And what if it's the beginning?"

"Then you know me . . . I'll be there when it ends."

"I know you will," Mona replied with a resigned look on her face. Then she glanced at the new bling on her finger and, at least for one small second, seemed to forget that her fiancé was about to do what he did best and jump into the center of the ring of fire.

▪

By the time Jake arrived at Bryant Park, a massive police cordon had been set up and was being guarded zealously by blues of all stripe. Forty-Second Street, on the north end of the park, was being used as a giant triage center with only ambulances allowed through at a steady clip. Jake approached a police officer guarding the crossing at Sixth Avenue and Forty-Second and flashed his badge.

"Sir! Not another step," the officer said.

Jake turned back to see the officer holding a straight-up machine gun with the muzzle aimed directly at him.

"Whoa, cowboy," Jake started up.

"Need to verify your identification," the officer demanded.

"How many dead?" Jake asked as he handed over his NYPD detective identification.

"Dunno. All I got is we're at top-level alert. DHS raised to severe, and there's feds pouring into Fifth, where command is . . ."

The man glanced at Jake's badge and then quickly back up at Jake. The cop was surprised, and Jake knew exactly why. It wasn't that this well-intentioned cop couldn't see he was staring at the same face in the picture. Jake's baby-blue eyes were distinctive and piercing. It was clear that he was a member of NYPD's large detective corps. But the Jake Rivett on his ID no longer existed. The Rivett in the picture had short hair, close to a buzz but ever-so-slightly parted on the right side of his scalp, with well-proportioned shoulders tucked neatly into a dark blue uniform. The photograph had been taken years before. Now, Jake Rivett's blue eyes peered out from a face that was almost gaunt. He was much skinnier. His hair was grown out to shoulder length and was casually tied behind him. He had gone about two weeks since his last shave. He wore all black, from the boots to the black dress shirt buttoned up to the neck. A shiny black leather jacket finished off the ensemble.

"Detective . . ." the cop stammered.

"Rivett."

"Right. Yes, sir." The cop handed Jake's ID back and lowered his gun. "Sorry 'bout that. At the other entrance you'll have a faster go-through."

"You know if Tony Villalon is here?"

"Don't know him. Chief Herlihy is."

"Can't miss her."

"Ya sure can't," the cop replied.

Jake proceeded past the cordon and paced up Sixth Avenue.

"Hey, Rivett?" It was the cop again. "Ain't you the guy who climbed the Statue of Liberty?"

"Uncorroborated," Jake answered with a slim grin.

"It's an honor, bro."

"Thanks."

As Jake gazed to his left at Bryant Park on his way to the command center, the flurry of activity had turned into an avalanche. Thirty-three now, Jake was a junior in high school when 9/11 occurred. He had only seen anything like this in archival footage. The chaos was almost overwhelming—a panic attack in and of itself. Every single city, state and federal emergency responder that one could imagine had descended upon the park. A true human wall of SWAT operators in full tactical gear guarded the site. Across the way, he noticed that the triage tents were filling up with doctors and EMTs. On the blacktop of Sixth Avenue were a few large groups of civilians, being debriefed by what appeared to be a handful of FBI agents. But it was the center of the park, the now-melted ice rink, that drew most of Jake's attention.

The heaping mass of metal that was formerly the truck resembled a fire pit on steroids. The middle of the pile still burned red hot with thick coagulated embers. Firefighters were assembled to tend to the mess but were not quickly extinguishing the scene. At first he thought they didn't want to wash away any evidence, but then Jake realized that a chemical accelerant must have been suspected. Most of the booths surrounding the ice-skating rink and the Christmas market were pockmarked with shrapnel from the explosion. Thirty percent of the windows on the back of the library, which sat on the east side of the park, were blown out. It looked as though a bomb had gone off because it had. But it was worse than that. The scene was primordial, not from modern day. In fact, it looked as if a volcano had erupted in the center of Manhattan.

▪

Susan Herlihy thought the same. Susan had only been Chief of Police for about twelve months, having replaced Tom Marks during the administrative upheaval that resulted when the prior mayor, Ronald Berg, suddenly and unexpectedly resigned. Susan was notable for many reasons. The most public fact about Susan was that she was the first woman to serve as chief in New York's history. The newspapers and blogs had reported this fact with gusto, but sometimes the reporting had an undertone of the department "embracing diversity" as if Susan wasn't there out of merit alone. The truth was that Susan wasn't there simply due to merit, but her gender had nothing to do with it—far from it. The reason Susan Herlihy was chief was that she was an absolute wrecking ball of determination and personality tucked into a pint-size body. She reminded Jake of a female Napoleon, standing there addressing her troops, hands on her hips and high heels scraping across the pavement with no wobble at all.

Jake arrived towards the end of her speech.

". . . Mayor's going to be coming to us as the nexus of intelligence." Susan glanced at her phone. "And I've got to talk to him and the FBI super, Pete Mack, in twelve minutes. Nobody's sleeping. There are no holiday parties. There is no shopping. There is only this." She paused for a moment. "I want the departments to link up. Hey, Fong? You and tech need to move to wherever the feds set up their signal room. Most likely down at Foley Square. Link with antiterror and intelligence. Markle and SWAT need a voice in that room as well."

"Who's pulling city cams?" were the first words out of Jake's mouth.

"Down at Real Time Crime Center," Susan replied. "A compilation is being put together. We've already streamed a bunch of it. One big box truck, all white. Comes in on the Queens-Midtown and just heads right up to Forty-Second Street and over. It's less than eight blocks . . ."

"One guy?"

"Looks like it. We're combing through the clips now for more . . . no ID yet. Rivett, where's Tony?"

"I'm not his keeper."

"That's clear. When you find him you tell him to call me. You, Tony, and Major Crimes are on this. Every-fucking-body is on this, but I need my own eyes and ears, and that's gotta be you two. Understood?"

"Got it, boss," Rivett said.

"Counterterror is always slow as goddamn molasses. Think they are a bunch of scientists. Right now we need old-fashioned gumshoe shit happening and triple timed—super, super fast. So go hit the detectives up. Figure out what we know about the truck. Work it backwards through registration, grab video . . . Find me an address. That should keep ya busy for a couple hours. I'll let you know what Mack and the FBI want after my meeting."

"Suse—"

"Chief," she corrected Jake.

"Chief, why is it that the more senior you get in the force, the more you sound like you're from Long Island?"

"You think nowsa time for a joke, Rivett?"

"Sorry."

"Get your game face on, people. I ain't sugar coating when I tell you the whole world changed tonight."

▪

Jake could see a group of detectives huddled together underneath a tent about fifteen feet away—some of his colleagues from Major Crimes, a half floor of the downtown boys from the office, and a whole bunch he didn't know at all. Before heading over, he paced through the crime scene.

The carnage was simply overpowering. Even for a man with a stomach like Jake's. He was used to darkness, and he was a pragmatist. He knew very well the world he lived and worked in. But that didn't make it any easier to stare at pools of blood and body parts. All Jake knew was that he needed to absorb what had happened in order to understand it. He continued walking through Bryant Park, a lone man operating against the current. The current itself was about forty-five individuals from the evidence department—"CSI" as they were colloquially known—all wearing white coveralls and canvassing the scene for evidence. Each technician was responsible for combing a three-foot radius. Rivett walked right through them—upriver, as it were.

Amidst all the earthen colors, he could have sworn he'd seen a flash of blue. But when he was standing above the spot he'd identified, there was nothing there. Rivett turned and continued scanning. That's when he felt it under his foot. There was something hard embedded in the wet grass. He stopped and addressed the closest crime-scene technician.

"You guys covered this, right?" Rivett yelled.

One of the technicians turned and replied, "Yes, sir!"

"So I can put hands on it over here?"

"With gloves, detective!"

Rivett did as he was told. He snapped on a pair of latex gloves before he went digging. Whatever the item was, he felt the earth around it stubbornly resisting at first. He kept digging, and his fingertips grasped the item, which was almost entirely buried six inches under the soil. Jake was finally able to expose a sharp corner of the object. It was a piece of aluminum. Jake worked the dirt on both sides of the aluminum with his fingers, exposing the item millimeter by millimeter. Eventually he created enough leverage to pull the metal chunk out of the ground. He flipped it around in his hands and immediately noticed the familiar white-and-blue bordering of a New York State license plate.

"Hey, who's got a bag?" Rivett yelled to the detectives ahead. Hearing Rivett's voice, Tony Villalon perked up and moved out of the huddle. He saw Rivett holding the license-plate shard and quickly jogged over to him with an evidence bag.

"What you got there, Rivett?" As Tony neared Rivett, he exclaimed, "No shit! A plate?"

"Think so . . . A piece of it. From the truck?"

"They're gonna wanna see this right away. Come on!"

Inside the detective huddle, a laptop had been placed atop a small folding table, and a streaming video program was pulled up. Dennis Fong —Major Crimes' tech guru—was already working through footage that had been pulled and sent over from the Real Time Crime Center, a networked command center that NYPD had set up in years prior for instantaneous responses to events such as these. While the RTCC wasn't as spectacularly accomplished as its name might signify, they had a lock on the various city surveillance systems that were set up around Manhattan. Their computers sucked in video footage from almost every municipal, state, and federal camera in the city. Just an hour or two after the explosion, RTCC had already edited a montage of the white box truck as it traversed into Manhattan and towards Bryant Park. The truck had first been picked up on video driving through the Queens-Midtown tunnel, indicating that perhaps it had come from the east. But Jake knew one could never trust first impressions. What was more remarkable, however, was it seemed as though Jake was in fact holding a piece of the box truck's license plate. Rivett's shard, now in an evidence bag, consisted of the last two numbers on the right side of the plate. As he and Tony crowded over the piece, they confirmed that its numbers matched the two numbers on the video of the truck.

"Here's the problem," Fong remarked in his generally deadpan voice. Fong held his cell phone up for Rivett and Tony to view. On the screen was a very clear picture of another truck with the exact same license plate number.

"Where'd that picture come from?" Rivett asked.

"Got it five minutes ago. Plate is registered. There was an address. And there is a truck, currently parked inside a moving company's parking lot in Queens, with the exact same license-plate as the one that seems to have blown up our park . . ."

"It's legit?"

"Hundred percent," Fong replied. "Which means that our plate here, is—"

"A fake," Tony answered.

"It's a . . . something," Jake said.

"Shitburgers," said Tony.

"Indeed," replied Fong.

"So we don't have a bead on whose truck this is . . ." Jake said.

"Well, RTCC's still working on getting more footage out of Brooklyn and Queens. And, look, we'll track the route in the morning and see if we can pull video from any other restaurants or stores. We definitely should be able to build backwards and figure out where the truck came from. Just might take a little time," Fong said.

"Back up a sec," Rivett broke in. "Fake plate's a huge deal. First of all, you gotta create it. That ain't an easy trick. Or you buy it. But those sellers are hard to come by. Why does a terrorist make a plan to use a fake plate?"

"To hide their tracks . . ." Tony said.

"But is that what terrorists do?" Jake asked. "Hide their tracks?"

"Only if they're protecting something," Fong replied.

"Right," added Tony.

"And it's not just the plate, Tony. It's everything. It's the size of this. The shrapnel. Chemical explosives. Whole thing is just a fucking nightmare scenario for us, and let's be honest, 'cause it's crystal clear."

"There's a cell," Tony said.

"There's a big cell." Jake nodded.

"Case is going federal as we speak," Fong added.

"I know," Jake replied. "We're about to become real little guys on the totem pole." Jake held the license plate inside the evidence bag in his hands. He turned it under a spotlight in their tent. "Hey, Fong. Got anything sharp on you?"

Fong pulled a razor blade from his pocket.

"Rivett! You can't do that . . ."

"Tell that to all the people that died here today, Tony."

"But if you break the seal of the evidence bag—"

"Get me a new bag." Jake didn't wait for permission. With a swipe, he ripped the bag open. But he wasn't done. Once the license plate shard was accessible, Jake held it just inches from his eyes.

"Got another lead . . ." He held the plate out to Fong and Tony, who gazed curiously.

"What's the lead?" Fong asked.

"The three ain't a three," Jake replied.

The final number on the license plate was painted to look like a three. But now that the men were looking closer, they saw what Jake saw. Something was wrong with the three.

"Last number on the plate—the three. See how there's an extrusion coming up through the white paint? The plate was painted and glazed over. That three started out life as an eight," Jake said.

CHAPTER THREE

OMER AMIN COULD FEEL THE makeup around his eyes dripping down his face and running across his lips and neck, but he didn't care. That's what dance-punk was all about—show up glam and end up however the heck you ended up. No one cared what you looked like at this concert venue, just that you felt something while they were feeling something too. Omer was only seventeen years old, but he'd been going to these gigs for about a year. He understood most of the implicit rules of the scene. You didn't have to wear an outrageous costume. You didn't have to wear makeup. You just had to be yourself. But Omer preferred to have his face covered in product. He didn't want anyone to know who he was, although there was no way he'd be recognized. His hiding was figurative. He wanted to be masked so that he could pretend he was someone else.

The venue was ExCulture and the band was called Thrasher Disco and they were one of Omer's favorites. Their music was darkly cinematic but pumped up with rhythm and tempo. It was the type of music that would be chosen for an action sequence in a dark fantasy film—for example, if the hero was escaping from a prison ruled by a dragon. Thrasher Disco had a lead singer, but he didn't often sing actual lyrics. Every once in a while, there would be a word that repeated itself, and the singer would lean down into the microphone and whisper in a guttural fashion. But, no, mostly the band's music was all about the way the beat made you feel. What was particularly impressive about Thrasher Disco was the fact that, within a ninety-minute set, there would be periods where the whole crowd transferred from mosh-pit combat to nothing less than a religious wave of rolling and bobbing heads. Most bands picked one or the other and ran with it. Thrasher Disco did both, and well.

Omer bucked around the dance floor without a care in the world, his sweat-wet hair whipping back and forth in every direction to the rhythm of the music. He would generally cycle into the mosh pit in the center and then out every twenty minutes or so. He'd stand back to the side, catch his breath, people watch, and jump back in. His favorite pastime was dancing. He didn't care about the stink, the grime, or the elbows that he'd randomly take on the dance floor. He didn't need alcohol and had no use for drugs. Dancing gave him everything he needed and more.

Omer had learned a few tactics in the clubs that kept him safe. Don't accept drinks from anyone—even water. Buy it in a bottle from behind the ticket booth. Don't be a hero. If someone was bumping into you too much and you didn't like it, just move away. And finally, help people if they needed help—ask yourself what you'd want to happen if the same occurred to you. These rules weren't hard to pick up, and the scene wasn't particularly lecherous. It was true, however, that ExCulture's crowd was drawn from absolutely all over the city. It wasn't creepy, but it was diverse, and sometimes things that were foreign were also scary. The fact of the matter was that Omer was more than capable of taking care of himself. He'd always been that way. Ironically, he'd learned the art of survival from his family. *His family*. Every single person inside this venue understood Omer's need to simply be himself. His family, however, did not.

Sadly, the show was ending. As the lights came on, Omer pulled his cell phone out of his pocket while waiting for the slow-moving crowd to exit the venue. There was a text from his mother.

"I know you're at Haseem's for dinner, but please come back for dessert," the text read.

Omer sighed. Now he'd have to rush. But he knew exactly why his mother wanted him home—the terror attack in Manhattan, apparently perpetrated by a Muslim. He'd heard about it just as he'd been walking into the concert a few hours before, but he had managed to block the terrible event from his mind until now. His parents weren't politically active but they were certainly current-events minded. He'd have to brace himself for their opinions.

Ahead, Omer's section of the crowd was finally reaching the stopgap that was the front door. An ExCulture promoter stood to the side, handing out neon-yellow flyers advertising the upcoming week of shows at the venue. Omer grabbed one and jammed it into his pocket without looking at it. He didn't have time. In fact, if he was going to show up within even a semblance of a reasonable timetable, he'd have to run. He sprinted from the venue and began to race north. He charged along the city streets in northern Brooklyn, headed over the Pulaski Bridge towards the Vernon metro station, and raced down the stairs.

■

When he emerged in Astoria, Omer finally caught a reflection of himself in a mirror. He wasn't the prettiest sight and he had only a few minutes to spare. Omer pulled himself into a public restroom at the subway station and quickly began to work. He pulled off his backpack and yanked out a roll of paper towels. First, he used a wet towel to wipe off as much of the makeup from his face as he could. He followed that up with soap and water and finally another dry paper towel for what remained. Omer leaned closely towards the mirror, examining his face and picking at pieces of glitter here and there. He ripped his sweat-soaked shirt off, pulled a fresh one from his backpack, and put it on. Dry. Much better. Finally, he unclasped two necklaces from his neck and yanked bracelets off both wrists. He dropped all of the items into the outside pocket of his backpack. He reminded himself that he'd have to sneak most of the jewelry back into his sister's drawer when he had the chance the next morning.

A few minutes later, Omer sprinted along Steinway towards home.

▪

Omer pushed the door open to find his entire family sitting at the dinner table. It was bizarre to find them so solemn, especially at such a late hour. They stared at him for a second before turning back to their plates. Luckily, Omer could immediately tell that the jig was not up. He breathed a sigh of relief.

Dessert in the Amin household was a forced affair that evening, decided upon by Omer's parents for reasons that remained somewhat unknown. Obviously, the events of the day weighed heavily. But although the Amin family lived in Astoria—only eight miles away from Bryant Park—their angst was nothing more or less than that experienced by hundreds of thousands of Muslim families all around the United States of America. The Amins had no direct connection to the massacre, only a guess of a shared religion with the attacker. But this attack was the biggest and most deadly act of terrorism on American soil in almost twenty years. That meant there would be repercussions for all Muslims, whether codified into law or simply dealt with throughout the course of normal everyday life.

All five members of the Amin family were present. The patriarch, Omer's father Moradi, was a genial fellow who had moved to America from Pakistan when he was five years old and settled in Texas. After high school, it had been difficult for him to find a solid job. It seemed like all of the job openings were at convenience stores and laundromats. He chose laundry or it chose him. Either way, Moradi started out way in the back of the house of an industrial dry-cleaning company. He steamed, folded, ironed, and eventually ran and repaired the machinery.

The rest of Moradi's time back in Texas was spent trying to find a wife. That wife was Azza, whom he'd met through the eighties version of online dating—headshots sent from the homeland. He and Azza were set up in a transcontinental relationship by his mosque in Dallas, and after a one-month-long trip back to Pakistan with his parents, he was engaged to be married. Between the two of them, Azza was much more headstrong than Moradi. She was also more religious. Arriving in Dallas was a shock. The city was nothing like Karachi. At least the heat was similar at times, but her biggest problem was assimilation. Everyone from Pakistan who arrived in the US wanted to buy a huge SUV and become as American as possible. She felt that there wasn't enough diversity for her to maintain her identity, and she was convinced that New York City was the answer. Luckily for her, at that point Moradi was just happy to have someone to have marital relations with on a regular basis, so off to New York it was. The young couple saved up all of their money for about a year and eventually moved, much to the chagrin of Moradi's family at the time. The problem wasn't that they were moving; it was that Moradi still didn't seem to have much sense of direction in life—beyond whatever goal Azza was pointing him towards at any given moment. In any event, they left Dallas. They settled into a small Muslim community in the northern point of

Astoria, Queens. About ten months after finding a tiny studio apartment on Steinway Street, their oldest son Murad was born.

Moradi went back to doing what he knew best: installing and fixing the mechanical systems in the back of dry-cleaning businesses. He started working for a Jewish man who owned six dry-cleaning stores and over twenty-five laundromats throughout three boroughs of New York City. Azza also did what she was best at—telling Moradi what to do. She had worn a hijab for every second she was in public since age twelve and didn't let up once she'd arrived in America. She quickly convinced Moradi to stop smoking, although it would take her ten years before he would stop drinking. Even then, she suspected he might have a sip of gin on Friday afternoons at work. Azza wasn't condescending about other people's beliefs. She had no problem with Moradi's boss being Jewish, nor with the other Muslim women in the neighborhood who would walk around with a scarf around their shoulders—or no scarf at all. The only person that she was truly strict with was Moradi himself, because Moradi was the man who was going to be responsible for getting their family out of the studio apartment and into one of the nicer semi-detached townhouses that sat on the side streets to the east and west of Steinway.

It was not entirely clear how Moradi and Azza were going to accomplish this goal until the great reinstall. The great reinstall began when Moradi's boss decided to upgrade the facilities in his dry-cleaning businesses and contracted with a steel-and-aluminum fabricator out of Long Island to bring all new, custom equipment into the stores. Moradi was responsible for working with the fabricator and the mechanics to make sure everything fit. At some point, Moradi realized that all of the old equipment inside these stores was destined for the commodity dump. The first day Moradi dropped off what he viewed as seven thousand dollars' worth of machinery and received a check for his boss for four hundred dollars, he complained to Azza when he arrived back at home. It didn't take long for Azza to decide what must be done. They took every single dime of their net worth and rented an industrial space down the block that used to be a car mechanic's garage. Then they started paying the liquidation checks themselves. Moradi continued working for his old boss for about eight more months. That's how long it took him in nights and weekends to get all the old equipment running again inside of Steinway Cleaners, their new business. Thus began the first building blocks of Moradi and Azza's version of the American dream: two Pakistanis who pulled themselves up by the bootstraps and owned and operated a profitable dry-cleaning business in America.

In addition to Murad, Moradi and Azza had two more children. Their second child was Omer, who was quickly followed by their only daughter Salma.

The three kids sat around the kitchen table.

"It's not the political system that's the problem," Murad was complaining. "It's the social system." Murad was in his early twenties and worked for his father. But while Moradi was a closet liberal, Murad took after his mother. He was stubborn and devout. Moradi and Azza had been most strict with Murad. They had forced him to go to the mosque much more than the next two kids. Or maybe Murad's attitude was just due to the oldest-sibling dynamic. Parents are afraid of everything at first, which makes them crack down. By the time Omer and Salma arrived a few years later, and eleven months apart from one another, the laundry business was more successful and more demanding. There was less time for discipline and less time for everything else—just work, food, and maybe a vacation every year or two down at the lakes in Texas.

Murad continued to dominate the conversation. His words came off like a rant—something he had been doing more and more lately. But no one in the family complained. Murad had always been outspoken. It was his nature. Instead of placating him, terror attacks such as the one that had occurred that day generally got him more riled up.

"The social system! Know what I mean?" Murad's rant was reflected by mostly blank faces, except for a slight grin from Azza. "You see, officially everything in America is perfectly diverse and equal. My dollar bill is worth the same as anyone else's dollar bill. That's what people will tell you. What nobody talks about, but everyone knows, is the way the world keeps brown people down. It's not that Americans are overtly racist or anti-Muslim. Nope. They just don't have the time to try to make new friends who are different than them. And you help your peeps out. So if all your friends are white Christians, then those people are the ones you're going to help out. They get the job offers, the dinner invites . . . It's small little cuts like that that form the thousand cuts, and then . . . well, then today happens."

"Conflation . . ." Moradi responded quietly.

"No way," Murad replied.

"Yes. You're conflating two dynamics, Murad. You're creating a connection that doesn't have to exist. Can't live your life looking at barriers and thinking you can't climb over them. That's not what I did. If we thought that, we'd have no business at all."

"Well, I agree with Murad," Azza said.

"You think terror is justified?" Moradi asked.

"No, I didn't say that. Neither did your son," Azza replied.

"Sometimes when you dance near the line, you fall over it. And anyway, you're either part of the problem or part of the solution," Moradi said.

"It's not justified," Murad replied. "I am just saying that these people, our people, don't have a lot of ways of fighting back against—"

"I'm sorry, but that's totally crazy," Salma popped into the conversation. A year younger than Omer, Salma was the most outwardly liberal. She was always in conflict with her mother. She also often disagreed with Murad, but they tended to simply ignore each other instead of fight. "When you say stuff like that, you *are* the problem! What do you get out of it? You're going to sit there and be an apologist for some terrorist? All those people had families. People that love them. There's nothing you can say about it that makes it close to right."

"How do you beat back a system that's designed to make you lose?" Murad asked.

"You"—she pointed to Murad—"saying stuff like that? You're the problem. You're the loser. You're the person that all the haters and racists think we all are."

"I don't have time for this," Murad replied angrily as he rose from the table.

"Where are you going?" Moradi asked.

"The business club. I told you."

"It's after eleven . . ."

"Mur . . ." Azza gestured, a subtle hint. "Say hello to the guys,"

"I will," said Murad. He stepped towards the front door. "And Omer, I don't know how everyone else didn't see this. But just one question: Why are you wearing a ring?"

Omer glanced down at his fingers. Sure enough, he'd forgotten to pull a ring from his left pinkie finger. The jewelry itself wouldn't have been a problem, if it hadn't been a bright-pink gemstone in a silver setting shining brightly for all to see. For a moment, one could hear a pin drop at the kitchen table.

Until Salma popped in. "You found it? Omer, where? That's incredible." She reached out with her cupped hands and Omer gave her the ring.

"Uh . . . in the hallway . . . just now," Omer said.

"I told you I was looking for my ring. Thank you!"

"No problem."

Murad stared at Omer for another moment before departing.

"Omer, how are you?" Azza asked.

"Fine," Omer replied.

"You haven't said anything tonight. What are your thoughts?"

To be honest, Omer had been barely listening to their conversation. He knew that his parents had called the family meeting for a reason. They were worried about their kids. Ironically, he guessed that he was the reason for the meeting. They were always pushing and prodding to understand what he was thinking, because he was the quietest one. But the real reason he didn't speak up was because he didn't care about geopolitics at all. If he could never have another overwrought discussion about race, religion, politics, or terrorism ever again? That would suit him just fine. Deep down inside, Omer was fuming. He was angry that something like this had happened that day, of all days, because he had been looking forward to the evening. Now he was just worried about Murad and the ring—and worry was the real problem that he spent most of his time trying to eliminate. Oh, and both of his parents and his sister were expecting him to say something now.

"Maybe the system's designed to make you lose, but at least it has rules. So there's still a way to win. The nice thing about rules is you can make them work for you like rungs of a ladder. Then you just start climbing up," Omer said

"Couldn't agree with you more." Moradi beamed with pride at his youngest son.

"Our poet," Salma said.

"I'm glad you're home," Azza said while nodding, seemingly satisfied.

■

Later that night, Omer was alone in the bedroom he shared with Murad. He went through his pockets as he prepared to go to bed. He realized that he still had the brochure from the club in his jeans. He pulled the flyer out and uncrumpled it. Another punk show was being advertised, this time with a lineup of regional screamo bands. Right in the center of the page was a picture of the headliner, a band he'd never heard of before.

The band's name was Mythics, and their lead singer was Jake Rivett.

CHAPTER FOUR

"IMAM, IS THIS NOT THE moment you've been waiting for?" the doctor asked.

Hanafi preferred not to be called Imam. He viewed the title as a pejorative. He saw himself instead as an alim, a scholar of the letters of the book. He wasn't interested in growing a congregation and being out in front of it, even though he did just that. According to Islamic literature—in which there was much agreement and even more disagreement—an imam didn't even need any special qualifications to be called an imam, except for having memorized the Koran. But no one was called an alim unless he had spent years deep inside an academic institution under the demanding tutelage of those who had done likewise. Hanafi hadn't done that, personally, but he still preferred the term. Then again, Hanafi had to remind himself, what did the doctor know of Islam? The doctor's ignorance was almost expected at this point.

The doctor, Maximilian Borin, had proven time and time again that he had absolutely no interest in respecting Hanafi's wishes. Dr. Borin was in his early sixties. He was very tall, close to seven feet. Besides his height, Dr. Borin would be uninteresting to look at if it weren't for his hair. His hair—dark brown with flaming fingers of grey-white—fanned out for at least six inches in every direction like a fro. Or perhaps he had been electrocuted by his own inventions a few too many times. In any case, Dr. Borin truly looked like a nutty professor if there ever was one. The two of them had entirely different objectives in life but were bound together by a common conduit. Once they were done, Hanafi would see to it that Dr. Borin was finally put in his place. For the time being, Hanafi would have to continue to deal with the man. But he still wished the doctor would stop calling him Imam.

"I've asked you to not call me that . . ."

"Sorry. I just figured . . . You know, you run the mosque."

"The problem is you're not very good at listening. Yesterday was not a good day. All of your theories and hypotheticals aside, it was a bad day—a very bad day. And since I'm the guy who writes your checks, you better start listening. This is life or death."

"That's a good point. About the checks," Dr. Borin said.

The two men were standing in the basement of Hanafi's Queens restaurant, Best Middle Eastern Diner. Best Diner, as it was referred to, was located three doors down from the mosque where Hanafi sometimes led prayer services. Hanafi delivered sermons, but he was more of a wonk than a politician. He was more often sought out by high-minded, regional imams in the tri-state area than by members of the general population. He could be incredibly convincing when it came down to the minutia of a religious argument but he was less well-equipped to comfort a mother worried about her sick child. Most of the followers of the faith in New York had never heard of Hanafi and never would. It was only when one began to dig deeper that the rumors would begin to be whispered. Alim Hanafi was a stone-cold closer. He took men, and men only, who were nearing full commitment to their religion and made them totally unbreakable soldiers of Allah. His basement prayer room was ground zero for his workshops, consultations, and the like—it was Hanafi's office. He owned the entire building, actually, all four floors. The top three floors above the restaurant were apartments. Most of the apartments were rented to Muslims in the area whose only relationship with Hanafi was that of landlord-tenant. But Hanafi certainly had tenants who were paying a much lower rate or were simply staying for free. He sometimes did this out of the kindness of his heart, and also when it suited him. The building itself wasn't fancy. It was practically indistinguishable from any other building on the street. The sign for Best Middle Eastern Diner had been there since the late eighties, hung before Hanafi had even set foot on American soil. Hanafi had many secrets, and one of them was that his building and the businesses he ran out of it made no money at all. They mostly lost money. And yet Hanafi's checks to Dr. Borin were always good, the electricity stayed on, and his subsidized tenants lived worry-free above.

Hanafi and Dr. Borin—an odd couple if there ever was one—stood in the Best Diner basement in front of a long row of filing cabinets and shelves. Hanafi reached for the bottom drawer of the far-left filing cabinet. He turned a key, opened the drawer, and pulled out a generic remote control. He pushed a button on the remote, and one of the shelving units slid to the side, creating a four-foot gap that led into a dark passageway.

Once Hanafi and Dr. Borin were inside the secret passageway, Hanafi sealed them off again. Borin turned on the lights. Track lighting on the ceiling illuminated a large workspace, hidden in an unpermitted space underneath Hanafi's building. The white room was much cleaner than the rest of the basement. It had a clinical look because that's what it was—a clinic, run by Dr. Borin. Dr. Borin was already hunched over his computer, gazing at a series of newly outputted reports.

"Abdel did exactly what was requested of him. Is it not phenomenal?" Dr. Borin asked, unable to conceal the glee running across his face.

"He didn't do it at the right time, Max."

"The next one will."

"There may not be a next one. And if there isn't, you won't be able to complete your research."

"But Imam—sorry, Hanafi. Hanafi, Abdel is our confirmation. Of everything. It might seem like a failure to you, but this is . . . this is everything I've ever worked for, proven, in the flesh."

"I think you've worked for more than a little lab in a basement. There's a bigger vision . . ."

"Right, right . . ."

"We each care about what matters to us. That's what makes us such a great team."

"I understand what you're saying. I do," Dr. Borin said. "I didn't mean to get so giddy. It's just . . . I didn't expect Abdel to break so early. I didn't expect it to . . . work so well."

"It needs to work perfectly, mot just well. Not too early. Not too late. But perfectly," Hanafi said.

"And it will," the doctor replied.

The two men turned away from the doctor's computer and rested their eyes on a machine at the end of the laboratory. The machine was the central focus of their lives and partnership. At the center of the machine was an ergonomic office chair that had been bolted to the floor. Four sturdy steel columns stood on each side of the chair, supporting a large white tube, which was suspended in the air and utilized a vertical dolly system that allowed it to be raised and lowered. Behind the chair was a haphazard stack of machinery—the guts of the thing, pieces of custom-manufactured electrical equipment and computers. The technology dated back to Dr. Borin's time as a graduate student, through his career in the pharmaceutical industry, and eventually his tenures at Penn State and Stony Brook. Connected by all manner of wire and apparatus, the whole machine had a Rube Goldberg quality. It had not been designed for mass production. It was simply made to work.

"So you won't even give me a little bit of credit, Mr. Alim-a-man?" Dr. Borin asked Hanafi.

"We're definitely onto something."

"Thank you. From you, I will take that as a compliment."

"No one can call you crazy anymore," Hanafi added.

"They were always wrong."

The doctor turned back to his computer and started to analyze spectrophotometer results. But that wasn't the only reason he turned away. He also didn't want Hanafi to see the tears welling up in his eyes. *He was so happy.*

"I'll be here for a while," Dr. Borin eventually said.

▪

Hanafi padded down the dark hallway and out of Dr. Borin's lab, using the remote again to close the door from the outside. He exited the prayer study room, paced through his basement, and then rose up the staircase that led to the restaurant. As he walked through the restaurant, Hanafi pulled out his cell phone. He had an app that streamed footage from Best Diner's surveillance cameras. On the app, Hanafi could see two young men standing idly by the building's entrance, silhouetted by street lamps. Hanafi was expecting them. He headed towards the front door.

"All good?" Hanafi asked once he'd unlocked the door.

The men all had slightly worried looks on their faces.

"I think so," said Darab, a sturdy man with a strong beard.

"Assalamu alaikum, Darab," Hanafi said as Darab passed through into the dark restaurant. The other man, Ataullah, entered as well, and Hanafi greeted him in the same way.

Hanafi turned. "Where's the last one?"

Each man shrugged. No one seemed to know. Hanafi gazed back out into the street. It was crucial that everyone showed up that night. If they didn't, it could mean that everything was over. He could tell that the men were nervous. Even Hanafi was nervous, which was a rare thing indeed. Life's troubles had always rolled off of Hanafi's shoulders like raindrops. He had an innate confidence that worked to his advantage. Very little bothered him, and when something did, it was never for long. The possibility of exposure in and of itself wasn't what worried Hanafi that night. He didn't think twice about his men's allegiance. He didn't care that thousands of men and women across all branches of the US government were searching for any and every shred of information about Abdel Hayat. Hanafi wasn't afraid of a SWAT team breaking down the door. He knew that day would come. It was just that there was so much more to do, and he didn't want anyone or anything to stop his forward progress.

Finally, Hanafi heard two feet pounding down the pavement in front of the restaurant. The final member of the club had arrived.

"Assalamu alaikum, Murad."

"Hello, Alim Hanafi. Sorry I'm late . . . Family stuff."

Hanafi wrapped his arm around Murad Amin's shoulders as he guided him into the restaurant.

CHAPTER FIVE

RIVETT DIDN'T HATE CHIEF SUSAN Herlihy, but that didn't mean he liked her. Unlike the rest of the puppies lapping up her every word in the briefing room, Jake knew it was best to hold Susan at arm's length. Susan had been a source of great misery for Jake. She'd demoted him. She'd threatened his career on multiple occasions. She was even responsible for blowing his identity once. But she was still the boss, and what had happened at Bryant Park transcended personal feelings. Jake was back at One Police Plaza after a short but merciful night of sleep with his new fiancé, and a joint task force had fully coalesced by the time of the morning briefing. Jake sat at a long table filled with Major Crimes investigators, including Tony and Fong. Multiple divisions of the NYPD were there, as well as the FBI, and in the back row was a serious group of individuals Jake had never seen in his entire life. As Susan introduced a representative from the Real Time Crime Center who was loading their newest montage of surveillance footage, Tony leaned over to Rivett.

"See those guys in the back?"

"Sure . . ." Jake said.

"We hit big time," Tony replied.

"Why? Feds?"

"OGA."

OGA stood for Other Government Agency, which was a generic slang nomenclature among the NYPD for any of the federal agencies that stood above the FBI. That meant the men in the back could be CIA, they could be NSA, or they could represent the other sixteen federal intelligence agencies that formed America's federal security backbone. Jake casually peered over his shoulder at the group. He was struck by their utter normalcy. The agents looked like well-dressed, well-meaning, traveling IT professionals. They didn't have the macho persona of some of the NYPD detectives, but they were certainly paying attention. Jake immediately recognized a razor-sharp clarity and determination in the OGA agents' eyes.

Jake turned back to the briefing, where the RTCC representative was beginning his presentation.

"We get our first bead on the truck going into Manhattan on the Twenty-First Street entrance to the Queens-Midtown Tunnel," the rep said. "He does pay the toll, in cash. The cameras at the tollbooths are 1080p, but the encryption is subpar. Sorry for the choppiness. We'll let the FBI and the profilers talk more about what we see here . . . But it's fairly clear that our subject is not incredibly stable."

On the video, Abdel Hayat seemed to be conducting a haphazard conversation with himself.

"I will drive to the center of Bryant Park," Abdel was saying. At first, the tollbooth operator thinks Hayat is asking her a question and she responds, but then he begins to speak over her. He's not listening. He simply repeats the same phrase about Bryant Park over and over again, at least four times, while the operator prepares his change. After the awkward moment, Hayat drives the truck away from the toll and into

Manhattan.

The rep continued speaking. "The rest of his path has been discussed. Our office will continue to widen our net. Obviously, we're most focused on getting data from Queens and Brooklyn. We're doing everything—canvassing, talking to the cloud camera companies to see if we can get all their geolocated imagery. We'll have another update at four today with at least ten to twenty minutes more footage. Please let me know if you're not already on the chain from us. Thank you."

Susan stood up again in front of the crowd. "I want to mention that we're doing our best to put the fear of God into any sources who have access to unreleased footage of Hayat. But it'll get out. Even the tollbooth footage will. I promise you that. There's also about a million news trucks parked outside the front steps downstairs, in case you're blind. The public, the press—they're all going to be on this like nothing else matters. Because it doesn't. Let's be clear. This is the largest terrorist attack on American soil since 9/11, so the microscope is on us and the zoom is way up high . . . Be prepared for it. Assistant Director Mack, talk to us."

Pete Mack, head of the FBI's New York City office, stood. Mack was an impressive man, broad shouldered and bald headed. If Rivett was the opposite of what a detective should look like, Mack was out of central casting. Mack was probably the most connected individual in the room. He knew everyone, all the way from Susan to the feds in the back. He had once been an NYPD detective, but was recruited by the FBI about fifteen years prior and had quickly risen up the ranks. As a man whose name was being whispered for even higher profile jobs, such as the advising of presidents, Pete Mack was well aware that this case would either doom or cement his legend once and for all.

"First off, my extreme gratitude to my team of analysts. I have a handful of them here with me, but we have literally two hundred people across the street who slept on the floor last night. I mean, they probably didn't even sleep. We are pulling from absolutely everything we possibly have to create a biography of this guy. Not a huge amount so far, but here's what we know." Mack took a deep breath. "Abdel Hayat is, I mean was, twenty-nine years old. We consider that on the slightly older side for a terror event such as this, but not alarmingly so. He was born in Pakistan in 1990, immigrated to the United States with his parents and younger sister in 1993. Father had a valid work visa and managerial job in IT, which eventually became a green card and then citizenship for the entire family. Father, mother, and sister are all still alive and living in Michigan. From everything we can tell, they are law-abiding citizens who have been expressing anger at what has happened. They told us last night that they hadn't seen Hayat in about four years. Hayat had behavioral issues which may be the result of an undiagnosed mental illness. From what his family related, he never talked to himself like he's doing in our tollbooth video. He wasn't necessarily psychotic, but in the years that they knew him, he was prone to angry outbursts and stubborn idealism. After high school, he wandered around the Midwest and would see his family once or twice a year. Eventually he told them he was moving to New York—said he had a job lined up at a restaurant. He moved. They do not know the name of the restaurant, nor did they have any of his contact info. He continues to call them for about a year, and then the calls stop. They report that it had been three years since they'd spoken to him, and our filtering of their phone and electronic records so far indicate that's true. We're still working on verification, though. Once Hayat arrives in New York, we begin to lose any record of him. He stops filing taxes, and his credit report shows no new accounts or addresses. He does not get a New York driver's license.

Any mailing addresses that we do have for him go back to Michigan, usually to his parents' house. He doesn't create a Facebook account or seem to use the internet at all. And after disappearing, he suddenly reappeared yesterday . . . and you know the rest of it." Pete Mack shuffled with slight unease. "Our number one goal right now is to rebuild Hayat's missing three to four years in New York. Where did he live? Who knew him? Who were his friends? There is no way this man labored by himself to put this bomb together. He was clearly working with others. So there's a cell. Or a group. Whatever they are, they are organized enough to keep one of their own living in our city without a shred of records, which is saying something in this day and age."

"Did he have a phone on him?" one of the feds in the back asked. "Can you track a device using triangulation?"

"Don't have an answer to that yet. There's been no physical evidence recovered that indicates he had a cell phone. Tower reads are being pulled as we speak, timed to the tollbooth appearance. Problem is this is Manhattan. If he were driving down a country road, we'd know if he had a cell phone. We may be dealing with over thirty or forty thousand devices in the five-minute span that we've requested. The processing is going to take a while."

"Excuse me . . ." Jake spoke from the middle row. "How is this guy able to live so dark in America—in New York, man?"

The group lost a half beat while Pete Mack tried to locate Jake.

"I've spoken to that . . ."

"Agent Mack, I understand the literal. I heard what you said. But think about how hard that is, up here . . ." Jake tapped his head. "Not just the fact that most people can't do it. Most people don't want to do it," Jake said. "Does that worry you?"

"This is Jake Rivett, one of our detectives," Susan added. "He's the one who figured out the license plate had been painted over . . ."

"The plate job was professional," Jake said. "And I just heard the new plate number came back to a stolen car from over a year ago. So I'll just say it. I'm sure you all are thinking it. But right now we've got a perpetrator who seems like he's been backstopped by nothing less than a damn intelligence agency. Right? All of it points to some sort of, like, super bad—not normals with jihad on their minds. Not just some regular guys who wanna do mass murder and use the internet to talk to their pals in the Middle East. It's all a step above all that."

"We share your conclusions, Detective Rivett," Pete Mack replied.

"Yeah, and finally, forget about where he lived. We still have no idea where this guy even came from on the morning of the attack. That's the lead we need and we got nothin'. We can't trace him ten minutes, let alone four years," Jake added.

"That's not entirely true," a voice announced.

A man began to speak from the back row of tables. Unlike Susan and Pete Mack, the man didn't stand. He handed a small flash drive to one of his underlings, who hurried up to the front to load a new file. Within seconds, a video played. High-resolution playback scrolled from the top down over Manhattan, like a live-action version of Google Maps. It took a beat before Jake realized that the video was satellite imagery and it was following a white box truck . . .

"What you'll see in this video is Abdel Hayat's truck driving through Brooklyn about four hours before the bombing. Oh, and I should mention that this technology is classified, but that seems less relevant at the current moment . . ."

Audible gasps punctuated the crowd.

"Don't worry. We weren't tracking Hayat. He wasn't on our radar at all. The eyes in the sky aren't up there all the time. One just happened to be over Manhattan yesterday, which means that we have fourteen hours of to-the-inch footage over a twenty-mile radius. The truck sat in a parking lot and didn't move until about eight o'clock in the morning. We do have information regarding this business . . ."

Onscreen, the video footage rewound quickly. Now the box truck sat idly in a large parking lot filled with other trucks. Early morning pink light flooded the satellite view. The technician hit play on the video again, and the whole room watched a small figure walk towards the truck and jump in.

"So what I would suggest to all of us, including the detective in the front, is that we do in fact have our first lead. We have an address in Brooklyn. It's a commercial truck rental shop. They've got a few parking lots—looks like at least a handful of mechanics working. But they ain't a conglomerate. It's a family-run thing. Russians. Axel Bossonov—"

"Bossonov?" Rivett erupted.

"Yeah. Why? You know him?"

Rivett was well acquainted with the Bossonov family. Their name brought him right back to the case that had made him famous within the department: the Flash Crash robbery of Montgomery Noyes. Axel and his nephews Roschin and Petrov were the only three criminals who'd managed to walk away from that case scot-free. Now here they were again.

"Yes, sir," Jake said. "Axel's the patriarch. He's older. Not so sophisticated . . . or at least we didn't think he was. He's got two nephews . . ."

"Roschin and Petrov," the man in back said.

"Right. We used to have surveillance on all these guys—two years ago. You remember them, Tony?"

"Of course," Tony answered. "Axel's old school, a boxer. Roschin's the young buck, the leader. And Petrov, if I remember, doesn't speak a lick of English at all. More of a workhorse."

"They basically run one of the biggest crime syndicates in the city. Thought I'd busted it up when we got Axel's former boss Vlad. But terror? That's just not part of their game plan," Jake said.

"We'll need all your files on them," the man instructed Jake.

"Let's be clear," Susan jumped in. "You're not operating in Brooklyn without my men working hand in hand with you. Right, Peter?" She looked to Pete Mack for backup.

"She's probably right," Pete Mack agreed. "Interagency means interagency. We're all in this together."

"Great. Then the blond kid comes with us," the man said. He pointed at Jake.

"And Tony," Jake added.

"No time to spare," Susan announced. "Just walk the warrants downstairs. I've already arranged to have a judge present in chambers twenty-four seven for at least the next week. Those Bossonovs are getting every single orifice cleaned out." Susan glanced at her phone. "I'm calling it now. Let's break till the afternoon working session. Back here at four." Susan was already halfway out of the room by the time she was finished speaking. One of her hidden talents was the utter domination of aggressive men. She did it by appearing to be more important than any of them. Perhaps she even was, but her fundamental trick was that she never allowed enough time for the question to be asked.

Jake stood up and paced to the back of the room. He knew

something important had happened. Beyond the niceties, he was very aware that he'd been chosen by the man in the back. He still didn't even know who he was about to start working for, but he knew he should probably shake the guy's hand. Jake observed his new boss for a brief moment. The man's version of business casual was a half step higher end than the rest of the feds. Still no tie, but his light-blue shirt had elegant texture and was pressed and tucked in. His grey wool pants were hemmed up high and tight over lime-green socks and fine leather shoes. But what interested Jake the most was his belt. The man's belt consisted of thick woven leather in a western style with an absolutely massive silver belt buckle pounded into the form of a bald eagle.

"Excited to make your acquaintance, sir," Jake said. "Just one question. Who are you?"

"Sheldon White. Please call me Mr. White."

"Okay, Mr. White . . . I'm Jake Rivett. NYPD. I work for Susan, but you already know that. And what do you do?"

"I kill bad guys, Detective Rivett," replied Mr. White.

▪

Jake Rivett was famous. As soon as he stepped out the front door of One Police Plaza, he immediately regretted his decision. He should have listened to Susan and chosen a different exit. Unfortunately, he'd locked his Ducati up in a small motorcycle parking zone at the very front of the building. Jake had to push himself through the throng of reporters waiting outside and calling his name. They were sticking their cameras in his face and screaming over one another like fans at a concert—while bombarding him with a volley of questions. It made matters much worse that he was a known quantity at One Police Plaza nowadays. A few news reports about Jake had popped up after the Flash Crash job, but when he'd singlehandedly taken down property mogul Arthur Metropolis, the cat was really out of the bag. He recognized the reporters and bloggers because it was always the same faces over and over again, and they certainly knew him. He was hard to miss. Jake could never figure out why the press was so interested in him specifically. It was deeply ironic. He had achieved more fame as a detective than a rock singer. He wasn't sure if that was good or bad.

"Detective Rivett, what's the latest on the Abdel Hayat investigation?"

"Why can't you talk to us, Rivett? Don't you think the American people deserve to know?"

"Will there be another attack?"

The last question hit Jake hard. He couldn't let them see that, though. He rarely talked to the media, and when he did, it was only when a superior required him to. It wasn't his job. Jake was sure he'd probably fail miserably if he answered any of these reporters' questions. He also knew that Pete Mack was about to brief the president, who was in turn going to address the nation that evening. It was the president's job to talk to America. Jake's was simple: Bash the case wide open.

Jake finally reached his bike and strapped his helmet on, but the reporters wouldn't give up. They crowded around him like a rabid mob, their hands gesticulating and jowls churning. Jake took a deep breath. He leaned down and grabbed the crowbar he kept attached to the bike's frame and whipped it in the air. He flipped the crowbar around in his hand, wound up, and smacked the steel tool against the pole that his bike had been locked to. It only took three loud reverberations before the reporters went silent. Without a word, Jake gestured with the crowbar ahead of himself, like a golfer parting the crowd for a shot. Once he had created a visible path, Jake ripped away from the circus that was One Police Plaza.

▪

As Jake slid into the parking lot of Axel Bossonov's truck rental enterprise, the cavalry had already arrived. The business was roped off with yellow police tape. Tony, Fong, a number of FBI agents, and a handful of SWAT operators stood on each side of the line, seemingly guarding the place. Jake strode up to Tony with a quizzical look on his face.

"Where's Mr. White?"

"They told us they're going to handle it inside," Tony announced dourly.

"Like hell . . ." Jake replied. He pushed past Tony and headed towards the small office inside the lot, where he could already see Mr. White and his sidekick, Shep Moseley. Both men were wearing blue FBI windbreakers, even though Jake knew they weren't FBI agents. Moseley was much bigger than Mr. White, with strong alpha muscles but a downright goofy face and set of ears. Moseley was essentially the muscle, the Pinky to Mr. White's Brain. Once Jake was inside the office, he didn't break his stride. He swept past the two mysterious feds, towards Axel, and got right into his face.

"Where's Roschin?" Jake immediately asked.

Mr. White and Moseley whipped their necks towards Jake.

"You know who I am, Axel?"

Axel Bossonov stared at Jake for an uncomfortably long moment. Rivett was, in fact, the very reason that many of Axel's loved ones were in jail or dead.

"Yes," Axel finally said.

"So where's your nephew? Actually, where are both of them?"

"Who you talking about? I don't know? How would I know?"

"Roschin and Petrov. The twins."

"They're not my employees . . ."

"We know they work here."

"Oh . . . maybe. Maybe independent contractors. Very complicated, running a business. Benefits, you know . . . I have a lot of nephews. Fuckall, I have a lot of kids. Hard to keep track of them all . . ."

Jake turned to Mr. White. "You can talk to this bozo, 'cause I won't. Totally old school. An expert at saying a whole bunch of stuff while saying nothing at all. Right, Axel?"

"You never really understand a person until you sit down and eat pizza with him . . ." Axel replied.

"The less they say, the more they know," Jake replied. "I'm gonna look around. I imagine that you already took a glance at the search warrant."

Jake exited the small office and paced quickly back to his Ducati.

"Jake . . ." Tony started, knowing exactly where Jake was going and what he was about to do.

Jake reached for the crowbar latched to the side of his bike and whipped it around in his hands. He surveyed the massive parking lot. The lot was filled with all manner of industrial trucks and vehicles parked in loose lines up and down the property. He was actually impressed with the sheer size of the place. Who knows how Axel had gotten his hands on this piece of land and all this stuff. Jake probably didn't want to know, or else he'd have to open up a whole new investigation. Ahead of Jake was a tall pile of junk metal, rising about twenty feet in the air. He sprinted towards the junk and climbed up the proverbial mountain. When he reached the top, he finally had a fantastic vantage point over the lot. The facility looked to be multiple acres in size, and Jake quickly realized that in addition to being huge, it was just a plain mess. It might take weeks for his detectives and the FBI to search the entire place.

Not only did they not have weeks, but something else was nagging at Jake. At the end of the day, he didn't believe that Axel Bossonov was a terrorist. Jake didn't even think that Axel would knowingly aid and abet a terrorist, even for money. That just wasn't in the game plan for mobsters like him. Jake knew these people and this area. The Russians, the Armenians, the Belarusians—none of them committed crime on behalf of any sort of god, unless that god was a new luxury car or sending their kid to the right summer camp. They committed crime, usually forms of fraud, mostly because it was an easy way to make a lot of money. Money got them what they really wanted, which was status, and getting involved in a terror plot would torpedo that status quickly.

While Jake thought, he caught a blur of motion at the far end of the business.

"Roschin," Jake murmured. Roschin Bossonov, clear as day, was dressed smartly and walking into the yard from a back exit. He headed towards a small shaded area, where a number of the company's workers were sitting. The employees were chatting and observing the police activity with a detached interest, as if they were watching a mildly entertaining TV show. Jake leapfrogged down the junk pile and practically sprinted towards Roschin, with Tony and Fong in tow. Jake held the crowbar, rapping it against his hands every few steps. He neared the plastic chairs where Roschin stood in front of a handful of auto mechanics and painters.

"Hey, Roschin. Such a treat to see you again," Jake said.

"Mr. Detective. Hard habit to kick."

"I thought the same thing, too. Where's your brother?"

"I dunno. I'm not his keeper."

"You two are like two peas in a pod. Where's Petrov?"

Like clockwork, Petrov appeared. He was also hustling back into the facility from the exit.

"There's the boy," Rivett said. "So what you guys been up to while I was gone? Just renting out trucks to terrorists?"

"Listen," Roschin said. "Terrorist scum need fuckin' die, detective. You know not what we do."

"That true, Petrov?"

Petrov—a quiet man who many might call mute—simply nodded.

"All right. Well, let me say that I take you on your word with that," Jake said. "So where do you paint the fake license plates?"

"Uh . . ." Roschin stammered for a moment, caught off guard. Then he quickly corrected himself. "What you talk about?"

Jake glanced at Petrov's fingers and forearms, which were splashed with paint. Jake was well aware that between the two brothers, Roschin was the one who talked and Petrov was the one who worked.

"Where's Petrov's workshop?"

No one in the entire crowd of men said a word, but they all seemed to be holding their breath. Jake knew he was onto something. He eyed a series of work benches inside the garage the men were sitting beside. He peered in. The benches were piled up with all manner of garbage—old sheet metal, car parts, license plates, pieces of electrical cabling, and cable brackets. Jake stepped inside with Tony and Fong. The two brothers followed him.

"What's all this crap?" Jake noticed that the work benches and lights were all clean, newer, and high-end with good wiring. But why were the tables covered in trash? He took his crowbar and with one large swipe brushed one of the work tables clean. Junk clattered in every direction.

Jake could finally see clearly that the top of the bench was covered in white-and-blue paint splatter.

"You guys just have an aversion to the truth, don't ya?" Jake asked.

"What? Is paint. We paint parts. All day long. Is our job," Roschin said.

"My guess . . ." Jake said and then continued, "is that, yeah, your guys may paint parts. But you're also painting plates every once in a while. Most likely right on this table."

"You can guess, but a guess is a guess. Is not a fact. Is a fact that you're still a moron."

Rivett didn't take kindly to Roschin's comment. There was a reason that Jake Rivett was Jake Rivett. It went way, way back—so far back that the only people who knew about it were his parents and Mona. But you didn't make fun of Jake Rivett—especially not if you were a Russian mobster engaged in every possible scam and illegal activity on this side of the East River. Rivett pivoted and launched himself directly at Roschin. The two men toppled backwards across the room, with Roschin reaching to grab on to one of the work benches to prevent himself from falling. Jake continued to propel Roschin backwards, jamming the crowbar up against his neck like a vise. After a moment, Roschin was pinned against a back wall of the small shack. Roschin's submission only lasted for a few seconds—as long as it took for Tony and Fong to yank Jake off him.

"Fuck you, detective. I know you got a short fuse. I seen it!" Roschin yelled. "What you got next? Gonna do a murder on me? That solve your crime and find your little terrorist?"

"Shut the hell up, Roschin. I'll solve the crime and then I'll deal with you," Jake spat back while Fong did his best to keep them separated.

"We're going back to the office, Rivett. C'mon! Now!" Tony yelled.

Jake stormed away with Tony, but Roschin was jogging behind them and trying to get in Jake's face. As they neared the front office, Roschin began to complain to Mr. White and Moseley.

"Your detective assault me! He assault me!"

"Rivett?" Mr. White asked.

"He's full of it," Rivett said. Rivett stomped past the agents and into Axel's office again. Once inside, Rivett addressed Axel.

"Bossonov, you've got a good thing going here. Good life, right? A business? But you think things are gonna stay this way? You think you and your nephews and whoever the hell else other goons you've got working for you are just gonna continue your merry little lives, driving around in your Mercedes while a terrorist cell is on the loose in my city? One that you helped? You are making the biggest mistake of your life. I know you're a gambler, but you don't wanna play with me. I am the wrong mark today, Bossonov. I don't know what it is you like to do for fun. Maybe you still get those boxing gloves out? Maybe you like to hit up your ladies of the night for a freebie? The boss discount? Who knows, maybe you just go home to your wife and Netflix and chill. I don't even care. But whatever it is you like to do, I am going to make sure that you never, ever, get to do that again. I am going to make sure you spend the rest of your life wishing you had done the right thing in this moment. All you got is this one time to change your future. You tell me the truth, right now? Then I'm out of your life again. Poof. Gone. Just like a bad dream."

Axel thought about Jake's proposal for just a moment. Then he spoke. "I don't know anything, Detective Rivett."

Jake was livid. But he had Mr. White behind him, so the crowbar he was holding in his hands was useless. There wasn't much he could do besides steam up while he stared at Axel. And he couldn't even stare at

Axel, because he hated him so much. So instead he gazed right past Axel at the wall behind him.

That's when Jake noticed the marks on the wall.

There was a line of small white plastic clips nailed into the wall above Axel's phone and computer. They ascended up the corner of the room and then stopped. They were brackets, designed to hold a piece of cabling. But where were the cables? Rivett glanced up at the ceiling. He saw that a small piece of the drywall was missing from the corner.

"You had cameras," Jake suddenly said. "Where are they, Axel?" He pointed to the broken drywall and the empty cable brackets.

Mr. White noticed as well, a sly grin appearing on his face.

Jake glanced outside the office. Roschin was walking away from the group, heading across the lot and towards the back exit.

"Roschin has the cameras, doesn't he?"

"Yes," Axel replied quietly.

Roschin began to jog. Jake stepped out of the office and immediately sprinted after Roschin, who saw him coming. Roschin began to run. Jake picked up his pace to match. Ahead, Jake could see that Roschin's car was parked just a few feet outside the back exit. Roschin reached his car—*a white Mercedes, of course*—and jumped in. He started the engine. Jake was still about twenty yards behind him and wasn't going to be able to catch up. Instead, he rotated his shoulder back as far as he could and heaved the crowbar directly at Roschin's car. The crowbar rotated in the air like a tomahawk before smashing through the Mercedes's back window. The window was blown to smithereens, glass blasting in all directions.

Roschin wasn't fazed. He turned his wheels to the left and jammed the accelerator, peeling out of his parking spot. He raced the Mercedes down the street. Seconds away from escaping, a police cruiser suddenly rammed into Roschin's car, T-boning the Mercedes from the side and immobilizing Roschin. Tony had smartly arranged for a few squad cars to guard the back gates. The preparation came in handy.

Jake paced up to the smoking car. He discovered Roschin pinned inside the driver's seat, finally defeated. Rivett glanced into the back seat of the Mercedes. Since the car's dark-tinted window was broken, he could see what was inside. Sitting in an open cardboard box in the back seat of the car, clear as day, was a full surveillance system. There were eight cameras, a whole bunch of wiring, the master HD recording unit, and perhaps what Jake and the joint task force were really looking for—a break.

CHAPTER SIX

KATINKA JOHANSSEN SPENT MOST OF her time in front of the computer. As an MD and former graduate student in bioengineering at Penn State, this was to be expected. But the ennui of underemployment had increased her screen time exponentially. It had all begun with her dismissal from her PhD program and the ugly incidents that had resulted from said dismissal. It had ended up here, in this rundown walk-up in Flatbush, where she conducted video therapy over Skype using a third-party app that connected doctors to patients in need. Katinka was forced to operate from her kitchen, where she strung a tie-dyed cloth to hide the rack of pots and pans behind her. At least she was still practicing. She still had patients. But the billing rates were anemic for a doctor with her level of training, and her living situation did nothing more than punctuate her dramatic fall.

Katinka's career had begun with such excitement. Instead of a regular residency after medical school, she had opted to create her own PhD program at Penn State. Technically within the engineering school, her new position stood on the forefront of an entirely new field of medicine—the use of mechanical technology to treat mental disorders. She had held her advisor in the highest esteem possible, having read all of his books and covered his speeches and papers religiously. But at the end of the day, what she hadn't been able to account for was the treachery hiding inside that man. She hated thinking about him, and yet she couldn't stop herself. For a woman who studied compulsions for a living, hating him was her compulsion. Katinka thought about him every single day, sometimes for hours on end, and sometimes without eating or drinking or showering.

Every once in a while, Katinka was able to focus on the work at hand. She wasn't running her own brand-spanking-new lab at a biotechnology startup as she thought she would be. But she still had to pay the bills, namely the rent and the internet, not necessarily in that order. She had a therapy session scheduled in twenty minutes, fifty bucks for forty-five minutes, and she didn't want to miss it like the other three she'd forgotten that week.

However, Katinka was still distracted by the television. Blasted all over the airwaves and the internet for the last few days had been headlines about the Bryant Park massacre. She only knew what was reported but couldn't turn her head away. The police had nothing, or at least they weren't releasing any information. CNN reporters stood outside of One Police Plaza asking questions, and none of the grim faces that emerged had any answers. One of them, wearing black leather from head to toe, simply stared coldly at the camera and didn't respond while reporters blasted him. As the man walked away, the CNN reporter turned back to the camera. "I believe that is NYPD Detective Jake Rivett, himself no stranger to controversy. You heard it from him and others. Or, rather, you didn't hear. The police are being very, very tight lipped right now. Meanwhile, the President of the United States has promised another update to the nation . . ."

Katinka scrambled to find a piece of paper on her small desk. Unable to locate one, she grabbed an old unopened bill and flipped the envelope to the back where she wrote down Rivett's name.

"Jake Rivett. Detective Jake Rivett," she said out loud.

She had a habit—some of her family members might call it an obsession—of writing down the names of people and things she wanted to investigate further. The license plates and descriptions of cars parked outside her apartment were one favorite. Another was obscure individuals referenced in articles she read online. Katinka herself had become quite the investigator. It had begun with the fire that had engulfed the lab at Penn State. The fire wasn't her fault. She hadn't started the fire, no matter what the school administrators thought. Her former mentor was definitely responsible. That much she was sure of. She couldn't prove it, though—not yet. But she wasn't done trying.

After the depressing update about the Bryant Park massacre, Katinka mindlessly began her daily web browsing routine, something that she would repeat hundreds of times per day. Clicking begets clicking. She started with the regular news sites, where she would get her fill of daily news. Then she would move down the ladder, to obscure video sites like VidLeak and her favorite psychology and nanotechnology blogs. Down in the rabbit holes of these online worlds were where she felt most comfortable. She was an active commentator.

When she saw the top post on the front page of VidLeak, a compilation of underground videos one would never find on YouTube, Katinka was startled. A new video of Abdel Hayat had just been posted four minutes prior. It was titled "NEWLY RELEASED VIDEO OF TERROR SUSPECT-WHAT IS HE DOING?"

Katinka quickly read the caption underneath the video. Apparently, the terror suspect had stopped at a 7-Eleven for breakfast on the morning of the attack. One of the employees at the store had gotten his or her hands on the video and uploaded it to the internet, bypassing the authorities completely. Katinka couldn't stop herself. She hit play.

Hayat was dressed well, in crisp slacks and a polo shirt. He wandered through the store, ostensibly looking for something to eat. He poured himself a cup of coffee, took a sip, and then left it sitting on the coffee stand. That was when the cashier began to take an interest, moving from behind his register and beginning to shadow Hayat. Hayat paced down another aisle of the store before grabbing a bag of chips, which he immediately opened and began to eat. The cashier spoke and the audio was clear as day.

"Are you planning on paying for that? What about the coffee?" the cashier asked.

"No," Hayat said quietly under his breath.

"Then you need to leave my store."

"What's your mission?" Hayat asked the cashier.

"To get you to stop shoplifting."

"I know my mission," Hayat said. "I will drive to the center of Bryant Park."

"That's great, man. But you gotta go."

"I'm going to leave. I'm going to leave. I'm going to leave." Hayat repeated the same phrase three times, and then he truly began to rant, his voice growing deeper and stranger as he did, until it took on an almost otherworldly tone. "Say it with me. I'm going to leave. Say it with me one more time . . ."

"Whaddya mean? No way. What's wrong with you?" replied the cashier.

"I'm going to leave. I'm going to leave anyway. I'm going to leave anyway. Say it with me. You're going to leave anyway. You're going to leave anyway. You're going to leave anyway. Say it with me. Three times. I know my mission. I will drive to the center of Bryant Park. I will drive to the center of Bryant Park. I will drive to the center of Bryant Park." Now Hayat was screaming, his face caught up in muscular spasms as he spat angrily at the cashier, who was amazingly holding his ground. "Say it with me!"

"Get out!" the cashier screamed back.

Katinka was stunned. The hairs on her arms stood up, and she felt a deep anxiety race through her body. There were many possible disorders that might cause a man to act like this. She didn't doubt that once the FBI saw this video, they would be investigating Hayat from numerous mental-health angles. But Katinka knew, deep down inside, that there was only one reason for Hayat's behavior. Her proof had nothing to do with him being a terrorist, his unstable performance in the convenience store, or even most of the words he muttered.

"Say it with me. Three times," she muttered under her breath. Say it with me. Three times. Those words—random connectors—were what scared her the most. Because she'd heard those words before. Many, many times. She'd helped develop the taxonomy behind those words. They were not meaningless. They were the key to everything.

Katinka scrambled to open up her video-editing application. She wasn't great at shooting and editing, but she knew enough to get around. She'd done it many times in the past. Thirty minutes had passed by that point, and she was well aware that she would miss her appointment with her therapy client. Her client could wait. This could not. She began recording into her webcam.

"This is Katinka Johanssen speaking." She paused dramatically. "I just saw the Abdel Hayat video—the one in the Seven-Eleven. I need to get this out right away, because there may not be very much time. The armchair psychologists will have a field day with this evidence. They will pick all the most obscure diagnoses out of the DSM they can muster, but I know what he's displaying has nothing to do with mental illness. Hayat might have a few screws loose, but I know who was turning them. Dr. Maximilian Borin is responsible for what you see. All you have to do is watch the video. First, one must examine the subject's intonation. Can you hear it? Go watch the video on VidLeak and then come back here. He is not repeating his own thoughts. Those are not his words. Those are not his ideas. The things coming out of his mouth are programmed. I will say it once, loud and clear. Abdel Hayat was brainwashed. He was conditioned. Abdel Hayat was brainwashed by Maximilian Borin. Say it with me. He has been brainwashed. Say it with me. You'll see . . ." Katinka kept speaking before eventually trailing off and staring out the window for a full twenty seconds before she realized that she was still recording. She stopped the recording and saved the video file as "THE TRUTH ABOUT BRYANT PARK."

Katinka logged into her own personal video channel on VidLeak. All of the past videos that she'd uploaded were there, along with their view counts. She had posted about twenty-five videos over the last year, all with sensational all-caps titles like "MAXIMILIAN BORIN IS EVIL," "I WILL NOW EXPOSE DOCTOR MAX BORIN," and "PSYCHO PSYCHOLOGIST, MAXIMILIAN BORIN." Her most-watched video had nine views.

Katinka uploaded her new video. Then she stared down at the name she'd written on the envelope earlier: Detective Jake Rivett. She loaded a new tab in her browser and searched for Jake's name.

CHAPTER SEVEN

THE CRIMES OF THE BOSSONOV family were exposed on video —the footage that Jake had recovered from the back of Roschin's car was voluminous.

The whole joint task force was back inside the command center at One Police Plaza. A dozen analysts, led by Rivett, had spent the entire night scrubbing through thousands of hours of footage. Thanks to the hard drives the Bossonovs had invested in, the authorities had close to a months worth of activity to work with. The results were clear. A majority of the video was incredibly boring. But for every hundred hours of mundane tow and rental truck servicing and leasing, there were fifteen minutes of prime criminal activity. Roschin seemed to specialize in the Photoshop work—printing fake titles and forging signatures. Petrov was better with his hands. He took care of replacing VIN tags, altering mileage, and, in one particularly important clip, painting and glazing license plates. The whole enterprise was relatively mundane. The Bossonovs were essentially operating an anti-DMV for a whole dark and shadowy part of the economy that most people don't know exists. But it was crystal clear here, thanks to the high-resolution video system they had chosen to put in. It never ceased to amaze Jake how eager some criminals were to immortalize their own misdeeds with surveillance cameras. But that was the nature of being an organized criminal—if you're a robber, you're more likely to get robbed.

"Petrov Bossonov personally did the work on Abdel Hayat's license plate," Jake announced while the footage played behind him. "He's the one that doesn't speak English—or at least he doesn't let on if he can. Has his brother do all the talking. But for what he lacks in speech, he makes up in craft. The man is meticulous, frankly. First, he's refashioned a metal stamping machine to flatten the number or numbers he wants to alter. Then, after taping a stencil to the plate, he uses another machine to extrude new numbers. Finally, he sands everything down just a little bit before painting, adding an epoxy finish, and finishing with a dirt sand."

Rivett was speaking to the entire task force, most of whom had only arrived in the last hour. He gazed past Tony and Fong to Susan and Pete Mack and, of course, the inimitable Mr. White and his right-hand man, Moseley.

"So where's Hayat in the video?" Susan asked.

"Funny you should ask . . ."

Rivett waved to Tony, who loaded a new file and hit play.

"It was the camera in Axel's office that we were really interested in. On the morning of the Bryant Park bombing, it was running, for sure. We all expected to see Hayat retrieve the truck that morning. Problem is . . ."

The surveillance video showed the elder Bossonov sitting by himself and fiddling with his computer before the glass door to his office opened and a man walked in.

"A man walked in to pick up the truck," Jake said. "That man wasn't Abdel Hayat."

"What the fuck?" Susan glanced at Pete Mack, who was locked in on the surveillance footage.

Onscreen was a white man, seemingly in his late fifties or early sixties. He was tall, with a huge mop of curly hair that had gone halfway grey. The man wore slacks and, strangely, what appeared to be a long white lab coat. Even though there was no audio, the man seemed like a chatterbox. He kept grinning and gesticulating with his hands as he and Axel talked. Axel picked up his telephone, quickly spoke, and then hung up. Finally the two men walked outside, and only the bottom portion of their legs and feet were visible on the video while they waited for the truck to pull up.

"Who's Einstein?" Mr. White asked.

"This is outrageous . . ." Pete Mack said.

The joint task force watched the screen in shocked silence. The problem wasn't necessarily that they weren't looking at Hayat. But the man they saw was nothing like the profile they'd been building of Hayat's cell. The more they learned, the more concerned they became.

"I don't think I gotta tell you this, Agent Mack," Jake said, "but a very weird looking white guy picked up our truck."

"He looks like my unemployed neighbor who mows his lawn four times a week with a weedwacker," Mr. White said from the back of the room. "Not a terrorist—a nothing. And *that* . . . scares the shit out of me."

Pete Mack jumped into action. "Start the facial recognition algos cracking. Get the best face scans you can from the video here, and get his image to absolutely everyone and anyone—Google, Facebook, Twitter, local newspapers, everything. I'll make sure NSA gets it, too. Sheldon, can your boys do something with this?"

"Done," Mr. White answered. "We'll pump it internationally through Interpol and then personally call our partner agencies. DHS should have it, too. We'll tell them to run it through every passport photo in the last ten years. If he traveled, we might be able to get him. My guess is he's an American. Looks like a doctor or pharmacist," Mr. White said.

"Thinks he's one, at least," Jake added.

"Beyond all." Pete Mack stood next to the monitor and rapped his knuckle on the screen. "Einstein is our number-one lead and our number-one person of interest right now. Everyone in this room get on the horn with your people. We must find Einstein."

"Agent Mack," Jake said. "You gotta let me go talk to the Bossonovs. I have a way with them . . ."

"They're in custody. My people are doing that as we speak," Pete Mack answered.

"Your people aren't me."

"Rivett, you need a break, not a new interrogation," Susan added.

"I don't take breaks."

"Kid, if it weren't for this being what it is, you'd be on a permanent desk break for six months with what I heard you did there at the lot yesterday," Pete Mack said.

Rivett flinched. His muscles contracted ever so slightly. Pete Mack was doing the thing he hated most of all. He was doubting Jake. Sitting next to Jake, Tony lightly placed his hand over Jake's arm to try to calm him down. Jake reacted badly, elbowing Tony angrily and standing up.

"Don't speak to me like that, Mack."

"Your request is to talk to the Bossonovs, yeah?" Pete Mack began. "The same guys you assaulted with your crowbar? Are you so stupid, so bereft of all due process, that you don't realize their lawyers can already use that against us? Your goddamn crowbar might've wiped ten years off their sentence. If you want to get tough with me, you're welcome to. I'll meet you outside. Then after we're done, no matter who wins, you'll never step into this room again. I'll make sure of that. So are you ready to go, or what?"

Jake took a deep breath. In the past, he might have reacted differently. But instead of doing what he was practiced at—escalate, up the ante, lash out—he thought about what Mona would tell him to do.

He shut his damn mouth and he sat down.

CHAPTER EIGHT

THANKFULLY, SHE WAS STILL WEARING the ring. Jake had barely spoken to Mona since two days earlier, when his proposal was punctuated by the horror of Bryant Park. As he entered their new apartment in Williamsburg, waves of emotion poured out of Mona. She ran towards Jake and jumped into his arms. They embraced.

"Are you okay? I didn't expect you back . . ."

"I'm fine," Jake nodded. "It got a little heated, and they told me to take the afternoon . . ."

"Oh, so you pulled a Jake Rivett."

"Hard not to be myself," Jake said as he grinned.

"If you cooled off a little, you might accomplish more."

"I'm passionate. It's what makes me tick."

"I'd put it differently," Mona said. "I'd say it's what *made* you. Doesn't have to *be* you. So what's going on? Are we getting them?"

"It's complicated," Jake said.

"Always is . . ."

"I'm telling you . . ." Jake shook his head. "This one's intense, Mona. Guy is like some ghost terrorist out of a movie, and we know he's got at least one person he's working with—an old white. Breaks the mold completely. It's gonna be a real puzzle."

"More attacks?" Mona asked.

"I don't know." Jake paused thoughtfully. "And that's what's been eating at me."

"Speaking of which, let's do just that. I was making some pasta. There's enough for both of us."

Mona pulled the pasta off the stove, drained it, and quickly mixed in some tomato sauce she'd been heating up. The two of them sat down at the kitchen table. Although they loved their new place, Jake and Mona lived in New York. That meant their apartment wasn't huge. In fact, it was tiny. The "kitchen table" was about the size of some people's bedside tables. There was just enough room for the two of them, with Jake's back pushed against a wall and his knees scraping the bottom of the table. On the wall above their table was a corkboard with important mail and bills. Mona had also pinned up a few photographs of the two of them, one with her co-workers at her graphic-design job, and one featuring Jake with his band, Mythics.

Jake was a fantastic detective, but he was also a great singer. To Jake, Mythics was nothing more than a hobby. However, the rest of the band thought Mythics could be something. There was evidence, too. They had been approached by agents and labels multiple times. But Jake had remained steadfast in his refusal to commercialize the band. That created a strange duality where they didn't perform all that often but had an avid underground fan base. Schaub, the drummer, set up their few performances per year. The shows were always at local establishments in the city, usually in the East Village or Brooklyn. Schaub did everything else, too. He was the one who updated their social media, uploaded songs to the streaming services, and coordinated all of their practices. Jake knew that Schaub wanted to expand Mythics and that he was the reason they couldn't. But what Jake loved about Mythics wasn't the music or the camaraderie, although he respected and enjoyed both. Ironically, what he loved the most about singing was that it helped him relax. And for a guy like Jake, that meant a lot.

"Are you still happy to be engaged to me?" Mona asked Jake as they started slurping down the pasta.

"Of course."

"Tell me more."

"You tell me. You really want to get married? Always said you didn't."

"I don't want to get married," Mona said. "But I do want to get married to you."

"I feel exactly the same."

"I know."

"So . . . when?" Jake asked.

"Take it down a notch, big boy," she said as she laughed.

"You know me. I go full bore—zero to a hundred."

"You don't want a very long engagement like everyone else?"

"I never want to do what everyone else does," Jake replied.

"I'll think about it." Mona shrugged. "We can go fast."

"I'm into that," Jake replied. "Crazy, though. I was a cop, thought you were a robber, and now we're getting married."

"More like ironic—since I'm sure you've done a lot more bad stuff than me."

"Only to bad people," Jake said. Then his mood darkened. "Like this evil bastard."

"Try to leave it—just for dinner."

"I know," Jake said. He pushed back from his chair and stood. Then he started pacing. "It's just so difficult. I gotta figure out who the white guy is. The one with the truck . . ."

"What truck?"

"Never mind." Jake knew he wasn't supposed to discuss the operational details of his investigations with Mona. But he simply couldn't avoid talking it out, and anyway, she wasn't the problem. The problem was that he was perpetually trying to connect the dots in his head. He was constantly going over the connections and evidence they had: *Hayat, the rental truck, the Bossonovs, Einstein . . .*

Unfortunately, all he was getting was a bunch of loose ends sparking around in the ether—and the result was the anxiety he was feeling.

"Jake. Please. You gotta stop for just, like, thirty seconds. Relax. I don't want you to go crazy. And neither do you, 'cause then how are you going to solve any more crimes?" Mona asked as she watched him pace back and forth.

Not a bad point, he thought. But he kept pacing.

Then, all of a sudden, there was a knock on the door.

"Rivett, ya in there?"

Both Jake and Mona knew exactly who it was. They could easily recognize the voice through the door. Jake quickly opened it to find his bandmate and good pal, Schaub. He was completely decked out in black-and-white leather, with slicked back hair and four long necklaces hanging around his neck.

"Ready to rawk?"

▪

Jake, Mona and Schaub hustled towards the club. Jake had completely forgotten that Mythics was scheduled to perform that night as the late-night closer at a rock club in Brooklyn called ExCulture. Obviously, this wasn't a convenient night for a performance. It was Mona who had convinced Jake to go. She knew him better than he knew himself. After an hour of screaming his lungs out onstage, Jake might actually be able to sleep that night. They dipped down the alleyway to the side of the venue and into the talent entrance with just minutes to spare.

▪

ExCulture didn't book the most popular bands. The venue couldn't pay for them. But what it lacked in finances was made up for in energy. If anything, ExCulture was a place that made a band in order for that band to never have to perform there again. There was an informality about almost everything, including the set lists and even the performers each night. That's why Omer Amin wasn't sure if there was another band to go or if the evening was over. He'd been standing to the side of the crowd for about ten minutes since the last act finished. The lights hadn't come up, but it was getting late. He'd stick around for a little longer, he thought, as he gazed around the crowd. The crowds were one of his favorite things about New York and these rock venues in general. People there truly did not give a fuck. The ethos was so different from his upbringing, where his father, mother, brother, and even his sister certainly did give a fuck . . . about every little thing. Omer wanted badly to morph completely into this world and leave his own behind. But he wasn't quite ready yet. For now, he simply watched. He rarely spoke to anyone at the clubs. He just danced and watched.

"Can I get you a drink?" a man standing next to Omer asked politely.

Omer glanced at the guy. He was just a few years older than him. Early twenties. Asian. But Omer kept to his rules of engagement. He never accepted drinks.

"No, thank you."

"Okay. No problem," said the man. "You excited about Mythics?"

"Wasn't even sure if they were coming on . . ."

"They will. They're classic—as close to a house band as this place gets. You come here a lot?"

"Not really. Just a few times."

"I love your makeup. I'm Ty."

"Thanks."

"And what's your name, my friend?"

Before Omer could respond, all of the lights in the venue collapsed to pitch black. Then a single spotlight burned onstage, and into the middle of the light stepped the striking local New York legend known as Jake Rivett.

▪

Rivett raged. Spit coated the microphone in front of him as he belted out Mythics' most popular song, "Out of the Mist," a melodic and actually somewhat poppy journey punctuated by interludes of deeply complex beats. "Mist" ended with a grotesque scream, as many of Mythics' songs did. It was Jake's trademark, a loud and cacophonous yell that was only appropriate in a place like ExCulture.

Screamo was the opposite of commercial music, and it was also Jake's favorite. Screamo had been his jam for a long, long time. For much of Jake's life, he had used music as a distraction from everything else going on around him—from his father's drunken rages to his early years in New York when he didn't know up from down and was struggling in the back kitchen of a restaurant in Chinatown. Now, finally, music was becoming something that he was able to sculpt to his own liking. That's how "Out of the Mist" had come into being. It was more accessible than Mythics' old stuff. It had a touch more Radiohead and a dab less darkness—not much less, mind you. But enough that the crowds were growing more diverse and the band's iTunes downloads were increasing. Jake didn't care about the money or the fame and never would. He whipped his blond hair around the stage like a mop cleaning the walls and the crowd went berserk for him. And in that very moment, Jake Rivett was an absolute, no-doubt, genuine-beauty, heart-throbbing rock star.

But at the end of the day, Jake wasn't there for the fans. He was there for the feeling. Performing was his only drug and practically his only drink. The more he lost himself on stage, the more he felt as though he had found his real self. While he was performing, he didn't perceive the audience. He only cared about how he felt. There were a lot of eyes on him that night, but he couldn't see any of them. That was the nature of the spotlight. He did what he wanted, and everyone else watched him do it. Jake Rivett was the piece of art.

▪

Besides the five hundred concertgoers, besides Omer Amin, besides the bartenders and proprietors and promoters, there was one more set of eyeballs watching Jake Rivett perform. Those eyes belonged to Katinka Johanssen.

At the end of the evening, Katinka stood in the alleyway beside ExCulture and waited for Jake. It hadn't been easy to find him, but it also hadn't been hard. Buried deep in the comments of a newspaper article about one of Jake's recent cases had been a mention of Mythics. Katinka had quickly connected the dots after that by locating Mythics' Twitter handle and hustling over to ExCulture. She stood out like a sore thumb amongst the cigarette smokers and loiterers in the alleyway. Maybe people thought that the skinny, solitary girl with the frizzy red hair was a groupie. But probably not.

A moment later, the artist door opened and Jake and Mona walked out. Katinka stared directly at Jake. She caught his eye and a chill came across her body. When he passed by Katinka, she grabbed his arm forcefully. Jake attempted to brush it off as Mona stepped ahead, unaware that he'd been stopped. But Katinka held on.

"I know who did it to Abdel Hayat."

Jake stopped in his tracks and stared at her.

"Who?"

"The doctor."

"Who's the doctor?" Jake asked. "Who are you?"

"I'm—"

"Hey! Now's not the time!" Mona had turned around and was yelling at Katinka. "Get away from him."

"Wait," Jake said. "What did you just say? Who's the doctor? Who are you?"

Katinka suddenly clammed up. She didn't answer. She could see that Jake was becoming annoyed, and his girlfriend even more so. Maybe this all had been a huge mistake.

"I— It's all in my videos."

"What?"

"It's in my videos," Katinka finally said out loud.

"I'm off the clock," Jake said. "If you know something about Abdel Hayat, call the hotline. Okay? You need to call it in."

"I . . ." All of a sudden, a look of horror came across Katinka's face. "You guys have no idea, do you? You don't know anything." Katinka's face turned red, and she raced out of the alleyway.

"Hey!" Jake yelled. He jogged towards the alley's entrance. But by the time he reached the street, there was no sign of the red-haired girl.

"C'mon," Mona said, following him. "Don't worry about that."

"She was talking about a doc—"

"I don't think that girl had any idea what she was talking about," Mona replied. "She was probably wasted."

"Yeah. Maybe . . ." Jake answered.

"You ready to go home now?"

"I think so. I'm . . ."

"Yeah?"

"Tired," Jake finally said.

And those words were truly music to Mona's ears.

CHAPTER NINE

JAKE WAS BACK AT ONE Police Plaza by seven thirty in the morning. When he walked into the office, he saw most of the joint task force crowded around a television. They were watching CNN. The news network was broadcasting a previously unseen video, shot in a convenience store, of the terror suspect before the attack. Jake quickly learned that the footage had been found by someone on the internet and was being broadcast by all the major networks.

"What I'd love to know, Peter, is how the goddamn internet gets this video before we do?" Susan asked.

"How would I know that, Susan? I'm not God."

"No, that's Mr. White," Susan said.

The whole room chuckled nervously.

"Much obliged," Mr. White said, barely looking up from his computer screen. Mr. White and his group continued to be somewhat standoffish when it came to cooperating with everyone else—but they were still undeniably part of the team.

"Seriously . . ." Pete Mack said, steamed up at the apparent indictment of the FBI's cyber investigation. "I can't stop some guy who owns a Seven-Eleven from uploading whatever he wants to upload. I can't force him to call us first. Let's move on and focus on what the profilers are saying about it."

"And what's that? That the guy's insane?" Jake said.

"We agree that when this video is analyzed in the light of the tollbooth video—which is not public, mind you—that a mental-health conclusion is becoming more and more likely. But mental health is not binary. We don't know what he was suffering from. We don't have a diagnosis. We don't have any medical records for Hayat . . ."

"And we don't have Einstein," Mr. White added.

"The doctor . . ." Jake muttered, remembering his strange conversation with the red-haired girl.

"What?" Susan said.

"Nothing."

"Peter, what happened with the Bossonov interrogation?" Susan asked.

"They gave us absolute shit. But now I think they're telling the truth, at least. Apparently the man we're calling Einstein, from the video, he showed up in person each time and never called in. He always called himself Daniel. He paid cash for everything," Pete Mack said. "They figured he was a local."

"If the doctor had a cell phone in his pocket, we may be able to triangulate it," Mr. White announced from the back of the room. "My guys are working with Pete's on that downstairs right now. But it's a real needle-and-haystack job."

"Where'd the new video come from?" Jake asked. He pointed to the 7-Eleven video playing on CNN. At the bottom of the video file, a watermarked image had been applied. But the CNN chyron obscured it.

"File was first uploaded to a site called VidLeak yesterday," Dennis

Fong announced. "Twitter got ahold of it in the middle of the night."

Jake paced towards Fong's computer. Fong had loaded VidLeak already and was playing the video again. Rivett watched as Hayat paced and ranted inside the 7-Eleven.

"What's VidLeak?" Jake asked.

"Just some video site. Anyone can upload anything."

"All surveillance video?"

"What do you mean? No. I know this site, actually," Fong said. "It's mostly real-life stuff—dangerous stunts, road rage, police chases, weird and random crap. Comes from all over. It's pretty much non-denominational."

Jake watched as Fong scrolled down the page. Along the bottom row of the VidLeak page was a series of thumbnails containing videos that had been auto populated by VidLeak's algorithm. Jake's eyes quickly scanned across them, but he didn't spot anything unusual.

"Who uploaded the video? The owner of the store? Is that confirmed?" Jake asked Fong.

"Yeah. Seems so. Our guys are already there interviewing him. We'll have the HD version in under an hour."

"Good."

As Fong was about to click off the page, Jake suddenly took a second look at one of the linked thumbnail images.

"Hey! Wait a minute," Jake said as he pointed at the thumbnail. "That one. Click on it."

Fong did as instructed.

The new video featured a woman who was staring at the camera. But she wasn't just any woman. Jake knew her face. It was the same red-haired young lady who'd accosted him briefly the night before. The video was titled, "THE TRUTH ABOUT BRYANT PARK."

"Play it," Jake said.

Fong clicked, and soon Katinka Johanssen's most recent VidLeak upload was being displayed across the task force's massive wall of screens. Katinka's angst-filled face filled the frame while she ranted.

"First, one must examine the subject's intonation. Can you hear it? Go watch the video on VidLeak and then come back here. He is not repeating his own thoughts. Those are not his words. Those are not his ideas. The things coming out of his mouth are programmed. I will say it once, loud and clear. Abdel Hayat was brainwashed. He was conditioned . . ."

"Why are we watching this—some conspiracy theorist?" Pete Mack asked.

But the whole room was still drawn to the video. The insanity of her presentation felt like a well-needed comedy break for the investigation. At the end of the day, it was all conjecture. What she said didn't add up to anything, and she had no proof.

As Jake vaguely listened to Katinka speak, his eyes quickly scanned across her VidLeak profile page. He noticed that she'd been posting videos for at least the last two years. Virtually every video had a similar thumbnail—just Katinka's face looking straight ahead at the camera. The uploads barely had any views. But there was a remarkable throughline to many of the videos' titles. They all referenced the same person's name.

"Maximilian Borin," Jake said quietly. He spoke louder the second time. "Maximilian Borin."

Fong glanced up at him. "Who?"

"Search for Maximilian Borin," Jake commanded Fong. The room realized that Jake was becoming unusually aggressive. What was going on? Fong loaded a new window, typed quickly, and tapped search. His results piled up on the main screen in the front of the room.

"Images," Jake said.

Fong clicked on the search engine's image tab. A professional portrait of Maximilian Borin stared back at the room.

"Holy mother of—" Sheldon White muttered. "It's the doctor. You found fucking Einstein, Rivett."

Dr. Borin was clearly the same person as the unknown man from the Bossonovs' security-camera footage.

▪

In under an hour, a veritable army of law enforcement personnel were ripping halfway across Long Island and heading towards the leafy college town of Stony Brook, New York. The FBI had pulled up tax returns and credit checks for Maximilian Borin, all of which listed his address as a unit in an apartment building adjacent to SUNY Stony Brook.

Jake read through the doctor's hastily created FBI biography as he sat shotgun in Tony's SUV, following two armored personnel carriers filled with SWAT members. Borin had spent most of his adult life in academia. For the last two years, he'd been an adjunct professor at Stony Brook. Before that, the bulk of his time had been spent as a full professor at Penn State.

"What are you learning?" Tony asked Jake.

"It's light on details . . . Distinguished academic. Full tenure at Penn State, but suddenly leaves the university a couple years ago. In the videos, the girl says she was his graduate student. We need her address— immediately."

"I know," Fong said from the back seat. "VidLeak just came back and gave us the IP without a court order, which is great. But her ISP's demanding a warrant. Susan's trying to get the judge to sign it right now. We should have her name in a few more minutes."

The convoy of vehicles—NYPD, FBI, ATF—careened into Stony Brook like a Mythics intro—no warning, all shock and awe. The SWAT captain, Jack Markle, jumped out of his truck immediately. Although a veteran, Markle was known to lead the charge. Without any ado, the whole SWAT team approached the apartment building ahead. The complex was older, without controlled access. Built like a giant U, each unit had a door that faced the central parking lot. SWAT only announced their presence while the doorbuster was swinging through the air.

"Police! We have a warrant!"

They bashed down the door in less than two seconds. The operators fanned into the apartment. Markle turned a corner with his gun up and in the ready position, but he quickly realized the place was unoccupied— and half empty.

"No one's here," Markle spoke into his radio.

A moment later, Rivett and the other detectives stepped inside. Jake took a look around.

"Shit," spit Rivett. "Where the hell are ya, Einstein?"

▪

As was becoming usual with this case, they had a whole bunch of questions but no answers. Jake wasn't in the mood for the slog ahead. He liked cases that cracked quickly. The faster they cracked, the faster they broke. But at the moment, all Jake could do was watch unhappily as NYPD CSI and tech teams began the slow and arduous process of documenting Dr. Borin's apartment. Sitting on a folding chair, Jake wasn't sure what to make of Einstein's lair. It seemed as though Dr. Borin had moved out quickly but not in a panic. The doctor certainly hadn't left the place abandoned. He'd packed up all his books but had left empty bookcases. Based on the stains on the counter, it appeared that he'd taken his coffee maker but not his microwave. He'd left a handful of heavy winter jackets, but—assuming he owned any—taken all his shirts. His toothbrush was gone, as was his shampoo. His washcloth remained.

Jake watched the teams work. He didn't feel like pitching in. He was dejected. He felt—actually, he knew—that they were losing momentum quickly. Something needed to change.

"Rivett!" Fong yelled, hanging up a call.

Jake turned to Fong.

"The girl. Her name's Katinka Johanssen. Got her address."

Jake's mood instantly improved. The investigation was driving on fumes, but at least it was still moving.

"Let's double-time it, Fonger."

CHAPTER TEN

MAXIMILIAN BORIN PACED AROUND THE kitchen of Best Diner, watching Hanafi prepare steamed dumplings in the fryer. Hanafi was a little bit of everything—preacher, landlord, boss—but he certainly wasn't a cook. That didn't stop him from using the kitchen, generally the fryer. For a sacrosanct man, his body was not his temple.

"The video is sure to give me a heart attack," Hanafi said.

"That has nothing to do with me."

"They will be here—law enforcement. Sooner or later. It's only a matter of time . . ."

"Why?"

"The girl. Didn't you see her latest post?"

"Katinka? No. I can't control what Katinka does. You knew about her a year ago, and you still chose to hire me . . ."

"Listen, Max. My mother used to tell me you are what you eat," Hanafi said. He stared at the bubbling fryer. "Ironic. But there's an absolute corollary. It is . . . you are who you hire. So it might not be your fault that this girl is posting her dirty laundry on the internet, but it's definitely your problem."

"I've already spoken to her. There's nothing else I can do."

"I know. I know that. I'm not done talking. I'm the one who hired you. And you came with your own obsessed fan. So both you, and her, are my problem."

"The girl is irrelevant," Dr. Borin said. "What matters is the machine. I think I've located a bug in the neural-control technology. It caused Abdel to initiate early. There's a fix, but I'll need a functional near-infrared spectroscope to be sure."

"What happened with Abdel was an awful mistake, but you're obviously doing something right," Hanafi said while remaining focused on his fryer.

"Should I repeat myself? I need a fNIRS."

"What's that?"

"It's like the big white tube—the MRI machine. But different. Better."

"How much?"

"Ten to fifty thousand."

"Out of the question," Hanafi snapped. "But I fully believe you can solve our problem."

"So all I get is moral support?"

"I'm not buying you another one of those brain scanners."

"It's necessary. It will measure brain activity while the subject is moving, instead of just sitting still."

"You're out of your mind. We're not installing any more machines. We're doing one last operation, and then we're leaving."

"I don't know if I'll like the Middle East. It's pretty far from my mother . . ."

Hanafi turned back to the fryer. He pulled out a basket of french fries and chicken strips dripping magnificently with blazing-hot oil. He allowed the oil to pour away for a moment before transferring the food to a tray sitting next to the fryer. Hanafi then went searching through the refrigerators for dipping sauce. "I only like the honey mustard," he said. "But the cooks never stock it. That's one of the best things you Westerners ever invented—honey mustard. It's even freaking *halal*. Can you believe that?"

"Hanafi, pay attention. The machine isn't ready yet. Abdel was proof of that. I can't guarantee the next operation is going to be a success without a functional scanner. I won't. I wouldn't be half the scientist I am if I did. I know you want a proof of concept and you only think in terms of your final objective. But I'm worried about my research, too."

"You're very conscientious," Hanafi said. "That's why we make such a good team. But let me remind you of something," Hanafi returned with the honey mustard and poured it all over his food. He grabbed a fried chicken finger and took a huge bite. "There are no buyers here for what you're selling. To you and me? It's brilliant. But to the rest of the civilized world? It's immoral. We only have one financier—the man from Dubai. He needs to know that your technology works flawlessly. We don't have the resources, or the time, to purchase any more equipment. The only way any plan, any objective, yours or mine, works . . . is if your machine works. Otherwise, our money disappears, which means our protection disappears. I am saving your life right now. Remember? No one here wanted you. No one would hire you. No one wanted your garbage. Don't forget."

"I won't. And I won't forget that I know everything about Abdel . . . and you . . . and this place. The feds might want to get me, but they'll be even happier to get you, Imam," the doctor blurted out.

Hanafi didn't even feel the knife in his hand. It was simply there. He paced towards the doctor until he was holding the blade an inch from Dr.

Borin's neck. "You will never say something like that ever again, Maximilian. You do, and you'll never speak again. And don't call me Imam."

"You need me," Dr. Borin said.

"Likewise."

"Sorry." Dr. Borin exhaled. "I'm frustrated. I feel so close. Abdel did exactly what he was supposed to do, but he didn't do it at the right time. The machine is penetrating . . . They're getting the message . . . But they're not entirely under our control."

"I know. But perfection is near." Hanafi finally retreated, holding the knife gently in his hands. He suddenly swung the blade through the air, ripping downward across the chicken with extreme violence. "Want a wing?"

Both men heard the kitchen door open. Murad Amin appeared. He had a jacket wrapped around his right arm and was panting as if he'd just run a marathon.

"Success, dear one?" Hanafi asked.

"Inshallah," Murad answered. "Absolute and total, Alim."

"Great," Hanafi said. "Chicken?"

"In a moment . . ."

Murad paced towards the large industrial sink in the back of the kitchen. He pulled the jacket off his arm and threw it into a trash bin. Then Murad began to wash his hands and arms.

Dr. Borin watched from the other side of the kitchen. Murad wasn't washing dirt off his hands. Each time he touched the soap, a large streak of red liquid accompanied his swipe. It took Borin only a moment before he realized that Murad's arm was coated in blood, which he was furiously wiping off.

CHAPTER ELEVEN

RIVETT AND FONG WERE TWO miles from Flatbush and Katinka's address when they saw the smoke. Jake's stomach immediately sunk. The slight edge of panic turned into a sledgehammer as Fong whipped the SUV off the Brooklyn-Queens Expressway and tore south. With each turn, their car seemed to be drawing closer to the plume. What Jake had already known for five minutes proved to be true the second they turned onto Katinka's street. There was a structure fire, and Jake didn't need anyone to tell him that Katinka's apartment was the locus.

By that point, the blaze was ripping through all four stories of the walk-up where Katinka lived. Jake jumped out of the SUV and raced past a firefighter who was doing his best to keep civilians off the street. Jake immediately located the Ladder 157 station chief, flashing his badge as he approached. The chief was consulting a number of his firefighters and a few local cops who had just arrived.

"It's a four-story brownstone, turn-of-the-century construction . . ." the chief was saying.

"Which one's the girl's apartment?" Jake yelled.

"What girl?" one of the cops asked.

"Think she's the third floor," the chief said. He turned to address Jake.

"That's what one of the neighbors said. Bottom two are cleared out. Fourth is empty. Apparently there was a young woman on the third floor, but no one's seen her."

"Third floor?" Jake asked. He stared up at the building. The side of the structure had burned to such a degree that it was practically painted in black ash. Smoke was still billowing out of the third-floor windows. Less smoke emerged from the second floor, and barely any came from the first. "It doesn't look so bad."

"Excuse me, who are you?" the chief asked. Before Jake could respond, the chief was attempting to swipe Jake out of the way. "You gotta move, man. I got a ladder from 174 comin' in behind you."

Jake could hear the ringing sirens of another massive vehicle backing down the street. The chief had moved on, but one of the firefighters pulled Jake aside.

"Detective, issue with this old construction is the facades are reinforced cement, but the walls, floors, and roofs are all wood. So we can't put guys on the roof, and we won't go inside till we have a few feet of clearance from the windows. They'll need to pour a bunch more water in before they make entry, if they even do. Building's a goner. At this point, our priority is protecting the block."

"I need to know if the resident's inside," Jake replied.

"There's been no sign of her. You'll probably have to wait on that." The firefighter shrugged before returning to his work.

Slightly miffed, Jake turned away from the busy firefighters and walked back towards Fong and the SUV.

"What's up?" Fong asked. "Is she in there?"

"Only one way to find out . . ."

Jake opened the back door of Fong's SUV. He yanked a bunch of towels out of a supply bin, along with a bottle of water. He began to pour the water over one of the towels, soaking it. Then he tied the towel around his head, covering his nose and mouth.

"You can't be serious . . ." Fong said. "I mean, you've had some bad ideas but this one is really the tops."

"Did I ask for your opinion?"

"Susan's going to kill me."

"No," Jake replied. "She's going to kill me—but not before I find that girl."

Fong reached behind his back, where Jake knew he stored a weapon at all times.

"Don't even think about it," Jake said.

Fong thought about it.

"Fonger, you are not going to stop me. And I know you're not going to shoot me," Jake said.

Then Jake turned towards the massive ladder ahead and began a dead sprint.

Jake didn't bother to climb the engine using the small stairs that led to the ladder platform. Instead, he clawed his way up the side of the engine and over a rail. He jumped past the surprised ladder operator, who wasn't able to stop him in time.

Jake began to climb up the engine's ladder, which was raised diagonally about fifty feet in the air. He could see a lone firefighter above, standing on the ladder and directing a stream of high-pressure water into the building's third floor. Jake reached the top of the ladder within thirty seconds and vaulted past the firefighter, who was unaware of his arrival. Before anyone was able to stop him, Jake flung himself off the ladder and into the open center window of Katinka's apartment.

▪

The moment Jake's feet touched down inside the building, his body was telling him that his time was limited. A thick fog of black smoke occupied the top two-thirds of each room, and tendrils of flame wrapped around almost every single surface of the apartment. Jake immediately dropped to the floor, where he found a few feet of visibility. He crawled through the apartment's living room towards the kitchen. As he passed the kitchen, he realized that the hallway to the back of the apartment and the bedroom was totally blocked by fire.

"Katinka! Can you hear me? Where are you?" Jake screamed.

There was no response except for the whip-like crackle of flames.

Jake rotated back a hundred and eighty degrees. He couldn't be sure if she was in the apartment or not, but he definitely knew it was time to go. As he passed the small kitchen alcove for the second time, Jake suddenly stopped crawling. Through the pall of smoke, Jake could make out a large mass on the kitchen floor. It wasn't moving. He moved another foot forward, and it became clear to Jake that the object was a woman's body. She had red hair. He didn't need to see any more. It was definitely Katinka, and he could tell she was dead.

Jake could barely breathe. Time was of the essence. As he crawled back towards the windows, he started to become disoriented. All of a sudden, it seemed as if the windows ahead were disappearing. Or maybe he was going the wrong direction? Jake felt his vision collapsing around him. The cone of light that was the center window of the living room got smaller and smaller until it disappeared. His true north was gone. What the hell was happening? Was it him, or was it the smoke? For the first time, Jake's adrenaline began to let him down, and he started to experience fear. Soon, he couldn't see anything at all. He continued to scramble along the living room floor. He tried to use his hands to orient himself, pulling his body along the length of the living room rug. He reached for the exterior wall . . .

What Jake wasn't able to see was the sharp corner of a coffee table positioned against the wall. His head bashed into the table and a wave of pain spread through his brain like a supernova blast.

Then Jake Rivett lost consciousness.

CHAPTER TWELVE

MONA.

She was the first person he saw in Heaven.

Or was it the hospital?

Jake lifted his arms slightly. He could feel an IV needle in his left wrist restricting movement, but he could shift his right arm. He felt gingerly around his head and discovered a huge bandage wrapped over his forehead—protecting his right eye and ear.

His vision of Mona flickered ahead as he fully opened his left eye. He was indeed in a hospital room. And yes, Mona was actually standing in front of him.

Mona saw that Jake was awake and burst into tears.

"Don't worry about me," were the first words out of Jake's mouth.

Wrong thing to say.

"Worry about you?" Mona replied between sobs. "How about me?"

"I'm sorry."

Mona finally leaned in to kiss Jake. She was apparently happy he was alive, but he could tell that she was oh, oh, so mad.

"I have two questions," Mona said. "First, how do you feel?"

"I feel . . . not horrible, actually. How long have I been out?"

"The fire was yesterday."

"What's the second question?"

"What the hell's wrong with you?"

"Yeah. You're right. I have some work to do . . . on myself . . ."

"I'm not going to marry someone with a death wish."

"I don't want that . . ."

"Then what's your problem?"

"I get blinded," Jake finally responded.

"You get stupid," Mona said. She started to tear up again.

"You're my priority," Jake said.

"Don't think so . . ." Mona shook her head. She finally straightened out. "We'll talk about it later. You were burnt. Big laceration on your face, but it just missed your eye. The doctors told me I'll probably be able to take over tomorrow."

"You're still going to take care of me?"

Mona nodded. "Then I'll figure out what *my* priority is."

"I . . ."

"Yeah?"

"I think I need to rest more."

"I agree."

"I love you, Mona," Jake said.

"Thank you," she replied.

"Do you?" he asked groggily.

She didn't answer, and he fell asleep.

■

"Only reason I won't put that guy in a hospital bed is 'cause he's already in one."

Those were the first words Jake heard when he woke up the second time. But now Mona wasn't there. Instead, the entire brain trust of the joint task force was assembled around Jake. Their expressions ran the gamut. Pete Mack was so mad that his face was bright red and all he could do was sputter. Tony and Fong were the most calm, probably because they knew Jake the best. Susan stood next to Tony, the hands on her hips mirroring her incredulous expression. Even in anger, her sass shone through. She was grinning like a shark who'd happened upon a family of minnows. Finally, Mr. White sat in a chair in the back of the room, with Moseley leaning behind him. Neither of them seemed willing to express any opinion at all.

"Katinka's dead," Jake said first.

"No shit, Sherlock," Pete Mack said.

"Don't patronize him," Susan cut in. "The only similarity Rivett shares with Sherlock Holmes is a terrible sense of fashion."

"So I'm right . . ."

"It wasn't really necessary for you to risk your life to figure that one out, Jake," Tony said.

"His life?" Pete Mack said. "How about the firefighters that had to go in there and save him? Did he think about them? I'm sorry, Susan, but if this guy is your best, then maybe the NYPD needs to step out of the way."

"Don't be hysterical," Susan replied. "You need me. But you're right about one thing—I don't think any of us need Detective Rivett."

"Hey!" Jake yelled. "Stop talking about me. There is no one angrier at myself than me. That's my problem to work out. But everyone in this room? We are *nowhere*. Absolutely *nowhere*! You wanna know what I was thinking, or are you just going to sit there and pile on? I thought to myself . . . If there's a one-percent chance I can find that girl alive, we're all going to be that much closer to finding the doctor and figuring out who

Hayat was working with. You want to yell and scream? Fine. Maybe it makes you feel better. Maybe it brings you up. Doesn't help us, though. Only thing that's going to move the needle is figuring out what's going on. Take me off if you want. Hell, do whatever you think you need to cover your ass, Susan. But this is still my case. The second I get out of the bed, this is my case. When I go to sleep, it's my case. When I wake up, it's my goddamn case."

"I don't cover my ass, Rivett," Susan replied. "I shake it in people's faces and dare them to try something. Don't start thinking anyone in this room doesn't want to find Hayat as badly as you do. Have some goddamn faith in the full power of the lawman. And in case you're not sure who the fucking lawman is—it's *me*."

As usual, Susan had a way with words that rendered the room silent for a few moments.

"Peter, let's go. Rivett, don't come back until I decide what to do with you," Susan commanded.

After Susan and Peter had exited the room, Tony approached Jake's bed.

"So you think they took the girl out on purpose?" Tony asked.

"Absolutely."

"I'm running everything we possibly can on the doctor. We got a lot more of his backstory. Still can't find him."

"Family? Relationships?"

"Mom lives way out in Long Island, middle of nowhere. Interviewed her this morning. Real God-fearing lady. Christian with a Jewish last name. Came from her late husband, I guess. She says there's very few friends and no girlfriend. Closest the doctor had to a girlfriend, actually, was Katinka Johanssen. But that's just because they used to work together and he'd talk about her. Mom says she hasn't seen or heard from him since he moved out of Stony Brook four months ago."

"I should be good to go tomorrow."

"Impossible," Mona's voice interrupted. She'd stepped back in the room.

Jake grinned. "Maybe you're right."

"I'm right," Mona replied.

"She's right," Tony added.

"I don't know, detective," Mr. White spoke up from his chair, an eyebrow raised. "You seem to specialize in proving everyone wrong."

CHAPTER THIRTEEN

THE FIRST TIME OMER AMIN heard of Pat Welch was a year prior, when Grant High School's soccer team was paraded through the cafeteria during lunch period. The school had been honoring the players for appearing in their state division's semifinal soccer match. Grant High School in Astoria wasn't known for much—certainly not their sports teams. The school did not prioritize athletics. In the back of the campus, there was barely space for one full playing field. Both the football and soccer teams shared the pitch, alternating practice times. Pat Welch was the captain of said soccer team and was perhaps the only sporting star that Omer could remember having ever emerged from Grant. Pat had singlehandedly scored fifty-two goals during the past season, more goals than any striker in their entire division. He was on track for similar stats that year. It was even rumored that Pat was going to NYU on a soccer scholarship after graduation, but Omer wasn't quite sure about that. The truth was that Omer had spent almost four years at Grant and had never spoken to Pat Welch. Omer had barely even thought about him—except to know that he was good at soccer.

It was sometime in mid-October when Omer realized he'd have to pay closer attention to Pat Welch. The realization began when Omer's class schedule changed. Instead of Omer waiting for Salma after school on the front steps, as he had for three years, Salma began to wait for Omer. Then one day Omer exited the school but couldn't find Salma anywhere. He finally located her sitting on the cement wall that separated the sports field from the sidewalk. From then on, Salma would wait by the wall instead of the front steps of the school. At first Omer didn't think anything of it, until the day he turned down the street and saw Pat Welch leaning over his sister. Pat whispered something flirtatious in Salma's ear and lightly touched her lower back before he ran back onto the field.

On that particular evening, the walk home had been fraught with tension. Omer wasn't happy about what he'd seen, and he let Salma know in no uncertain terms.

"What are you doing? You can't talk to that guy. You know how pissed off our parents would be if they knew," Omer said.

"You're going to stop right there," Salma said. "You don't get to say that."

And she was right. Even as he had said the words, he wasn't sure that he actually meant them. But Salma wasn't done.

"I'm the one who protects you. Don't get preachy with me. Don't think I don't know about how you steal makeup from me, and who knows what you're doing with it . . . Actually, what *are* you doing with my makeup?"

"I go out to the shows. You know that—"

"Whatever. You know what? The point is I don't actually care what you're doing, because I know you're a good person. I know you wouldn't do anything to get yourself or anyone else in trouble. And I trust you. So do you trust me?"

"Obviously. Yes. I do," Omer replied. "I just don't want Dad finding out. And even worse would be Mom or Murad."

"Well, there's nothing for them to find out, and they're not going to find out anything anyway."

"So what's the real deal? Is Pat Welch your boyfriend?"

"We just talk," she said.

And talk they did. From that afternoon onwards, it became clear that Salma and Pat were becoming a thing. After another month, Salma began to stay at school until soccer practice was over. That was fine with Omer, because he didn't like being home for long periods of time. So he'd wait until Salma was done hanging with Pat, and then the two of them would walk home together.

▪

It was the last few days of the fall semester, just before the holiday break. Omer noticed that Pat was standing on the sidewalk next to Salma —in his school clothes. That was very uncharacteristic.

"Hey, Omes," Pat said.

"Pat," Omer replied with a nod.

"Since the holidays are coming up, I was going to walk with you guys. Gonna have to be away from my girl for too long!"

"Salma, you think that's a good idea?" Omer asked his sister.

What was unsaid between the two siblings was not just their family dynamic, but also the close-knit nature of the community they lived in. The streets were somewhat anonymous, but not fully. The Amin family was well known due to their prominent and public-facing business. One never knew if the clerk at Zaman's, or the guy working on cars at the corner of Steinway and Thirty-First might notice Salma and Pat walking together and take enough issue with what they saw to bring it up to Moradi. It was a long shot, but it was possible. Omer was naturally risk averse. He did everything he could to avoid conflict and make sure the spotlight was never on him. He knew that his father might not particularly care. But fury would rain down upon the siblings if their mom found out—and Moradi knew better than to try to lie to Azza. All of this was unsaid but nonetheless realized by Salma. That's why she came up with the idea that Pat Welch was going to be Omer's friend.

"You guys are friends," Salma announced. "I'm just your sister . . . and I walk with you, too!"

And with that, Salma had implicated Omer in the plan to keep his sister's budding romance safe from prying eyes. The three of them padded down the sidewalk westward, towards the Amin family's cleaning business.

"So if we got married, would you still be Muslim?" Pat asked in a remarkably earnest way.

"Of course," Salma said.

"That's just ridiculous," Omer said. "You're sixteen years old."

"We're not getting married," Salma said.

"Yeah, dude, are you cray?" Pat said. "But wait, what about our kids? I'm Catholic, you know . . ."

"Hypothetical kids . . ." Omer muttered.

"How many do you want?" Salma asked.

"A lot."

"The whole thing's impossible," Omer said.

"Huh? What about pure love? Your family wouldn't deny pure love, would they?"

"Yes. They most definitely would," Omer said.

"I don't know, actually." Salma thought about it. "Each of us are so different. Omer's mostly afraid of our family values . . ."

"Hey!" Omer protested.

"It's true. Murad . . . He's like the enforcer of them. But I feel like I'm the one they all listen to. Dad would be fine. Mom would have a fit. She probably wouldn't talk to me for a year. But I know she'd keep loving me. By the way, I'll always be Muslim. That's never changing. But the world changes around us, and I'm not the person who's going to tell anyone else what to do with their life. Omer knows that."

Omer nodded. He couldn't really focus on their conversation anymore, because Steinway was coming up, and it was already making him nervous.

"Don't you think Pat should head off now?" Omer asked.

"He's your friend . . ." Salma shrugged. "That's up to you guys."

"No way!" Pat said. "I'll hang out with my pals all the way to their house."

"Don't think so," Omer said as they turned the corner. "This is the place. It's not worth it, Salma."

"Fine," Salma replied. "If I don't see you beforehand, good luck at the game tomorrow," she said to Pat.

"I'll see you. I promise. Later, Omes," Pat said. He stuck out his hand in a fist bump towards Omer, who awkwardly tried to cup it into a handshake. Pat shrugged the encounter off. Then he wrapped his arm around Salma in an awkward side hug. As he pulled his hand away, he brushed down her arm and their fingers intertwined for a brief moment. Pat turned and headed back the other direction.

Omer and Salma continued padding down the sidewalk towards Steinway Cleaners.

"Omes?"

"It's cute."

"Not my name," Omer said.

"It's a good thing. You could take a couple lessons in coolness from Pat," Salma said.

"You really think you know what you're doing?"

"He's kind and funny, and at the end of the day he's right. We shouldn't create artificial barriers."

"I know he's right. Doesn't mean dating him is the right thing to do."

"I'm not worried, Omer."

"How come?"

"Because I have you."

They finally reached Steinway Cleaners. Salma pulled open the door and gestured dramatically for Omer to enter. He did. They danced their way inside.

▪

What neither Omer nor Salma knew was that someone was watching them. A few blocks back, a man stood inside a convenience store. He'd been spying on the three young adults for the last five minutes of their walk. The man didn't need to watch them, of course, because he knew two of them very well. But Murad Amin had certainly learned something new about his younger siblings—one was dating a white boy, and the other was protecting them.

CHAPTER FOURTEEN

RIVETT ONLY HAD ONE GOOD eye. The other was wrapped up with a pound and a half of surgical gauze and he'd promised the doctors at Weill Cornell Hospital that he wouldn't cut it off himself. Meanwhile, Mona had quickly learned that Jake made for a terrible patient. He had been instructed to spend at least three days in bed, but after one night of sleep, Jake was already sitting on the couch in the living room. He was surrounded by a potent mix of hospital-prescribed painkillers, Gatorade, Chinese food, his laptop, and reams of printed pages of evidence from the Hayat investigation.

As promised, Rivett was still on the case. That morning, he had called Tony at home to catch up on the investigation, and Tony wasn't stupid enough to try to knock Jake Rivett out of the box. He had revealed to Jake that the joint task force had successfully utilized a cell-phone tower triangulation technique, mastered by the CIA after 9/11, to track down Dr. Borin's number. The method worked by cross-referencing data from the three closest cell towers to the Bossonovs' rental lot and loading every device present at the same time Dr. Borin had appeared in the surveillance video. The hard part was identifying and eliminating all of the erroneous phone numbers that were scooped up by the algorithm.

The process could take as long as a month or two during a normal investigation, but the feds had completed the task in less than forty-eight hours. It was confirmed that Dr. Borin had a cell phone in his pocket when he spoke to Axel Bossonov. However, the joint task force's overall assessment was that Borin rarely used the phone. It seemed he hadn't contacted anyone out of the ordinary, or really anyone personal at all. In one year, Borin had sent less than ten texts. He had not used the browser function on the phone, nor downloaded any apps. As for his calls, they consisted of a long list of big-box stores, taxicab companies, and takeout restaurants.

Tony had emailed Jake a secure PDF with Dr. Borin's phone records, along with the FBI analysts' conclusions and research notes. Jake had been up all morning reviewing every single line item on the list, but he'd found nothing that made him doubt the team's conclusions. The work wasn't fun, but Jake knew it was necessary. He didn't love the slog. It just sometimes happened to solve cases.

He continued checking the entries from Dr. Borin's logs. He was looking for anomalies, but he was especially interested in numbers that the FBI's investigators had yet to assign an identity to—about ten percent of the calls. Nothing interesting was coming to the surface, except Jake did keep running across outgoing calls to an unknown number with a 631 area code. The analysts had been unable to figure out who was behind the 631 number. It wasn't Mrs. Borin's number, it didn't belong to any of Dr. Borin's few friends or former colleagues, and it wasn't coming back as a business. The number was registered to a prepaid wireless carrier. Although he knew the FBI would already be working on the carrier, Jake's interest was piqued. Where was 631? Jake loaded a map and discovered that 631 encompassed the entire eastern portion of Long Island. Hadn't

Tony mentioned that Borin's mother lived out there in the boonies? But the analysts said it wasn't her number . . .

Jake sighed. It was hard to focus with only one eye. He placed the records down and stared out the window. One of the nicest features of their new apartment was the large bay window in the living room, which afforded a perfectly framed view of the Brooklyn Bridge leading over the East River to Manhattan. Jake studied the beautiful pointed arches of the neo-Gothic suspension bridge for a while, until his vision became blurry from fatigue.

"Frustrated?" Mona asked from the kitchen table. She was working from home.

"Beyond," Jake admitted.

"Maybe it's time to take a nap. Rest your eyes."

"I hate naps."

"Sometimes people need to do things they don't like in order to get to where they want to be."

"Just like you taking care of me?"

"Bingo."

Jake leaned back on the couch for a brief moment. Then he shot back up.

"Can't let another attack go down . . ."

"It's not all on you, Jake."

"Can't sleep. Can barely eat. I'm nervous. Everything about the case bugs me. Hayat's dead, but he has no past. Someone went to extremes to hide him from society. Then with the doctor, it's the opposite. He's too normal. Who owns a cell phone and never browses the web? How does that happen? So is he a nothing, or is someone protecting him, too? Was Katinka right? Is the doctor creating some sort of terror machine? Is that what he's all about, or is it a means to an end? And most importantly . . . where is he?"

"Maybe you're looking too hard."

"What do you mean?"

"I mean . . . people want clean and easy reasons for things. It's what feels good. But that's not how the world works. Just like us. Think about how we tell our story to people we've met."

"We say we met at a party."

"Exactly. It's not a full-on lie. We sort of did. But the truth is, like, so much more spaghetti. It's messy. Lots of moving parts. You were investigating my ex-boyfriend but ended up respecting him, and meanwhile I was just about to go full-on criminal. But people don't really care. Their eyes gloss over after a sentence or two, even though it could fill a book. So we just go with the simple answer, even if it's not the full answer."

"What's your point?"

"You're probably not going to find easy connections. Maybe there's nothing there. Maybe Hayat was just a hermit. Maybe the doctor is just a boring dude, angry and out of a job. Maybe Hayat met him on the street and paid him to rent a truck. Maybe there's no conspiracy. In fact, there's probably no conspiracy."

"But maybe there is . . ."

"I see I'm really making an impact here," Mona joked. "Can we change the subject?"

"Sure."

"Do you feel up to coming to my sister's tomorrow?"

"Tomorrow?"

"Yes, Jake. Tomorrow's Sunday. You haven't been in a while. If you're so sure you don't need my help anymore, that means you're probably well enough to come see Adriana and the girls."

"You see her pretty much every Sunday . . ."

"Jesus. You do need a nap."

"No, Mona . . . Hold on . . ." Jake scrambled towards the pile of phone records in front of him. He scanned through the list as quickly as he could, looking for the 631 numbers. "Maxine Borin," he finally said. "It's gotta be . . ."

"Who's that?"

"Maximilian Borin's mother. Also named Max, which is weird but not the point . . ." Jake continued scanning. "Yes!" he finally yelled out. "Maybe Maxine Borin goes to church—same time every Sunday. Then when she's back, her son calls—not her main line, but some burner he gave her. Everyone saw the 631 number, but they weren't looking at it the right way. It's not the number itself that matters. It's *when* Borin calls. Every single call is on a Sunday morning between ten twenty-eight and ten thirty-one in the morning. It's so consistent. And . . ."

"Yes?" Mona asked.

"Tomorrow's Sunday."

"But you, Jake Rivett, aren't available," Mona replied.

Jake sprung from the couch. He stretched his neck. He paced into the kitchen. He turned towards Mona with a large kitchen knife in his hands and a maniacal smile on his face.

"Cut the bandage off, Mona."

"You promised the doctors . . ."

"If you don't, I will."

CHAPTER FIFTEEN

THE DAYS BLURRED. RIVETT WASN'T sure if it had been five nights or a week since the Bryant Park bombing. It didn't matter. Fuzzy was the status quo—the days, his eyes, the case. What mattered was that he could somehow pull it all into focus. As Jake sat shotgun in Tony's SUV and watched the urban blocks of the city deteriorate into the splotchy forest of Long Island, he realized they were at the very worst part of the investigation—the *nadir*. Most detectives would be afraid now. Jake was different. He felt anxiety on the way down, but once he was there and actually swimming at the bottom, he became more calm. He welcomed the feeling. In a way, it was similar to how he felt onstage—except that a song only lasted for a few minutes, whereas a case could go for months. That's why Rivett loved being a detective.

"How's Susan?" Jake asked.

"As if you want to know . . ." Tony replied.

"She hate me?"

"Yes—very much so," Tony answered. "But . . ."

"Yeah?"

"Deep down inside, I'm pretty sure she loves you."

"Like a brother?"

"More like a pet."

Jake chuckled. "Is she gonna let me back in the room?"

"No idea. And I'm not doing your dirty work on that."

"Does she know we're going to see Borin's mother?"

"Mr. White signed off. With Susan, it was more of a 'you know, dear' . . . I left out the part where you're with me."

"Smart. A Unodir," Jake said. Unodir was short for *UNless Otherwise DIRected.* It was one of Jake and Tony's favorite memo subject lines to write when they wanted to begin an operation.

"That's how I get promoted," Tony replied.

"You get promoted. I get sick pay."

"Same, same."

Rivett and Tony soon entered the small hamlet of Farmingville— located at just about the center of Long Island.

"Some balls on Maxine Borin to say her son called from different numbers . . ." Jake said.

"It's a hunch, Rivett."

"Cracked cases with much less."

"Maybe we'll sit down with this nice old lady and get nothing at all."

"Truth," Jake admitted.

"We'll know soon enough," Tony said. He tapped on the small clock on the SUV's instrument panel. It was ten twenty in the morning.

"How far out are we?"

"Six minutes."

"Can't be late," Rivett said. "Fong's ready on the other side, right?"

"Yeah—he and Moseley. They're at the AT&T substation right now. Everything's ready for the live trace. If he calls, think he'll talk?"

"Normally I'd say no way, but just like the real Einstein, nothing this guy does makes any sense to me," Rivett answered.

The sky was turning from blue to purple above them. Rivett gazed out the window, deep in thought, as it began to rain. It was always glorious heading east, towards the sea, when a winter rainstorm began. The clouds were an obvious tell, and a beautiful one. As the first raindrops splattered down on the windshield, Rivett felt himself becoming even more zen. There wasn't going to be an audience at this time, at least not in the room—not except for Tony and Maxine. But he was still going to perform.

▪

Maxine Borin's house was everything Rivett expected and more. Her small wood-paneled cape home was painted a pale yellow and situated in a modest neighborhood. Most remarkable to the two detectives was her front yard. It was accented by dozens of lawn ornaments of all shapes and sizes. Mrs. Borin didn't stick to a particular theme. There were garden gnomes, windmills, flamingos, giant mushrooms—you name it. Rivett had to stop and gawk for just a moment. Then he remembered there was a time crunch and that it was go time.

Knock-knock. Rivett rapped his hand on the door. He was surprised to hear an elderly lady's voice yelling back almost immediately.

"What do you want?"

"Police, ma'am."

The door opened and Maxine Borin stared out. She was in her eighties, wearing a maroon cardigan festooned with sequin patterns and black pants. A pair of reading glasses hung from her neck, and she pulled them up to gaze at Jake and Tony.

"Anthony! You're lucky. I just got back from church."

"Hi, Maxine," Tony replied, glancing at Jake. "This is Detective Rivett.

We're here for a routine follow up." Tony grinned his friendliest grin at Maxine.

"All right. Well, you two can come in . . . but just because you're here, Anthony. You were such a delightful guest last time. Want some more cookies? I can make lemonade."

"Oh, we already ate—"

"We'll take some cookies—happily. And maybe just water?" Jake said.

"You can't have cookies without milk or lemonade. Milk?"

"Lemonade, please," Jake replied.

Once they were inside the home, Rivett quickly eyed the interior. Maxine's house was filled with tchotchkes. The walls were framed with large glass cabinets full of everything from expensive crystal glassware to cheap plastic birds balancing on small cones. Maxine's living room was clearly organized for Maxine to live in. Her well-worn La-Z-Boy sat in the middle of the room with a small table next to it filled with calendars, a rotary telephone, pillboxes, and TV remotes. Jake clocked the telephone. Most likely, that was the phone number the FBI already had—not the one they were looking for.

Maxine pulled a Tupperware bin off her dining room table. It was filled with homemade cookies. Jake thought to himself that either she had plenty of visitors or she wanted plenty of visitors. While she placed the cookies on a plate, Jake scanned across a series of framed photographs on the wall above her Laz-E-Boy. A number of the photos clearly displayed Maxine with her son, Maximilian. Only one photograph seemed to feature a man whom Jake assumed was Maxine's husband—the three of them sitting on a small dock in front of a lake.

"Maxine, did you name your son after you?" Jake asked.

"Almost didn't. But I won. Always do."

Jake chuckled. "What do you mean?"

"Well, my late husband really thought that was a bad idea. Not like *he* wanted a junior. I think he simply didn't want Maxie to be *my* junior. Bless his heart."

"How'd you convince him?"

"Put him in a choke hold," Maxine said dryly.

Jake and Tony stopped for a moment to check her face. Then Maxine burst out laughing. The detectives joined in.

"That's him?" Jake pointed to the photograph by the lake.

"Yes." Maxine nodded. "That's Jerry Borin. He was trying to teach Maxie to swim. But Jerry wasn't good at much, and Maxie never did what he was told either. It didn't go well. He never did learn to swim, actually. Always felt bad about that." She held up the cookies. "Cookie?"

After accepting their cookies, the two detectives followed Maxine around the room until she finally sat down. Jake could see that she was just an arm's length from her house phone. He pulled out his own cell phone and set it on his lap. Idly tapping the home button, Jake learned it was ten twenty-eight—just two minutes until the call, if there was going to be one.

"So, really, Mrs. Borin, the reason that we're here is—"

"I prefer Ms. Borin now."

"Okay, Ms. Borin. Reason I had Tony come back today is just because we're having a hell of a time finding your son. Nothing's working. I thought that I could talk to you, 'cause I heard you're an honest lady who just wants to help. You haven't heard from him at all?"

"My lovebug used to call. He also used to visit from Stony Brook, but not in a while." Maxine shook her head. "Last I think I heard from him was five months ago . . ."

Rivett glanced at his phone. The digits flickered to ten twenty-nine. "What if there was an emergency? You obviously love Max. He loves you. How are you supposed to contact him if you went to the hospital or something?" Jake asked.

"Well . . ." Maxine paused. "Hadn't quite thought about that. That's a really good question. I figure whenever I see him next, he's going to hear it from me."

"When did he leave the Stony Brook apartment?" Tony said.

"He did?" Maxine seemed confused.

"He didn't tell you?"

She shook her head in confusion.

Jake spoke up. "Is it possible that he's abandoned you, Ms. Borin?"

The question hung in the air. Maxine took a deep breath. Jake caught her glancing ever-so-slightly towards the kitchen. "That's just a ridiculous question. Anthony, is this man being silly? Maxie would never, ever, abandon me. He loves me. And, anyway, he wouldn't be allowed to. Mother's in charge. He knows that."

"But he doesn't call. He doesn't come see you. And he hasn't told you where he is . . ."

"Jesus, Mary, and Joseph. You don't seem so smart," Maxine exclaimed and then sighed. "Forgive me for taking the Lord's name in vain. You don't understand what I'm saying. I don't need to know where Maxie is to know that I'm the most important thing in the world to him."

Jake was having trouble stalling. The phone beside Maxine still hadn't rung. Maybe this wouldn't be his Sunday. The call records they'd pulled were very, very specific. If the call came, it was never more than a minute or two on either side of ten thirty. Jake knew he was missing something. But what was it?

"I think . . . Listen, Ms. Borin. I'm not religious. Least not as much as you. My mother was and my father wasn't, and sometimes I'm more like him than I care to admit. But I do believe there's *something* out there. So maybe we just take a moment of silence here and think about the things that we have in our lives and how much they mean to us. How's that sound?"

"That sounds wonderful, detective."

Jake cut Tony a look. Without further ado, the three of them closed their eyes and sat in silence in Ms. Borin's living room.

That's when Jake heard what he needed to hear—*no, not God.* Instead, he was aware of the slightest sensation. He could perceive a buzzing— somewhere between a vibration and a sound. He knew what he was sensing. It was a phone. But where?

"Lemonade," Jake erupted.

All three of them opened their eyes.

"I forgot!" Maxine said.

"Don't worry, Ms. Borin. I'll get it."

Jake stood and paced into the kitchen. He knew Maxine was shuffling in behind him. But once he was in the kitchen, he could hear the buzzing much better. Although the noise was muffled, Jake could tell the vibration was emanating from one of the kitchen drawers. He began to pull the drawers and cabinets open, one by one, until he reached a counter-height drawer to the right of the sink. He yanked it open to find a small flip phone. An unknown number was calling.

Jake didn't think. He opened the phone and spoke.

"Is this the doctor?" Jake asked.

"Yes, and, uh, who's this?" Maximilian Borin answered.

"Where are you?"

Click. Dr. Borin hung up.

CHAPTER SIXTEEN

EARLY ON MONDAY AFTERNOON, OMER stepped off the front steps of Grant High School and began his daily walk towards the sports fields. He knew that Pat had a game today and Salma would be spectating. When Omer turned onto the sidewalk that ran down the length of the school's property, he heard someone yelling his name.

"Omer!"

Omer recognized the voice immediately. It wasn't just any someone. He lifted his head and noticed that one of his father's dry-cleaning vans was parked at the entrance to the school—and Murad was yelling at him out of the open window.

"Hey, brother! Want a ride?"

Omer stepped towards the van, resting his arms on the window frame.

"I'm okay. It's not far. What are you doing?"

"Deliveries. But I'm done. Figured I'd zip over here and might help out my little kid siblings for once. Where's Salma?"

She was just down the block, but thankfully still out of sight from Murad.

"Don't know . . ."

"Don't you guys walk home together?"

"I meet her here." Omer shrugged. "Maybe she's still in class . . ."

"All right. Well, I'll give you a ride, then. Get in." Murad reached over to the door and opened it.

"I should wait for her, I think."

"Come on, Omer. I gotta get going. I'm doing you a favor. *Get in.*"

Faced with no particularly logical reason why he shouldn't take his brother's offer, Omer jumped into the van. Murad began driving around the block and away from the school. Omer was relieved to see that he was taking a route that completely avoided the sports field on the south end of the property.

"How's school? How are the chicks?" Murad asked.

"It's good." Omer shrugged. "I'm not too worried about girls."

"That's good. Maybe if you study, you'll be able to do more than me. Driving Dad's van around all day . . . Though it ain't terrible. Gives me freedom. Get to see the whole city filled with all its miserable people."

"Right," Omer said.

"What about Salma?"

"What about her?"

"You're keeping track of her, right?"

"Of course. I'm her brother."

"Yeah. So am I," Murad said. He slowed down, waiting for the traffic passing on the left to proceed past. With a sudden turn of the wheel, Murad ripped the van into a U-turn. "Omer . . . You and me might have a different sense of what it means to take care of our sister. A woman never walks over a man. Do you understand me? Especially not a sister."

"What do you mean?" Omer stumbled. He saw that Murad was driving directly towards the sports field. Murad jammed his foot on the accelerator of the van, his eyes narrowing, and aimed directly at the bleachers to the side of the athletic field.

"You know . . . Tell me what I mean, brother."

"What are you doing?" Omer gripped a handle in the van, glancing at Murad nervously.

Murad accelerated. The speedometer moved up slowly, from twenty to twenty-five . . .

Ahead, Omer could make out Salma chatting with Pat Welch. His arm was around her waist.

"When were you going to tell us about Salma?" Murad yelled.

"Slow down! Stop it!"

"When?"

"I don't know! I'm sorry!" Omer began to cry as the van crossed the double yellow lines in the center of the street. It seemed to Omer that Murad was planning on crashing directly into the bleachers.

At the very last millisecond, Murad whipped the wheel back in the right direction. He swerved the van into its lane and passed by Salma and Pat—who had noticed nothing at all.

"You know the rules, Omer. I didn't make them up. They are bigger than any of us. Salma can't date anyone without permission and chaperones. She definitely can't date a non-Muslim. I'm very disappointed in you. Thought that you cared about our family, but maybe you're just as bad as she is—because you've been protecting her. Maybe you've been idle, but I won't be."

"I'll talk to her, Murad," Omer promised.

"The time for talking is over. You talk. I take action."

"You won't hurt her . . ."

"You don't decide what's going to happen."

"And Dad?"

"Dad will do whatever Mom says. Whatever I might want to do, Mom will be ten times worse."

"Please. Let me handle it. I'll make sure she never sees the soccer player again. What can I do so you'll let me?" Omer knew his brother was a loose cannon. He needed to buy a little time to figure out what to do.

"Maybe there's a world where I'll let you take care of it, just for a little . . . But if not, I'm going straight to Mom."

"What do you want?"

"The business club. At the restaurant. You know?"

"Yeah . . ."

"We need some help. There's a delivery, and I need an extra hand."

"So I help you, and you won't mess with Salma?"

"As long as you solve the problem."

"Deal, brother," Omer agreed.

■

After a brief dinner with the family, during which Murad gazed at Salma menacingly but did not say anything, Murad and Omer headed out again in the van. Their first assignment, Murad told Omer, was a pickup to the east. Omer wasn't exactly sure where they were going. Murad himself had never been there. He only had an address, as well as an invoice for two containers.

"Can I put it into navigation?" Omer asked Murad.

"No!" Murad yelled.

"Why?"

"Just don't. I pretty much know how to get there."

They headed east into Long Island, eventually exiting the highway and turning down a road framed by warehouses. At the final building, a skinny man stood underneath a lone streetlamp, playing on his cell phone. The two brothers parked and exited their father's van.

"Joey?" Murad asked.

The skinny man didn't say anything. He just nodded and stepped towards a small access door to the warehouse. He entered the structure and disappeared into the darkness.

"Are we supposed to go in there with him?" Omer asked.

"I . . . I don't know," Murad finally responded.

They stood out in the cold and misting rain for about a minute.

"Maybe I should go in," Murad said.

"Are you sure? Is it safe?"

"They've already been paid for . . ."

At that moment, the massive warehouse door began to rise. They had their answer. Once the door was open, the two brothers could make out a forklift heading their way, holding a square plastic container filled with a viscous liquid. The container itself sat inside an aluminum cage designed to provide extra support. The whole contraption was about the size of a washing machine.

"Turn the van around," Murad instructed Omer.

The skinny man operated the forklift. He drove the container towards the van and then stopped and waited for Omer to back it up.

"Can two of us carry it?" Murad asked.

"Heavy but doable," the man said.

"And you're Joey, right?" Murad asked.

"Doesn't matter."

"Okay," Murad answered after a moment. "But there's two containers, right?"

"Correct," the man answered.

Omer jumped out of the van and ran around to the back. He opened the doors. Omer and Murad stood on each side of the container and lifted it into the back of the van. There would be just enough room for two containers and nothing more. It took about twenty minutes for them to fully load the van with the mysterious cargo. When they were done, Murad handed the invoice and written address to the skinny man.

The man grabbed the paperwork. "Thanks," he said. "Did you write down this address?"

"No." Murad shook his head. "Only what's on there."

"And no phones, right? No Google?"

"As instructed," Murad confirmed.

"Good," the skinny man said. He reached into his pocket and pulled out a lighter. He flicked the lighter and lit the invoice. The three men stood in the dark and watched the fire engulf the invoice. The paper burned until it transformed into a piece of ash, which was picked up by the wind and carried off into the mist.

"Good doing business," the skinny man said. "Remember—you were never here. I was never here. We never met. This never happened. That's how my people operate, and we expect our counterparts to do the same—*or else.*" With that, the skinny man walked back into the warehouse, and the bay door slowly rolled shut.

"Or else what?" Omer asked Murad, a tinge of anxiety in his voice.

"What do you think, Omer?" Murad said. "Don't sit around worrying. Just follow his instructions. I know I will."

"What is this stuff?"

"Chemicals."

"For what?"

"Our product."

"And what's that, Murad?"

"You're just helping out, brother. You're not a member of the club. So shut up and remember our deal, all right?"

▪

"This is your brother?" were the first words out of Alim Hanafi's mouth when he saw Omer pacing behind Murad and into Best Diner. It was well after midnight.

"Yeah. Like I told you . . ." Murad said.

"What's your name?" Hanafi asked.

"Omer."

"Are you a man of faith, Omer?"

"I'm a Muslim," Omer said as he nodded, but then he shrugged in a decidedly noncommittal manner. He'd promised his brother that he'd help out, not alter his life philosophy.

"A good Muslim?" Hanafi inquired.

"Sure," Omer said.

"Absolutely," Murad added. "You don't need to worry about my brother. He's a solid kid. Knows when to keep his mouth shut. He has respect."

"Fine," Hanafi said. "Because we need your hands, but we don't need loose lips. Everything's coming to a head. So, young Omer, the only reason you're allowed in the club is because of Murad. I don't know you. But I do know Murad. Very well. And . . . I trust him." Hanafi turned to Murad. "And the pick-up?"

"The van's full," Murad said.

"Excellent timing. I've received word that our investor has arrived."

"The man from Dubai?" Murad asked.

"Yes. He's in New York," Hanafi said. "Bring the chemicals

downstairs."

Omer and Murad opened the back of the Steinway Cleaners van. They lifted one of the plastic containers and painstakingly carried it down to the basement. It was tough going, like moving a dishwasher, with only inches to spare on each side of the stairs. Hanafi could have helped, but instead he simply watched from the bottom level. Once Omer and Murad reached the basement, the brothers were able to lay the container on a dolly and push the liquid down the hallway. They placed the container in a large storage room filled with all manner of industrial restaurant supplies. Then they repeated the process one more time. After the final trip, Omer followed Murad into the prayer room in the basement.

"Tea or cookies?" Murad asked.

"Sure," Omer replied. Omer gazed around the room. There was nothing particularly out of the ordinary about the space. It had the same familiar look—austere, yet faithful—that Omer knew from most prayer rooms.

"So what's the technology you're working on? What's in those containers?" Omer asked.

Murad cut Omer a sharp look, but Hanafi jumped in.

"Fuel," Hanafi quickly replied. "And the technology is proprietary. Can't talk about it with you—not yet. That's the truth about innovation. Once it's out there in the ether . . . you lose it. And then there's no saying whose hands it will end up in—"

All of a sudden, a bookcase in the back of the room began to rotate into the wall, revealing a secret passageway.

"That's all for now, gentlemen," Hanafi said. "Go on home. I'm sure you're tired. And thank you, Omer. It was wonderful meeting you."

Omer and Murad stood up. As Hanafi attempted to hurry them out and close the door, Omer caught sight of Maximilian Borin emerging from the bookcase. Omer was fascinated. Behind the doctor, he was briefly able to see what looked like an operating room. And in the center of the room, Omer saw a man sitting on a chair that was bolted to the ground.

Then the door to the prayer room closed in front of Omer's face. And with a click, the door locked behind them.

▪

The man in the machine was Darab. He had a rough face with a thick but short beard that covered the numerous valleys of his face. He had lived in the building above Best Diner for about eighteen months—fully paid by Hanafi. Hanafi watched the doctor prepare the machine. Darab didn't seem particularly nervous, but the doctor did. That made sense. Darab had been working with the machine for months. At that point, he wanted what the machine was pushing. But Dr. Borin, on the other hand, needed the machine to do exactly as it was designed to do. No one in the club wanted another Abdel Hayat situation on their hands.

"Are you nervous, Darab?" Hanafi asked.

"No, Alim," Darab shook his head. "Excited."

"You are so well prepared, dear one. I am proud of you."

Darab and Hanafi watched Dr. Borin tinker with the large machine in front of them. Officially termed a neural-control interface device, Hanafi simply called it "the machine." He didn't need to know how it worked, although Dr. Borin always tried to explain it. He just knew that the machine was the result of Dr. Borin's entire academic career. It was not a mind-control device like in the movies. It could not literally move the subject's legs and feet. What the machine did was deeply imprint a thought, which eventually transformed into nothing less than a directive, within the subject's mind. What Hanafi and Dr. Borin had discovered was that each subject required slightly different preparation. Neither Abdel nor Darab had been inclined towards martyrdom. However, Abdel had been more devout—initially. A hypothesis was growing between Hanafi and the doctor that a blank slate such as Darab was actually better than a zealot like Abdel. Only further testing, and action, would confirm or disprove their hypothesis.

"How many more sessions will I need?" Darab asked.

"Not many," replied Dr. Borin as he worked behind the long tube positioned above the chair. The top portion of the machine, hanging over Darab, was a reconditioned MRI device. Dr. Borin wanted to replace it. It was old and slow, but it was still quite functional. Dr. Borin's pioneering work in neural-control interfaces had begun when he was first trained as a radiologist. He had realized that the live brain scans created by MRI machines had other applications beyond simply identifying tumors. For example, the machine could identify the periods of time—perhaps even in fractions of seconds—when the subject's brain was most susceptible to suggestion or learning. The machine, in effect, was capable of an exacting form of hypnosis. During the brain's most malleable moments, Dr. Borin's machine would use a combination of audio and electrical stimulation to present new ideas. The technique was similar to the old slip-frame technique of flashing a cup of soda for one frame into a movie theater full of thirsty people. But now, due to his innovation, Dr. Borin was able to flash ideas into his subjects' brains at the exact moment they would be best absorbed.

After a few more moments, Dr. Borin was done. He made sure everything was hooked up before nodding at Hanafi. They moved to each side of Darab and locked his arms in place. The doctor carefully applied multiple Skintact electrodes to Darab's chest. The restraints around Darab's arms could withstand quite a bit of force—but they were medical, not medieval. A dedicated-enough mind would be able to yank free of them. They'd had that problem numerous times with Abdel, but so far Darab had proved to be an easier subject.

"Ready, Darab? The session will be three hours. Remember, you'll hear a loud beep every fifteen minutes and then a long, extended chime at each hour."

"I'm more than ready," Darab said.

"You're doing the hard work," Hanafi said, "not the machine. You're well on your way towards the infinite. We're just helping you get there faster."

Dr. Borin reached up and slowly lowered the MRI over Darab's head. The doctor stepped over to a computer and ran his custom software. A simulated voice spoke to Darab while Hanafi and Dr. Borin quietly left the room.

"Hello Darab. Please say it with me three times," the computerized voice began. "I will drive to . . ."

CHAPTER SEVENTEEN

MAXIMILIAN BORIN WAS IN THE wild, but he was trapped. Two days prior, Dr. Borin had called his mother's cell phone from a new number—one Jake and the joint task force had not known about. Within three minutes of Jake answering Maxine's phone, Dr. Borin's new phone had been turned off. However, three minutes was an eternity. The feds now had the coordinates for the doctor's physical location, and thus Jake had become responsible for the biggest break in the case yet.

Dr. Borin had returned to his apartment in Brooklyn late Monday night, and he'd been holed up in the small unit ever since. Susan and Pete Mack had decided, smartly, that Borin was worth much more to them if he didn't know he'd been found. The owner of Borin's building had been more than happy to help the feds enact their plan. The landlord allowed Dennis Fong and Shep Moseley access to the HVAC system in the basement of the building. The ultimate odd couple, Fong was a hulking man with zero-percent body fat, a shaved head, and a clipped, reserved personality. Moseley, on the other hand, was a social glad-hander who dressed in preppy corduroys and never combed his floppy hair. Moseley, as Mr. White's second-in-command, was there to supervise while Fong actually did the work. In this case, it had only taken Fong thirty minutes to push a fiber-optic camera attached to the end of a thin remote-controlled plumbing snake up three stories of heating vents and position it to stare directly into Dr. Borin's living room.

■

Jake, Tony, Fong and Moseley sat inside a large Con Edison van located a block away from Dr. Borin's apartment. For the last few hours, they had been treated to the still-life reality show that was Dr. Borin's life. He hadn't even left the apartment for food. However, things were quickly becoming more interesting. As Tuesday afternoon arrived, it became clear that Borin was preparing to leave the apartment.

The joint task force was ready for this eventuality. In fact, they were more than prepared. Tracking Dr. Borin was set to be one of the most impressive surveillance operations that the NYPD, in cooperation with the FBI, had ever conducted. There were fifty—*yes, fifty*—men and women operating in the streets around Borin's apartment. Every single one of them was highly trained, meticulously costumed, and camouflaged—and they were all working together as one large amoeba. There were numerous ways to conduct a surveillance operation, but the most exhaustive and effective technique was waterfall surveillance. The basic concept of waterfall surveillance was that instead of rotating a handful of surveillance operators around a target, the team used so many agents that it would be extremely unlikely for the target to spot one repeated face during any twenty-four-hour period. The benefit of waterfall surveillance was that it was almost impossible to counter. The negative was the massive manpower and communication required. As a result, waterfall surveillance was only conducted by nation-states, and even then only on the highest priority cases.

When Maximilian Borin exited his apartment and stepped onto the sidewalk, there were already ten sets of eyes on him. Practically every single person on Borin's street was employed by a law enforcement organization. That's what made waterfall surveillance so effective. Borin could spend valuable time and energy trying to figure out which one person, if anyone, was watching him while not realizing that the answer was *everyone*.

When Dr. Borin turned the corner away from his block, he passed by a homeless man sitting on a stoop and warming his hands over a small camp stove. The man had strewn his belongings out on the stairs and had been there the entire night. He'd proudly collected about eighteen dollars. He was also an FBI agent. For every block that Borin would walk that day, no matter how far he traveled, he would be passed or followed by anywhere from one to five agents. Should Borin decide to board a bus, taxi, bike, scooter, or Uber, the team was ready. In addition to the fifty agents on foot, another thirty-five were spread out in twenty different vehicles within an eight-block radius—on mopeds, bikes, cars, and trucks.

In the meantime, Jake and the others in the Con Edison van kept up the pace a few blocks behind Dr. Borin. They tracked him via reports, not visuals. Borin was walking through Brooklyn, heading north towards Queens. After about an hour, the team concluded that this wasn't a simple jaunt to the grocery store. They were excited. Dr. Borin walked for about two more hours before finally reaching the northern section of Astoria and entering an area where the main artery consisted of Steinway Street. Finally, he began to slow. He seemed a bit more comfortable, perhaps having convinced himself that if he was being followed, he'd shaken everyone. *He had not*. After another few minutes of darting back and forth across Steinway, Dr. Borin stepped into a restaurant.

Within fifteen seconds, a nondescript Honda Civic parked across the street from the restaurant. The car had blackened windows and shiny aftermarket rims. Everything about it fit right into the neighborhood, including the man with slick gelled hair yelling into his cell phone and smoking a cigarette while frenetically tapping ash out of his rolled-down window. While the driver spoke, the woman next to him used her cell phone. She turned and asked her companion to smile for a photo, which he did begrudgingly.

But instead of taking a photo of the man, the woman's phone was trained on the restaurant across the street. Her high-resolution photographs were quickly routed to the entire joint task force, from Jake in the van to Susan, Pete Mack, and Mr. White at One Police Plaza. Within seconds, the entire team was focused on the next target of their investigation: Best Middle Eastern Diner.

CHAPTER EIGHTEEN

MURAD AND OMER AMIN WEREN'T all that different from one another. Both wanted lives quite different from the ones they lived, and both had secrets. One of Murad's secrets was cigarettes. He was a pious man in almost every aspect, but his sin was the cigarettes that he'd begun smoking when he was fourteen and never stopped.

Murad's sin, or what Hanafi would call *haram*, had a side effect— wandering. It was usually walking, but sometimes it was also joyriding in his father's vans. It all came together to make Murad the eyes and ears of the neighborhood. When he wasn't at the mosque, the dry-cleaning business, or Best Diner, Murad was wandering around Steinway. He liked to walk and smoke, hiding his cigarette behind his leg or simply throwing it to the ground if he spotted anyone who might disapprove.

Murad enjoyed moving. It made him feel free. He liked to think he could keep going one day, never returning back to his normal surroundings, and end up somewhere other than where he was. He would daydream about this future version of his life, God willing. He would loosely strategize about how to get there. His thoughts always began with criticism of the disgusting regularity that surrounded him before morphing into an imaginative dream of the rich and sumptuous world he might soon occupy halfway across the globe. He would think of himself as a financier in Dubai or an arms dealer in Syria or the owner of an exotic-car dealership in London.

Usually his breaks were quick, but sometimes Murad would walk or drive for hours at a time. The longer he was gone, the more he didn't like what he saw and the deeper his aspirations would become. However, at the end of every sojourn, with a cigarette or two or three absorbed into his lungs, Murad would always find himself looping back down Steinway again. He knew every crack of the sidewalk and each crooked shopkeeper's sign. This was his terrain. If a new store was opening up, he'd track its progress on a daily basis. If a bum showed up on the stairs of the mosque, he'd take a mental note. If a trash can had fallen onto the street, he'd call the sanitation department to have it fixed up. It might be ugly, but this was his place and his people. He paid attention, and he took pride in knowing and seeing everything.

CHAPTER NINETEEN

"BREACH, BREACH, BREACH," NYPD SWAT Captain Markle screamed over the radio.

After a night of waiting for Dr. Borin to reappear from Best Middle Eastern Diner, the decision had been made to go kinetic. The restaurant had been the target of twelve hours worth of multi-agency surveillance and research operations with a few schools of thought as to the next steps. Susan had toed the line, standing in the middle of the issue, because any other position would make her less supreme. Pete Mack and the FBI continued to support a wait-and-see approach. But like a magician, Mr. White had pulled satellite footage from the past, which appeared to show the loading of explosive materials into the back of the restaurant. His evidence cemented the need for a raid as soon as possible. As Mr. White had put it, it was time to shock and awe those bastards into submission.

Listening to Markle announce the breach, Jake sat side by side with Pete Mack and Mr. White in the back of an unmarked white van three blocks from the target location. Fong was driving, with Tony and Moseley manning the communication equipment on the other side of the van. No one in this vehicle was particularly risk averse, especially Jake. He was tired of sitting in vans and wanted to be in on the action. Although they ought to have waited a full five minutes, it was only thirty seconds before Jake spoke up.

"Let 'er rip, Fong," Jake said.

No one disagreed.

Fong yanked the van into gear and it began to scream towards the front door of the Best Diner. Within seconds, the generally quiet street had descended into absolute law enforcement mayhem. And soon hundreds more police vehicles would descend upon the scene.

"Think the whole cell's here?" Jake asked Pete Mack while they ripped into the belly of the beast.

"Neighbors said they saw Hayat around the building. Owner knew him. This is the place. With some luck, we'll get the doctor and the owner, this guy Ali Hanafi, all in one."

"I don't like luck, because it hates me."

"I'm with you, Rivett," Mr. White said. "But sometimes when it's your turn to ask a girl to dance, you gotta buck up and do the damn thing before you lose her."

The van arrived in front of Best Diner with just feet separating it from the front door. All of the men unloaded quickly and barreled into the broken-open door of the restaurant, following on the heels of the last SWAT team member.

▪

"Clear!"

Jake sprinted through the ground level of Best Diner, steps behind the SWAT team. He was witnessing it all as they were, and what he was seeing wasn't good. There was no one in the restaurant and no one in the kitchen. He began to hear radio reports from the second and third floors. Besides the tenants, there was nothing—nothing suspicious and no weapons. And worse, there was no Hanafi and no Dr. Borin.

The more Jake heard SWAT scream the word "clear," the worse he felt. He could tell where this was going already, even as he watched one of Markle's lieutenants spread plastic explosive over the lock of a reinforced door in the back of the restaurant. After a brief moment, the lock blasted open, and the team descended the stairs into darkness below.

Once in the basement, SWAT operators alternated to the left and right throughout the hallway, banging open doors and covering angles. But, again, the place was completely empty.

Jake observed the basement. The first space was a religious room. A series of prayer rugs lay on the floor. There was a cheap fold-out table with some food on it. Against the wall were filing cabinets and a bookshelf that was lightly stocked with religious magazines and books and not much else. Jake glanced around, but the room wasn't giving up anything.

"We'll have to look at all the documents."

"My people will be on it within the hour," Mr. White confirmed, walking up behind Jake.

The second space, further down the hallway, resembled a storage room. It also doubled as an overflow pantry for the restaurant above. Filled with old kitchen equipment and dry goods, there was no sign of the two large containers that Mr. White's satellite footage had recorded being carried into the restaurant.

"Inspector will come down here. If there's anything he can cite, he will," Pete Mack added while examining the boxes of food that were piled against one side of the room.

"Think we were all wrong?" Tony asked.

Rivett didn't reply. He was deep in thought.

"Whole place was covered," Pete Mack added. "Half the block's been under waterfall . . . How can we have missed them? Only thing I can think is maybe they rolled out the back the second the doctor went in, an hour or two before we were set up. Maybe they slipped us right off the bat . . ."

Perplexed, the men stepped out of the storage room and walked back towards the basement's prayer room. As they were about to turn up the stairs, Jake glanced into the prayer room a second time.

"The bookcase," Jake said.

"What about it?" Tony asked.

"Same as the one in the supply room, but nothin's on either of them."

Jake took a few steps towards the bookcase situated against the far side of the prayer room. He ran his fingers against the edge of it, where the metal met the wall. He attempted to push the bookcase, which was practically empty, but it wouldn't slide easily. Rivett backed up and slammed his shoulder into it with all his might. At first heave, it didn't budge. The second time, Jake only succeeded in causing the side panel of the bookcase to collapse into itself. Stepping back, Jake realized that he'd ripped the edge of the bookcase about two inches from the wall. He stuck his fingers into the crack and could feel a half-inch gap between the wall behind the bookcase and the room's visible wall. The seam was carefully fabricated—designed on purpose.

"Get me my crowbar," Jake said.

Within moments, a handful of the brawniest SWAT operators in the city were in the basement with multiple crowbars—working on the secret doors that existed behind not just the prayer-room bookcase, but also the one in the supply closet. After a few careful levers, they finally managed to open the hidden door in the prayer room. They discovered that it had been locked and was controlled by a hydraulic system.

"It's a clean room," Jake said as he stepped into Dr. Borin's laboratory.

The lab appeared ransacked. All sorts of computer peripherals, electronics, and manuals were strewn across the floor. There was nothing in the center of the space, except for four square steel panels that were bolted into the ground. Against the walls were shelves and cabinets, and there was even a small stainless-steel sink and counter built into one side of the room.

"The fuck was going on in here?" Jake asked.

Everyone could hear him, but no one had an answer.

Jake picked up one of the books on the floor and turned it over in his hand.

"*Diagnostic MRI: Sixth Edition*," Jake read out loud. "This is probably all Borin's stuff. At least now we've got cause to shut the whole building down and check out every square inch." Jake tossed the book on the floor.

"Rivett! You got to see this!" Pete Mack yelled from the hallway.

Rivett stepped out of the lab and into the basement hallway to see Pete Mack waving wildly. As he rounded the corner into the supply closet, he saw that SWAT had also successfully pulled away that room's bookcase.

But instead of a hidden room behind it, there was a subterranean passageway.

Somewhere between a hallway and a tunnel, the space was about six feet wide and existed outside the foundation of the building itself. It seemed to be a channel in which gas, water, and power lines, along with additional plumbing and wiring conduits, could run. Perhaps used in the initial construction of the structures along the street, the passageway was a forgotten underground relic. It reminded Jake of the tunnels that he and Mona explored when they met. Interestingly, the passageway didn't seem to end at Hanafi's building. Instead, it ran down the entire block, consisting of a hodgepodge of property lines, building systems, and structural retrofits.

Jake and Pete Mack sprinted down the passageway, using their cell phones for illumination—with their guns out and at attention. The men passed by multiple crumbling building foundations before finding their path blocked. A new-construction cinder-block wall stopped up the tunnel completely and a steel door was closed in front of them.

Rivett tried the handle—*it opened.* Whoever had come through last had not locked the door.

Stepping through, Jake and Pete Mack found themselves inside another supply room in another basement, except this time everything was sanitized and utilitarian. The building seemed to have been built within the last ten years. Jake realized it must be the new mixed-use building that occupied the corner of the street, about three hundred feet from Best Diner. The two men sprinted up the stairs towards a door marked with an exit sign. Once out of the basement, they raced down another hallway with half a dozen unmarked doors. At the end of the hall was a pair of prominent double doors. Jake pushed open the double doors, leading with his gun. He found himself in . . .

A gym.

The doors opened to a large room filled with high-end gym equipment. Up-tempo pop music was blasting. A couple dozen trendy but sweaty men and women exercised on ellipticals, treadmills, and the like. They stared back in shock at Jake and Pete Mack—*and their weapons.*

After a brief pause, the patrons began to scream and flee in a wild and fearful pandemonium. Jake quickly lowered his gun and pushed it into his holster. Pete Mack did the same while pulling out his badge.

"FBI! Don't worry! We're law enforcement!" Pete Mack yelled to absolutely no avail.

CHAPTER TWENTY

DARAB WAS STILL IN THE machine. Behind a curving rack of dress shirts deep within the Amin family's dry-cleaning establishment, Darab sat on a chair. The MRI tube above him hummed, with various parts of the machine pulling power from multiple outlets surrounding it. Darab was largely motionless. He wasn't unconscious. Instead, he was just locked in. The electric pulses and audio content of Dr. Borin's machine was designed to stimulate Darab when he needed to be stimulated and placate him when he needed to be placated. Like a toddler in front of a screen, the machine kept Darab happy.

Omer watched from halfway across the store with macabre fascination. Hanafi and Murad hadn't explained specifically what was happening, but Omer wasn't stupid. He'd picked up on everything. His brother had discovered that their invention was in danger. They'd spent the entire night moving out of the Best Diner building, sneaking through an underground tunnel to avoid being detected. This time around, Hanafi had accepted Omer into the group without a second thought. Perhaps he was desperate. Omer wasn't sure. Anyway, Murad had implied that Omer didn't really have a choice in the matter. The safest place for their small crew to assemble was in the back of Moradi's business—Steinway

Cleaners—so that's where they had gone. Murad had ushered them in just fifteen minutes after the store had closed for the day. At this point, Moradi had no idea what was happening. Hanafi, Murad, and Dr. Borin sat on plastic folding chairs in a small circle, watching feedback from the machine. Omer stood behind them, unable to look away from Darab. While he had only caught a glimpse before, now he was afforded a full view of the science experiment that was taking place. Omer could hear Hanafi and Dr. Borin bickering as they observed the process. He also knew another member of the club, Ataullah, was working inside one of Moradi's two vans that were parked in the small lot behind the business.

"Timeline's moved up, obviously," Hanafi said.

"Darab's compliance instructs our timeline, obviously . . ." Dr. Borin replied.

"Doctor, this is about much more than your science experiment."

"One enables the other."

"What you do is a means to an end. The end's what matters."

"The greater the means, the better the machine, the more impressive the ends."

"We're done experimenting," Hanafi said.

"Maybe," Borin nodded, his attention still firmly focused on the screen monitoring Darab's vitals. "But you're not in charge."

This statement caused Hanafi to flare his nostrils. "Watch yourself, doctor," he said.

"Don't get indignant. The man from Dubai writes your checks," Dr. Borin said. "He wants the technology perfect, and that's what he'll get. I'm not rushing just so you can go blow up Times Square and get us all caught. The goal is bigger than that. I know it. You know it, too, but you won't admit it."

"Times Square?" Omer asked nonchalantly, but no one replied to him.

"In case you are actually this incredibly, unbelievably dense, doctor, I'll lay out our situation." Hanafi raised his voice. "There is no more grand plan. We're in the back of a fucking dry cleaners. We are fully exposed. I don't see anyone from Dubai here right now. I make the decisions, and you can either go along with it or—"

"Or what? You can't do anything without permission."

"Or I'll have Murad break your neck."

"Happily," Murad added.

"You guys have nothing without me."

"Your machine," Hanafi said as he gestured to the tube above Darab, "is about to have its final test. But we're not sending Darab by himself. Too risky. Once the cycle is over and the van's ready, we'll all go with him. He'll drop us off a few blocks away and we'll observe to make sure he is successful. All I need from you, doctor, is to make sure that your man does his one and only job and presses the button."

"He'll press the button." Dr. Borin nodded in affirmation.

▪

That evening, the group stood in the back of the business next to one of the Steinway Cleaners vans. The back doors were open. Ataullah had completed his work, and the massive fertilizer container had been transformed into nothing less than a weapon of mass destruction.

"Where's the other one?" Omer asked Murad.

"The other what?"

"The second container. We picked up two . . ."

"Less questions," Murad replied.

Omer was pissed. He hadn't asked for any of this. But he felt he was in deep—*too deep*.

"Then why do you need me?" Omer asked.

"We don't," Hanafi jumped in, having overheard Omer. "You've done enough. It's time for us to part. You should go home and take care of your family."

"But . . ." Murad began to speak. "Taking care of our family means that you keep all of us safe. Right, brother? Not a word to anyone."

Omer turned to his brother. "What about you, Murad? Are you keeping us safe?"

"I have a long journey ahead. It doesn't end here. Tell them I love them."

"Where are you going?"

"I'm finding my place in the world."

"You're going into the machine?"

"No, no." Murad shook his head. "The alim and I are taking the machine to those who need it most. The machine is our message. As it spreads, so does our power. Goodbye, Omer."

Omer thought better than to ask any questions. His brother was obviously going crazy. All of them were, including the tall white guy. Nothing made any sense, and in this moment, Omer had a huge desire to do as Hanafi instructed and go home. That was perfectly fine—inspired, in fact. He would do what they asked. He wouldn't say a word. With some luck, doing nothing might help Murad disappear from his life forever. Without a look back at his brother, Omer padded away from the parking lot and into the night.

CHAPTER TWENTY-ONE

THE SPOTLIGHTS WERE SET TO maximum glare. The brightness would scare most mortals, but Susan Herlihy was well-suited for the pressure. Susan took a deep breath as she glanced down at her notes. Pete Mack didn't want to do what she was about to do, and Mr. White wouldn't have touched something like this with a ten-foot pole. But they had both agreed it was the right thing to do. The Bryant Park investigation was officially unsolved and unofficially a disaster of epic proportions. That morning's failed raid was the cherry on top. The most frustrating part, to Susan, was that it wasn't the police department's fault. Not really. The terrorists, the cell, or whatever you wanted to call them—they were extremely good. They were many notches above anything the city had seen since 9/11. But there was one more tactic the joint task force had not tried. That was why it came down to Susan, the tiniest of all the women in the brutal land of the cop man, to face down the press corps all by herself. She would put the joint task force out there with the hope that someone, anyone, might be able to help them. She arranged her notes on a podium, hastily set up in front of a blue banner printed with NYPD and FBI insignia, and then began to speak.

"There have been media reports of a police action this morning in

Astoria, Queens," Susan began. "The reports are correct. There was a raid. The NYPD, working with the FBI and other federal, state, and local authorities, identified a potential meeting place of individuals who are suspected to be involved in the Bryant Park bombing. Unfortunately, the suspects we were seeking managed to escape. That's why I'm here now. This investigation has reached the point where we need your help. There are at least two armed and extremely dangerous individuals loose on the streets at this very moment. We know their names and have their pictures. They are the prime suspects in the Bryant Park bombing, and they are likely responsible for many other crimes. Should you come across these individuals, do not be a hero. Simply call nine-one-one or contact your local authorities. We will take care of the rest. I address you with the deep regret that we haven't been able to find them yet. But the best way to further our mission of serving and protecting the citizens of New York, and America, is to tell you exactly who they are. Make no mistake, they are running. They are afraid. And after tonight, with the help of the public, I hope their free time is severely limited."

Two easels stood next to Susan. The contents of each were covered by a draped cloth. Susan reached up and yanked down both shrouds to reveal two poster-sized photographs.

"This is Dr. Maximilian Borin and Ali Hanafi. To them, and to anyone harboring them, you will never escape the long arm of justice. We will not rest until our city is safe again." Susan took a deep breath. She stared over the press assembled in front of her. "I know you have questions. I'm ready to start answering them."

CHAPTER TWENTY-TWO

OMER AND SALMA AMIN SAT next to each other at the table in their dining room, working on homework. Salma was focused. Omer wasn't. The family television was on, tuned to CNN, and Omer couldn't pull his eyes away. The network was broadcasting a press conference about the Bryant Park bombing. As the lady on camera revealed large photographs of the FBI's two most wanted suspects, Omer gasped.

"What?" Salma asked.

"Nothing . . ." Omer stammered.

"Fine. Then why are you being so weird lately?" Salma asked. "Is it because of Pat?"

"The whole Pat thing is a huge mistake."

"Excuse me? You're touchy today."

"Don't worry about me."

"Omer, that's not fair. We've been over this. If you don't think I should be with him, you have to tell me. You owe me that."

"Well, then, yeah. Of course you shouldn't be dating Pat. But I know you won't follow my advice," Omer said. "Even though I'm your brother and I'd only tell you what was best for you . . ."

"Where's this coming from?" Salma asked.

"You're impossible," Omer retorted.

"Whatever, brother." Salma placed her pen down and stared intently at Omer. "You can keep thinking you protect me. But that's not true. I'm not the only person hiding something in this family. In the end, I'm the one who protects you."

Omer knew what she meant. He glanced back up at the television. An anchor was speaking while the network played previously recorded footage from a week ago. "The NYPD's new approach to their investigation is far different from only a week ago, when we weren't able to pry anything out of them at all." Onscreen, video played of a week's worth of tight-lipped officials. The cuts were quick. The president was nonspecific. The chief of police silently pushed past media throngs. The FBI refused to speculate. The final shot, just a throwaway, was of a blond-haired detective muttering "no comment" as he jumped on his motorcycle and drove away from the federal building downtown.

"That was then," the CNN anchor said. "This is now." They cut back to the press conference and the chief saying, "This is Dr. Maximilian Borin and Ali Hanafi. To them, and to anyone harboring them, you will never escape the long arm of justice."

Omer watched the television with rapt attention.

"She seems pretty serious," Salma said. But Omer was already standing up and hustling into his bedroom.

Once he was safely in his room, Omer shut the door and crouched down by his desk. He dug through the bottom drawer. He was looking for something very specific and very yellow. It took a few minutes of searching, but he found it. He pulled out a crumpled yellow advertisement from ExCulture and smoothed it out with his hands. He looked at it. The flyer announced the band Mythics, along with a picture of their lead singer, Jake Rivett. Seeing it again, he was certain this Jake Rivett was the same guy from the CNN footage. Jake Rivett was both a detective and a screamo rocker.

"Do you need this?"

Startled, Omer turned. Salma was standing at the doorway holding her makeup case.

"I, uh . . ."

"I know you put on makeup when you go out to see the bands," she said and then paused. "Well, do you?"

"I'm not going to see a band."

"Then what are you doing?" Salma nodded at the flyer in Omer's hands.

"Can't tell you."

"Fine. I respect that. I'm sorry I got mad at you."

"You're not wrong."

"What's most important to me is that you're true to yourself. You should only do things that you're proud of. Don't let anyone else tell you what to do, and don't be afraid. Be the person you want to be. That's what I'm going to do, because that's how I'm going to be happy."

"I know, Salma. Thank you. You're totally right, which is why I gotta go . . ."

Omer took a step towards the door.

"And Salma?"

"Yes?"

"I love you."

CHAPTER TWENTY-THREE

"SHE'S GONNA BE MAYOR ONE day," Jake said.

Rivett was back in their apartment and sitting on the couch with Mona. The two of them watched Susan's press conference.

"Why do you say that?"

"Because she's voracious," Jake said.

"Like a dinosaur?"

Jake nodded. "She always goes for bigger and bigger prey."

"She looks tired. Are you getting any closer?" Mona asked.

"I'd like to say it's a matter of time," Jake replied. "But that might be a lie." He noticed a sullen expression on Mona's face. "What's wrong?"

"I worry about you."

"You don't need to."

"Maybe." Mona nodded. "I worry about me, too. But do you? You come home and just expect me to be perfectly happy with the fact that you're out chasing terrorists."

"No. I don't expect that. But . . ."

On television, CNN was playing a montage of clips from the investigation. Jake couldn't help but grin as his own face flashed on the screen as he jumped onto his Ducati.

"But what?" Mona asked.

"It'll be over soon," Jake said.

"You just said that might be a lie."

"Got me."

"Maybe one day you could ask me how I'm feeling. You could come in and say that you're sorry for how scared you make me every single stupid day this thing drags on."

"I'm sorry, Mona." Jake paused and then continued. "But . . ."

"Spit it out," Mona commanded.

"You knew who you were getting involved with."

"Jesus," Mona muttered. "How full of shit are you? For the first month that I knew you, Jake, all you did was lie to me. You told me you were someone else. Yeah, eventually I accepted who you really were—a *cop*. But that's not even the problem. The thing is, your whole life is like that clip on CNN. You're always running away. No matter what it is, whether it's your family, your job, or us—you're doing your best to break the rules. You love being a detective and I get that. But you also use it as an excuse. You don't know what to do with yourself when you're not charging at something. If we're going to get married . . ." Mona began breaking into sobs. She seemed both sad and livid at the same time. It probably wasn't any one thing. It was everything.

"We're going to get married, Mona."

"Oh yeah?" Mona said between tears. "Then when? When's the date, Jake? Did you look at any of the emails I sent you about venues?"

"I . . ."

"I know you didn't."

"There's the Hayat—"

"The case, the case. Guess what, Jake? After there's this case, there's going to be another one—and then another. I've figured it out. I know you. You'll jump from case to case for your whole life without ever touching the ground. But if that's really your plan . . . you're going to find that one time when you do come home, I won't be here anymore."

"I'm home now, aren't I?"

"Are you?"

"I love you. Nothing changes that. And this case is different. It really is. You know that, too, deep down inside. And after it's over, I'll look at all the wedding venues in the world."

"Did you tell your parents yet?" Mona asked him.

It wasn't that these were impossible questions to answer. It was just that Mona knew the answer already, and he wished she hadn't asked.

"No," Jake finally responded.

A long silence punctuated their argument. Jake didn't like fighting. It reminded him of his own childhood. But he also didn't like silence. Maybe that, too, reminded him of Albany. Mona stood and grabbed two empty wine glasses off the coffee table. She brought them into the kitchen and began scrubbing furiously, focusing her anger on the sponge. Jake watched her grind until his cell phone rang in front of him.

"It's Schaub," Jake said.

"Do whatever you want," Mona replied.

Jake declined Schaub's call. "He's been reaching out—for practice. We're supposed to have that show coming up. I'll cancel."

"Don't cancel for me."

"Really?"

"Band is a better therapist than I am. And you . . . You are in need," Mona said.

"I'm not that bad."

"You're obviously the most objective observer of yourself, Jake."

At that moment, Mona stared at her own phone on the kitchen counter. It was vibrating. Schaub was calling her next. She picked up.

"Schaub?" She listened for a moment and then stared at Jake with frightened eyes. "I don't want to hear this," she said. "I know he will."

Jake rose from the couch, and Mona handed over her phone. He tapped a button to activate FaceTime between him and Schaub.

"Sorry, dude," were Jake's first words. Jake always felt an inherent tension with Schaub and Mythics, primarily due to the fact that Jake was both the face of the band and its most unavailable member.

"Nothing to be sorry about, ol' pal." Schaub's raspy voice echoed through FaceTime.

Jake could see that Schaub was sitting in his own apartment. It was messy, just as Jake's used to be.

"I got this case, dude. You know—Bryant Park. Not sure if I'm gonna be able to make it next weekend. I'll try. You know me. I usually get done —"

"Jake, chill your roll. It's all good. You know the band motto."

"What's that?"

"When Rivett's happy, everyone's happy."

"Hadn't heard that one before . . ." Jake scrambled which glancing at Mona who stuck her tongue out at him.

"All right, listen up. I got some weird shit that happened," Schaub said.

Jake watched as Schaub flipped the FaceTime perspective to his front-facing camera. Schaub had a laptop open, perched precariously on top of a plate that was balanced on an ash tray. The laptop's browser was open to Twitter—Mythics' profile specifically.

"Can you see it?" Schaub asked.

"No. What?"

"We got a message—from a fan. But it's for you. And . . . it's not about the band."

"What do you mean?" Jake asked.

Schaub zoomed in on the band's message feed. There was a new message from a user with the handle *ShyScreamo.*

"Guy named Shy Screamo," Schaub said. "He says this: 'Jake, I didn't know how to contact you. I know where the doctor and Hanafi are.'"

"So it's a tip?" Jake asked.

"I guess. Yeah, it's a tip," Schaub replied.

"We're getting thousands of them . . ."

"Just thought I'd tell ya, bro. He said a few more things," Schaub continued. "'I know about the machine. I know about the tunnel under Best Diner. I'm going to the Charcoal Stop off Ditmars right now, and I'll be there for three hours if—'"

"Wait a minute . . . He mentioned a tunnel?" Jake asked.

"Sure did," Schaub repeated. "'I know about the tunnel under Best Diner—'"

Schaub didn't know it, but the phone call was already over. Jake raced out of the door without even a word to Mona, who began to cry as the loud revving of Rivett's Ducati faded down the street.

▪

Rivett walked into the Charcoal Stop diner a man on fire. SWAT was at One Police Plaza and loading up, perhaps twenty minutes away. As was his nature, Tony had insisted that Jake wait for backup—at least for the beat cops, who were just a few minutes out. But as was Jake's nature, he'd rejected the request. He scanned the twenty-four-hour restaurant and its red-and-white leather stalls, looking for *ShyScreamo*. It was almost ten o'clock, and there wasn't much activity in the diner. Within seconds, it was clear who *ShyScreamo* was—the olive-skinned teenage kid sitting in the booth by himself with no food or menus on his table. Rivett marched over and sat down.

"You're Shy Screamo?"

Omer nodded.

"What's your name?"

"Omer."

"How'd you know about the tunnel?"

"I saw it," Omer replied. "I helped move everything out of it."

"Who are you? How do you know them? Why'd you decide to contact me? Where are they right now?" Jake hit the kid rapid-fire.

"I . . . hate what they're doing. That's why I messaged you. I . . ."

"What?"

"I want to do the right thing. I don't want people to die."

"How do you know them?"

"My brother, Murad—he's with Hanafi. There's a club. They call it the business club, but it isn't business. Well, I didn't know that. Not until recently. My brother spent all his time there."

"Where?"

"At the restaurant—Best Diner."

"Go on . . ."

"Murad forced me to help them. They needed hands. We moved all that stuff through the back tunnel and out of the gym. Hanafi has a contact at the gym. The owner or something. He got a key. We just pushed it all out the back and into one of our vans."

"Pushed what?"

"The machine and the other stuff."

"What machine?"

"Aren't you a cop? Aren't you looking for the doctor?"

"There was a machine in the lab?"

"Yeah—the doctor's mind-control machine. The one that makes terrorists," Omer said without pause.

Jake took a deep breath. The pieces were coming together.

"Dr. Borin made it?"

Omer nodded. "Yeah."

"How's it work?"

"I . . . I have no idea. Darab was in it."

"Who's Darab?"

"Another guy from the club."

"Did they use the machine on Abdel Hayat?"

Omer shrugged his shoulders. He didn't know.

"How'd Hanafi meet the doctor?"

"I don't know, man."

"You said 'other stuff.' What other stuff did you move through the tunnel?"

"A bomb."

"Where's the bomb?"

"In the van—my dad's van," Omer said.

"Where?"

"They're driving to Times Square."

"Times Square? Now?" Rivett had felt many things, but never the awe-inspiring mainline of adrenaline that ran through his veins in that moment.

"Yeah—in our dry-cleaning van. It's white. Says 'Steinway Cleaners' on the side."

Rivett stood. He felt disoriented for a moment while his brain processed what he'd just heard. Perhaps he should be securing Omer and waiting for backup to arrive, but there just wasn't time. He stepped away from the booth and headed for the door.

"Hey!" Omer yelled. "What am I supposed to do?"

"Stay here," Jake replied.

"And what?"

"Wait for the cops."

"To arrest me?" Omer asked.

But Jake had already exited the Charcoal Stop and was sprinting towards his bike.

Inside the diner, Omer glanced around. The only person who had taken even the slightest interest in his conversation with Jake was the waitress. She ambled over.

"Still waitin', honey?"

"Uh, no . . ." Omer said.

"Want a menu?"

"I gotta . . . run."

He raced out of the diner as police sirens began to wail.

CHAPTER TWENTY-FOUR

RIVETT TOOK THE QUEENSBORO BRIDGE as though it were a giant slalom—dodging left and right around cars while shredding the middle lane. He was pushing ninety-five on the Ducati. His heart bumped with anxiety as he contemplated the danger he was about to encounter. Yes, he was scared, but situations like this were why he existed. While he drove, he spoke to Tony, who was in the joint task force office waiting for Susan to arrive. Jake learned that Pete Mack was downstairs at One Police Plaza coordinating with SWAT and police dispatch. Within minutes, every single beat cop in the entire city would be looking for the white Steinway Cleaners van. Jake was confident they would find the van quickly. But the big question was how much lead time the terrorists had on them. Because once the van arrived in Times Square . . . *show's over.*

■

Pete Mack watched Captain Markle and the rest of the SWAT operators armor up for war in the basement of One Police Plaza. Each member of the team was an intense specimen of brains and brawn. Working for NYPD SWAT was definitely the major leagues. That's why there was nary a word between the operators as they quickly and efficiently attached their battle rattle. Bulletproofs vests, helmets, ammunition belts, arm and knee padding, and all manner of sidearms and weapons were strapped on, loaded up, and locked in within minutes. An armored personnel carrier would take most of the men, but two large SUVs would also be used as point and patrol. The carrier was better for a siege, but the SUVs were easier to maneuver if the action was unpredictable. Pete Mack watched Markle with pride. The captain had his men well trained. There was no panic in the room—only determination.

"A well-oiled machine," Pete Mack commented.

"Slow is smooth; smooth is fast," Markle said.

"How long till we go?" Pete Mack asked.

"Ninety seconds," Markle said. "We?"

"I'm coming."

"Hell you are, sir."

"There's no debate, Markle," Pete Mack said, pulling a bulletproof vest over his head.

It only took a few more moments for the first SUV, with Markle sitting shotgun and Pete Mack in the back, to rip out of the large exit bay of One Police Plaza. Their car was quickly followed by the second SWAT SUV and finally the armored personnel carrier. Lights spun and sirens blared as SWAT raced towards Times Square.

▪

Jake finally reached Manhattan and piloted the Ducati south on Second Avenue.

"You get it yet?" Rivett barked into the microphone at Tony.

"Nothing yet, Jake. Where are you?"

"Close. I'm gonna be there first because I got the bike. Nothin'? Not even from RTCC?"

"We're on video conference with them now, too. There's a bunch of white vans. Analysts are working hard. No dry-cleaning logo. No Steinway . . . Are you sure—"

"Of what?"

"Sure the kid's story checks out? They lost him."

"How'd you lose the fuckin' kid?"

"Guys came two minutes later but he was already gone."

"Fucking track my Twitter," Jake yelled.

"That's going to take a few hours, bare minimum. Think. Are you sure? You don't think this kid sold you some bullshit?"

"I . . ."

Jake thought about Tony's question as he took a right turn on Forty-Seventh Street. There was a traffic jam ahead, but that didn't stop Rivett. He abruptly swerved the Ducati onto the sidewalk and bounced down the pavement. As he sped along, he caught sight of a white van out of the corner of his eye. His head whipped back to make sure he'd seen what he thought he had. He twisted forward again. A young couple approached on the sidewalk, pushing a stroller. At the last moment before collision, Jake pivoted the bike back onto the street. There was a large parked truck ahead. He jacked the brake on the bike and rapidly decelerated, his back wheel drifting to the side. The Ducati began to slide under him. Jake was losing control. Instead of resisting, he allowed the bike to pull him down onto the pavement. His body somewhat protected by rudimentary side bars, the bike sparked against the street and slammed into the back of the truck ahead. Once he had stopped, Jake rotated, smacked both of his palms down onto the asphalt, and pulled his body out from underneath the bike. He remained crouched behind the truck.

"Tony. You there?" Jake whispered into his radio.

"Yes?"

"I got them."

Jake hid behind the truck, waiting for the light ahead to turn green. Once it did, the pile of vehicles—in which he had previously been stuck—began to move again. He slowly stood and nonchalantly held his cell phone out as if he were checking an email. Thirty seconds later, the white van approached and slowly passed by the truck Jake was positioned behind. Jake stuck his phone past the rear bumper of the truck and snapped a few pictures of the van. He stared at the photos on his cell for a brief moment before forwarding them to Tony. As he had expected, the side of the white van read "Steinway Cleaners."

▪

In Times Square, an impromptu and massive evacuation effort was taking place. There were about twenty policemen assigned to Times Square at any given time of the day, and they were doing their best to clear everyone out. It was chaotic and haphazard, but more squad cars arrived with each passing moment to make the job easier.

▪

On Forty-Seventh Street, just a few blocks away, Jake reached for the Ducati. With three heaving pulls, he dragged his bike out from underneath the truck. He rotated the Ducati upright and checked it out. The bike looked fine—superficial damage only, just like him. Jake hopped on, started the bike up, and navigated back into traffic. He was ten cars behind the white van and following surreptitiously. Traffic was moving slowly, so he drove on the line to close in. He could finally see what the problem was. An avenue ahead, two cop cars had stopped the flow of traffic, and the police were directing all vehicles to choose south or north.

"Tony, why do you have the po-po blocking the street down here?" Jake yelled at Tony through his helmet mic.

"I made the call, Rivett." It wasn't Tony on the line. It was Susan. "Last thing I'll allow is more innocents going down like before," she said.

"Well, Susan, did you ever consider the fact that we're on a city street full of innocent people?"

"It's not Times Square," Susan replied back to Jake. "But you aren't wrong. So what're you gonna do about it, cowboy?"

"What I do best."

"Thatta boy," Susan replied.

Jake revved his engine and proceeded forward until he was just behind the Steinway Cleaners van. As he reached into his shoulder holster for his gun, the van suddenly swerved right and stopped. Jake followed, inches from the van's bumper. The back of the van didn't have windows. He hoped he was still invisible. He could hear the right side door of the van sliding open—towards the sidewalk. Jake jumped off the Ducati and peered around the van. The first person he saw was none other than Maximilian Borin, followed by a man he didn't recognize. Dr. Borin stared directly at Jake. They locked eyes.

Then the pandemonium began.

Jake lifted his gun towards Dr. Borin while the doctor and his companion sprinted past the front of their van and back into traffic.

Bang. Bang. Jake fired two shots, missing with both. Now the men were in the middle of the street, so Jake couldn't shoot without risking collateral damage. He rotated towards the van door. He was able to glance inside and spotted three more terrorists, their faces a mix of fear and menace, before the door slammed shut in Jake's face. The vehicle pulled away.

The van careened down the street, ramming into a pickup truck and sideswiping a Prius.

Rivett scanned across stopped traffic for Dr. Borin and the other suspect. He spotted the doctor's distinctive head of hair turning down Sixth Avenue. Jake was about to give chase when he remembered the Ducati. The bomb in the van was more important than the doctor. Jake jumped back on his bike and followed.

"Got two runners on foot, heading south on Sixth! One's the doctor!" Jake screamed into his headset.

"Got a SWAT unit on it," Susan replied.

Just as Rivett passed over Sixth Avenue, a large black SUV carrying SWAT operators came flying southbound with fury, lights whirling as it pursued the two runners.

"Where's Markle?" Jake yelled.

"He and Mack are already in Times Square with the rest of SWAT."

Ahead, Jake saw the Steinway Cleaners van accelerating towards the police barricade at Times Square.

■

There was only supposed to be one of them left in the van, but now there were three. Hanafi, Ataullah, and Darab stared through the front windshield of their vehicle at the two squad cars that were blocking the end of the street.

"Alim, how are you getting out?" Darab asked Hanafi from the back. His sweaty fingers were trembling on a small detonator remote in his hands, which was connected by a wire to the chemical-explosive payload.

"I don't think I am, dear one," Hanafi said. "Pedal to the metal, Ataullah."

"Yes, sir," Ataullah—driving—complied.

Hanafi gazed back at Darab. It was a damn shame, really. He could tell that Darab was one hundred percent ready. The machine had made sure of that. And yet, if the alim was going to go down with them, there was no way he wasn't going to be the one to press the button.

"Give me the remote," he instructed Darab.

Darab didn't move. He looked down at the remote, unwilling to meet Hanafi's gaze. "No, Alim. I know my mission. I will reach the center of Times Square. Say it with me. I will reach the center of Times Square—"

"Say it with *me*," Hanafi interrupted. "Your mission is to give me the remote."

When Darab looked up again, he saw a pistol staring at him in the face.

"We don't have an individual purpose, dear one," Hanafi said, aiming the pistol at Darab.

But instead of handing over the remote, Darab took a swing at Hanafi with his fist, only partially connecting. Just as Hanafi was about to start grappling with Darab over the remote, his attention was directed towards the front of the van.

Ping. Ping. A spiderweb constellation appeared on the front windshield as the police ahead of them began to open fire.

"Duck!" Hanafi yelled.

Ataullah was already doing just that. He was unscathed, driving the van with barely an eye on the road, most of his body crammed down onto the driver's side floor with his leg jackknifed against the accelerator. The two patrol cars ahead were close. The van accelerated. There was no time to brace for the collision, but Ataullah did his best to navigate the van into the dead center of the two-foot gap between the squad cars. The cops fired their last shots before diving out of the way as the van made contact. With a catastrophic roar, the metal animals did battle in the middle of the street. While the cop cars were reinforced, the van was much heavier. It tossed one of the vehicles to the side and scraped past the other, emerging through the gauntlet with a massive gouge along its left flank. The side door of the van swung open wildly, giving Hanafi and Darab a clear view of Times Square.

"Turn, turn!" Hanafi screamed, noticing their target was in sight.

Ataullah ripped the steering wheel to the side, but he was losing control of the van's wheels—the front axle had taken major damage. The van rocked back and forth, creaking from the strain of the previous altercation, as it bumped up and onto the central island of Times Square. Ahead, packs of civilians were still sprinting away to safety.

"Forward, forward!" Hanafi yelled, instructing Ataullah to hit the pedestrians ahead.

Ataullah slammed his foot down on the accelerator, juicing the van with everything it had left. The van surged forward.

Smmaaashhhhhh.

With no warning at all, a large black SUV T-boned the van directly into the center of Times Square. The van flipped onto its side, boxed between the red stairs of the tourist amphitheater and the SUV itself. Although Hanafi was dazed, he found himself perched above the van. He was hanging out the side, which was now the top, and he watched as multiple heavily armed men in black surged out of the SUV with semiautomatic rifles raised.

■

Rivett witnessed the collision from a hundred yards away. He didn't slow down. He saw Markle emerge from the shotgun side of the black SUV, gun high and ready, hurling commands at the terrorists in the van. Three other SWAT operators and Pete Mack flanked either side of the SUV, hidden as well as they could be behind the open doors. Rivett reduced the throttle on the Ducati and began to slow as he finally covered the distance.

When he was about twenty feet from the van, one of the men inside made a break for it. The man held his arms high up in the air—as if surrendering—with no weapon. SWAT did not shoot. But he was running directly towards Jake, their paths about to intersect. For a brief second, Jake was able to concentrate on the man's face. It was definitely Hanafi. But Jake didn't have much time, because once Hanafi was just a few feet away, someone started shooting.

Markle jumped back behind the protective bulletproof glass of the SWAT SUV as the van's driver opened fire with a pistol from the inside of the van. The shooter was aiming through the van's front windshield, attempting to pick off the officers standing in front of him. Without hesitation, SWAT opened up on the driver. Their metal piercing bullets made quick work of whoever was targeting them.

Hanafi saw Jake ahead and pivoted, sprinting to the side. Jake course corrected with Hanafi, leaning his bike into an arcing path in pursuit of the running terrorist. Jake didn't worry about colliding with Hanafi. Instead, he drove right into him. The spinning wheels of the Ducati made contact with Hanafi's feet, flinging him down onto the pavement. Jake maintained control. The Ducati sheared the side of Hanafi's leg as it slowed to a stop. Jake jumped off and pounced on Hanafi, who was moaning on the ground.

"It goes without saying," Jake said as he pulled out a pair of handcuffs and pinned Hanafi's arms roughly behind his back with his knee. "You're under arrest, Hanafi." Jake latched the handcuffs on to Hanafi's wrists, securing him.

Even though he was about to see the long arm of the law up close,

Hanafi was laughing.

"What's so funny?" Jake asked.

Hanafi smiled at Jake. "The machine," he muttered.

"What about it?"

"It's perfect. Darab was prepared to die."

"Who's Darab? The driver?"

"No," Hanafi said. "In the back."

Jake followed Hanafi's gaze back towards the van, which was surrounded by the SWAT operators.

"Oh, n—"

Jake Rivett didn't even have time to scream before the explosion erupted in the center of Times Square.

The blast was absolutely gargantuan. The molten fire from the chemical explosives inside the van reached as far as Jake and Hanafi on the ground. The firestorm was like a rekindling phoenix. It never seemed to end, multiplying on itself and snatching any and all pieces of debris, trash cans, car parts, city signs, and the like in its massive wake. The explosion was a tsunami of pure force, and the shockwave traveled well past them. And then, as quickly as it all began, it started to dissipate—leaving only an expanding cloud of pitch-black dust masking the entirety of Times Square.

Blown flat to the ground, Jake couldn't hear a thing and could barely breathe. But he opened his eyes and knew he was still alive. Hanafi lay on the ground next to him, mumbling quietly to himself. Jake tried to pull himself up into a sitting position. It was excruciatingly difficult, but eventually he did it. He shook his head, trying to clear the concussion that swirled through his brain.

Jake gazed into the center of Times Square. There was nothing there.

No van. No Pete Mack. No Markle. No SWAT.

There was nothing, except for a massive bomb crater.

Rivett couldn't control himself. The tears began to stream down his face, and he let out a primal scream. "*AAHHYYAAAAAAAA!*"

CHAPTER TWENTY-FIVE

MURAD AND DR. BORIN SPRINTED through throngs of tourists in midtown Manhattan. A few blocks from Times Square, they had heard the explosion like everyone else. The noise and vibration from the huge blast was impossible to miss. After the boom, the black SUV with the flashers pursuing them was forced to stop, because hundreds of civilians were sprinting across the street in panic. Murad glanced back to see multiple SWAT operators disembark from the vehicle. The assault team spread out across the street—guns out—slowly filtering through the crowd in pursuit of them.

"What's the plan?" Dr. Borin asked Murad.

Murad glanced down at his cell phone. "The plan is . . . keep running!" Murad exclaimed.

Murad and the doctor turned another corner and raced down a side street. They were now out of sight from every member of the SWAT team and would be for another fifteen or twenty seconds.

"You're telling me Hanafi was going to just leave us for dead?" Dr. Borin asked.

"Hanafi's not in charge."

"Well, *I* don't know what to do . . ." Dr. Borin panted.

Murad managed a laugh. "You aren't either, doctor."

A few paces ahead of them, an anonymous grey metal door with no handle opened. With only a lock visible to the street, this was a building maintenance door—one of dozens along the street—to one of the giant glass-and-steel skyscrapers that populated the area. A man in his forties with a rough complexion, in all black and wearing a chest bag, held the door open and stared at them. The man's face wasn't welcoming, but he didn't seem shocked to see them, either.

Dr. Borin pivoted to avoid the open door. He was surprised when Murad sprinted right in. Without a second thought, Dr. Borin followed.

CHAPTER TWENTY-SIX

OMER DEFTLY NAVIGATED THE SHADOWS. One could not grow up brown in America without this skill, but it was especially important for Omer tonight. He traversed back and forth across Queens, trying to decide what to do next. He'd ducked out of sight from twelve police cars in the neighborhood within the last hour. That was about twelve more than he'd seen in the month prior. The cops were not just passing through. They were looking for someone and he knew that person was him. Even though he'd connected to Twitter through an anonymizer called Tor, Omer had turned off his phone and thrown the device in the trash. That being said, he knew he wasn't in the clear—far from it. He was sure the police would quickly figure out who he was. He really wanted to go home, but he didn't know if he should. He didn't want to bring any more trouble to his family than he had to.

As Omer padded down the sidewalk in the middle of the night, the bright lights of an electronics store beckoned. Although the establishment was security-gated, the store kept its televisions on all night long, casting an eerie and fluctuating glow over the street. Omer almost passed by until a chyron running on the bottom of CNN caught his eye: "TERROR ATTACK IN TIMES SQUARE; MULTIPLE FATALITIES."

Omer stopped. He fully rotated towards the bank of televisions.

The van was the first thing he saw. It was impossible to miss. Well, half of it. Right on CNN was a live image of his dad's van—complete with a charred but identifiable logo reading "Steinway Cleaners"—smoldering in the middle of Times Square. So much for not bringing trouble to his family. The televisions weren't playing any sound, but Omer didn't need to see or hear any more. He was looking for a sign, and this was it. He kicked off down the street. He was twelve blocks from home, and he needed to get there before the rest of the world did.

▪

Omer tiptoed up the stairs of his house, attempting to be as quiet as possible. The second he reached the inside entranceway, he dropped the charade. All of the lights were on inside the living room, and his father, mother, and Salma sat solemnly at the dinner table.

"What's going on?" Omer asked innocently before taking one more step and discovering the answer himself.

Murad and Dr. Borin stood in the living room. Murad was holding a gun.

"We're a family that eats together, Omer. So we've been waiting for you," Murad replied sarcastically.

"The cops are going to show up . . ."

"No shit. Salma's lucky you're back."

"That's it!" Azza Amin stood up from the dinner table. "I'm going to bed. And you . . . Murad . . . You are leaving."

"Mother, I promise you . . ." Murad started towards his mother. He jabbed the gun in the air, spiking the weapon back and forth in Azza's direction. "I won't hurt you—never, ever would. But you can't leave. Not until Omer and I have spoken." Murad pivoted towards Omer and pointed the gun directly in his face. "What'd you do, Omer?"

"The fuck did you do, Murad? You're a murderer now? A terrorist? Is that how you want to be remembered? That's how you're going to protect our family?" Omer screamed at Murad.

"We had a deal."

"We *have* a deal," Omer said.

"You broke it. You squealed."

"I did nothing."

"What do you think, doctor? You're the mind guy. Is he lying?"

Dr. Borin stared at Omer. "He'll do."

"Not what I asked," Murad said.

"I'm cutting to the point . . ."

"So if you weren't talking to the cops, where were you?" Murad yelled at Omer.

"I was out. I was at a . . . concert."

Moradi and Azza gasped simultaneously.

"I'm not talking about your concerts, pretty boy. The only people who don't know about that are our parents. I'm talking about you tipping off the detective from that band—the one on TV. Jake Rivett."

Omer glanced at Salma, who had a pained expression on her face. No one said anything for a moment.

"He was going to kill Pat," Salma finally said tearfully.

"And now what's he going to do?" Omer asked.

"I told you to get out, Murad!" Azza yelled at her son again. She stood up and paced towards him. Murad held the gun in the air to try to stop her, but Azza kept pushing.

"Sit down!" Murad yelled.

"Shoot me! Shoot. I will not sit down. You're inside my house." Azza had tears in her eyes as she bum-rushed Murad. He didn't shoot, instead grabbing her in a bear hug with the gun still in his hands while she tried to whack him with her forearms.

"Mother, please. I love you."

"I love you too," she wailed.

"I'm the brave one. I'm the one who's going to change our destiny. Isn't that what you wanted? You hate the same things I do. Why are you trying to stop me?"

Behind them, Dr. Borin answered a phone call and listened.

"We'll be right out," the doctor said. He hung up and nodded at Murad. "The man from Dubai is waiting. They want to go."

Murad shoved Azza away suddenly. She fell to the ground between him and Omer, and Murad trained his gun back on Omer.

"I promised you, Mother, I will not hurt you. I keep my promises. Even this kid . . ." Murad gestured with the gun at Omer. "Although I do want to hurt him, I won't." Murad paused for a moment. "We'll let him do it to himself. We got to get out of here before the place turns to hellfire. Only good thing about all the police is they might need some uniforms pressed, Dad. Make sure you give 'em a business card."

Murad grabbed Omer roughly by the arm and shoved him towards the door. Dr. Borin followed.

▪

On the street outside the Amin family's house, a black SUV idled. The passenger door opened slightly, and Omer could make out a young man's pristine, model-like face inside. Murad roughly pushed Omer into the back seat. Once he was seated, Dr. Borin tapped something metallic onto the side of Omer's neck. Omer only felt the slightest pinprick, but within seconds a toxic chill spread through his veins. He turned towards the doctor and saw a syringe. He blacked out as the knockout agent took over.

▪

Moradi Amin turned on the television after Murad and the strange white man had left with Omer. The horror of the Times Square bombing was all over the screen. Moradi only shook his head in shell-shocked despair. He couldn't believe that after everything he'd accomplished in life, this was the result. His family's entire life story was about to become international news. Why had Allah reached down with his fingers and touched upon them like this? What had he done? How quickly the American dream could turn into a nightmare. Times Square was covered in cameras, and the entire attack was there in full HD. Moradi could only watch in horror as his own company's van, with the logo for his laundry business plastered on the side, drove into the middle of Times Square before engaging with a SWAT team and blowing itself to smithereens. The broadcaster was now a detective agency as well, of course. They'd pulled the logo off the van, expanded and sharpened it, and had a correspondent standing outside the family business in Astoria, just down the street. What's more, an unruly crowd of men—mostly white, mostly angry— stood protesting in front of the building. Moradi knew his creation was in jeopardy. He'd built the cleaners inch by inch, dollar by dollar, and day by excruciating day. Now, out of the blue, it stood at the center of a terror firestorm.

▪

Moradi ran down the street. His business was only a few blocks away, but the distance felt infinite. By the time he arrived, the crowd had grown exponentially from what he'd seen on television. Plenty of reporters and news media were approaching the scene, but the only true ruler that evening was chaos. The police hadn't shown up yet, although Moradi could hear sirens. As he stepped foot onto the block, he heard glass breaking for the first time. It started with a single brick, thrust by an adrenaline-pumped man in the shadows, but quickly one brick turned into many. One by one, the windows of Steinway Cleaners were systematically smashed. The rioters began to use other items—crowbars, baseball bats, flashlights, whatever—to break out the glass from the windows and gain entry to the business. Some of them were there to steal, others just to gawk. But as Moradi finally reached the front of his store, he saw a group of men pouring gasoline over the clothes inside. He stepped up to the doorway and began yelling.

"This is my property! I demand that you vacate the premises! You will be arrested!" Moradi screamed at the top of his lungs.

"This is yours?" one of the men asked him.

"Yes, it is. Now you will get out!"

After the first punch arrived, Moradi didn't say anything else. The rioters jumped him in a frenzy, pushing him to the ground and kicking him repeatedly. He curled into the fetal position, pain stabbing his body with each impact.

Within thirty seconds, the assault was over. Moradi snuck a glance from between his fingers to confirm that the cops had arrived. After they pulled the last rioters off him, two cops hauled Moradi himself off the ground. The crowd parted, and the police began to yell orders and engage in crowd control. The cops carried Moradi from the sidewalk to the street, where their squad car was parked. Moradi realized that although the police were pushing the rioters away from Steinway Cleaners, nothing was being done about the fire. Flames licked through the entire first floor of his business.

Finally, Moradi was guided into a sitting position on the back bumper of a police vehicle, guarded by two lukewarm blues. Through his two black eyes, he could only watch with sadness while his life's work burnt to the ground. It was quite a macabre sight. The fire burned red hot and no one was there to stop it. The police didn't seem to think it was their job, and he didn't see any firefighters on the scene yet. None of the numerous newscasters seemed to be upset by what was happening, either. They turned their backs to the fire and filed their reports—Moradi's misfortune all the better background for their breaking news.

CHAPTER TWENTY-SEVEN

THE LAST SIGHT OMER AMIN expected when he finally opened his eyes was a stunning skyliner view of the Manhattan sunrise. But that's what he saw—a vista of the city framed by floor-to-ceiling glass. Omer had never been in a room like this before in his entire life. He perceived that he was sitting in an ultra-modernist apartment way, way up in the sky—about fifty stories in the air and soaring over Gotham. This place was out of *Architectural Digest* and the future, combined. A hedge funder's dream, the apartment must have been worth untold millions of dollars. The room was extremely sparse. There was basically nothing in it besides wide-plank light-wood floors, white walls, and the view. Omer craned his neck left and right. That's when he discovered a second fact. He was strapped into a chair. He looked at his hands. They were each handcuffed onto a large office chair, which seemed to be bolted to the ground. Then Omer looked up and—*damn it*. There was that white MRI tube. Omer finally realized he was sitting underneath Dr. Borin's machine.

The door opened. Murad and Dr. Borin entered first, followed by two more men. Behind them, Omer spied an immaculate living room—complete with modern art, oversized furniture, smoke-grey marble, and a sprinkling of antiquity-era sculptures. Then the door closed. Omer gazed at the two new men's faces. The first he didn't recognize—a man with a rough face, wearing black activewear, a chest bag, and sneakers. He seemed to be a bodyguard. Omer recognized the second man. It was the same face he'd noticed inside the SUV that had picked them up at his family's house. The man was young and was of Middle Eastern descent. His deeply cut cheeks and designer duds made him look like nothing less than a fashion model. He was clearly in charge.

"You're the man from Dubai?" Omer asked.

The man nodded with a slim grin. "Dubious description," he said.

"Everyone was waiting for you," Omer replied.

"It seems I've arrived in the nick of time."

"What are you going to do to me?" Omer twisted towards Murad as he asked the question.

"It's just like Dad always says . . ." Murad announced. "You're either part of the problem or you're part of the solution. What do you want to be?"

"Do I have a choice?"

"I won't let you be a problem," Murad said, "which is why we are going to allow you to be part of the solution—a big, big part."

"What do you mean?"

Dr. Borin stepped behind Omer. He tinkered on a laptop set up on a small table.

"Do you want to kill?" Dr. Borin asked suddenly. When no one replied, he asked again. "Omer, do you want to kill?"

"No . . ." Omer replied. "Who? What do you mean?"

"Of course you don't. I've been waiting for over twenty years for this moment," Borin orated while he configured the machine. "I think we've done it. Darab proved that. But we need you for the final test, with our benefactor here watching. You're the dream. I know you don't want to do what you will eventually, but I must remind you of something. Before you met me, you were destined to be nothing. Now, you will be part of one of the greatest scientific evolutions in human history. That can never be taken away from you. Never!"

"You're totally out of your mind," Omer said. "What's the point? Why go through all the trouble? Aren't there enough terrorists out there who want to be suicide bombers?"

"You'd be surprised," the man from Dubai said. "But your job isn't to ask questions."

"No, indeed," Dr. Borin said. "Your job is to be the P.O.C."

"What's a P.O.C.?"

"You, dear brother, are our proof of concept," Murad finally answered.

Murad and the man from Dubai slowly helped lower the MRI machine over Omer's head while Dr. Borin continued to tap on the controls to his invention. After a few more seconds, Omer could hear their movement stop. He couldn't see anything at that point, the incredible panoramic view now blocked by the off-white plastic surface of the MRI machine a few inches from his eyes. He was strapped in and immobile. That's when the curiously attractive female voice began to speak. Her words were clearly emanating from speakers near his ears, but it sounded as though she were inside his brain. And all she was saying was the same thing over and over again . . .

"His name is Rivett," the woman said. "His name is Rivett. His name is Rivett." She repeated herself over and over again. Finally, she said, "Say it with me."

Omer didn't reply.

"Omer," she said. "Say it with me."

"His name is Rivett," Omer whispered.

CHAPTER TWENTY-EIGHT

SUSAN HERLIHY WAS CRYING. RIVETT stood in her office and wasn't sure what to do. He'd never seen Susan cry before, but then again he wanted to cry, too. The loss of Pete Mack and Jack Markle, as well as the other members of the SWAT team, was utterly devastating. Jake had always wondered what it would take for Susan to seem vulnerable. Now that he knew, he wished he didn't.

"I'm sorry," she finally said.

"Don't be. It's not your fault."

"I'm pissed."

"Me too," Rivett confirmed.

"I wish I could tell you to pull a Rivett on this guy . . ."

"On Hanafi? Still can. Happily. With gusto."

Susan shook her head.

"We can't torture him. But I can certainly get rid of him," Mr. White added from the corner of the room.

"Maybe later, Sheldon," Susan answered, only half joking.

"You're the boss," Mr. White replied, only half serious.

"You know I love myself a cowboy, Rivett. I almost married one once."

"I know. From Galveston. But he talked too much and was a scaredy-cat."

"You have a good memory," Susan replied. "That's why I always liked Pete Mack. He was the opposite. He was cautious, but at the end of the day he suited up. Balls of steel and he never advertised it. You could have learned something from him. Just remember, Jake—you're being taped, and there's about five guys from each agency watching outside. Don't get hot under the collar. Get answers," she concluded.

"Roger that, Susan. Don't worry. Things are going to turn around."

"Funny thing to say right now . . ."

"We got Hanafi. That's why."

"He'll be slippery," Mr. White added.

"Yeah. But at least there's a crack in the egg. You know?"

"I do." Susan nodded. "Don't lose the yolk."

"So . . . now?" Jake asked.

"Now."

Rivett walked out of Susan's office and down the hallway towards the interrogation room. He passed by Tony and Moseley, who nodded. Tony gave a thumbs up to indicate that all of their recording equipment was working.

"Break a leg, Rivett," Shep Moseley said.

Jake could easily identify the correct interrogation room, because it was the one with the police officer standing outside and packing a submachine gun. The guard moved aside.

Jake entered and took his first good look at Ali Hanafi. Cult kings fascinated Jake. He called them kings because the members of a cult always end up not just following but also revering their leaders. Whenever Jake met a cult king like Hanafi, he was always surprised to find them quite ordinary—at first. Usually their mildly pleasant exterior was simply camouflage for their intelligence and cunning. That's why he was staring at an utterly ordinary man in almost every respect. From the ten extra pounds around Hanafi's waist to the slightly formal yet ultimately casual polo shirt he was wearing, and with day-old stubble but still stubbornly parted hair, not much drew the eye about Hanafi. At the same time, he was certainly a valid foe. Somewhere along the line, Hanafi had managed to organize and carry out two major terror attacks in New York City without even a scent of his plans escaping into the ether.

The second Jake stepped into the room, the battle was on. Jake also knew he was in a losing position. He—and, by extension, the world—needed what Hanafi had and Hanafi knew it. There was only one way to break down a man like that. The guy needed to think he was winning.

"How you doing?" Jake began nonchalantly.

"Fine," Hanafi said. "Do I get a lawyer?"

"Do you want a lawyer?"

"Yeah. I already told them that."

"They're getting you one. I know you've been read your rights, so I'm not going to repeat them."

"Rights . . . What a joke. Did they read my brothers their rights in Guantanamo?"

"You had brothers in Guantanamo?" Rivett asked. "I didn't know that . . ."

"No," Hanafi said. "I guess cops don't get metaphors."

"What makes you think I'm a cop?" Jake asked as he sat down at the table in front of Hanafi.

"Huh?" Hanafi was startled for a moment.

"Just messing with you."

For a brief moment, Hanafi allowed himself to smile.

"Fuckin' Five-O, through and through. Son of a cop, too. How's that for ya? Real New York, huh?" Jake said.

"Had me there for a second . . ."

"Alim . . . That's what you like to be called, right? Alim Hanafi?" Jake said. "You know, I'm not here to try to drag you over the coals and pull every single piece of information out of you. I'd like to. I really would. But I'm not going to, because I can't. You wanna know why?"

"Why?" Hanafi asked.

"Because it wouldn't work. You're smart and you know it. And I know you know it. So, really, I'm just curious. I want your point of view." Jake took a long breath before the next words came out of his mouth. "What do you get out of all this?"

"I could tell you, but I couldn't make you understand."

"Try me."

"You and I . . . We're like two completely separate alien races—oil and water. We can't combine. Only one wins, and the other loses. That's the only way this goes. I'm just a little part of it."

"Are you talking about, like, religion? I'm not so good with that."

"Religion, culture . . ." Hanafi shrugged. "Resources, geopolitics . . . All of it."

"That's a little wishy-washy."

"Huh?" Hanafi asked.

"You strike me as a little more than just a buzzword guy . . . *Religion, culture . . .*"

"You want to know about me personally?"

"Yes."

"There's a light at the end of the tunnel for me."

"Not anymore," Jake said.

Hanafi shook his head. "I told you that you wouldn't understand."

"You called yourself 'a little part.' I feel like you're a big part of everything. From all our intel, it seems you're the big boy in the room. You're the boss."

"Every boss has a boss, detective."

"So who's yours?"

Hanafi shrugged.

"Sorry. My bad. That's my job, isn't it?" Jake asked.

"You're the cop," Hanafi confirmed.

"I really do want to understand. I know I don't, but I wanna. So you planned and carried out multiple terror events just because of an overall culture war?"

"It's a bit more complicated than that."

"Enlighten me."

"I told you—I'm part of something."

"So who else is out there?"

"There's nobody in New York. That's not what I'm talking about."

"No one?"

"Nope. You got us all, but not before we got some of you . . ."

"How do I know you're telling the truth?

"I'm sitting here in the heart of your government, detective. What do I have to lose?"

"Maybe two of your guys?" Jake pulled his cell phone out of his pocket and swiped through a number of photos on the phone. "You left out the part where these two got away," Jake said. He showed Hanafi a grainy surveillance photo of Dr. Borin and Murad running down the street in Manhattan.

"Don't know them," Hanafi said.

"I do—Maximilian Borin and Murad Amin. Quite the odd couple, if you ask me. How'd you find the doctor?"

Hanafi didn't reply.

"My guess is it wasn't during your annual checkup," Rivett joked.

"I'm done talking. You're not my lawyer, and you're not my friend."

"The doctor is the one who made the mind-control machine, yeah? The one you ran on Abdel Hayat?"

"I don't know anything about that," Hanafi said.

"Right, right. I forgot. Sorry. I have a problem with listening. Everyone tells me that." Rivett stood up. His hands gripped the chair he'd been sitting on. "I want you to remember something, Alim."

Hanafi listened.

"You're the one who ended this conversation, not me," Jake said. "Me? I could go on talking for days. I told you I'm not so big into religion. But I'll talk to you about it—happily. I'll talk about sports. Music. Man, there's one I can talk for days about. Weeks, really. Motorcycles. Art . . . at least a little. Hell, I can even talk to you about love. But you gotta talk back. Talking's a privilege. It's like a relationship. Needs both sides. You don't wanna talk? That's fine. Some people call me dense, but I'll get the picture eventually. Then I'll be gone. But . . . When I'm gone, you might never have another conversation again. Not with someone who can change your future. The day will come when the only person you'll be able to talk to is yourself." Rivett slammed the back of the chair against the table that Hanafi was sitting behind. The noise ricocheted around the room like a bullet with no way out. "And when you're sitting in Supermax up in Colorado, in your tiny little cell . . . When you're talking to yourself . . . That's when you'll finally realize that you're completely insane."

▪

"More I get to know him, the more I like the kid," Mr. White said. He was sitting in a glass conference room in back of the command center alongside Susan. They were watching Jake's interrogation.

"Rivett's a wild man," Susan said. "But that's his secret to staying employed. He makes you like him."

Mr. White nodded, his hand tapping on a keyboard in front of him. Sheldon White was good at multitasking. His personal motto was "multa bene facta"—*many things done well.* The credo had served him very well for over thirty years as a CIA agent. As was standard, not even inside this room was the CIA's presence overtly advertised. But everyone knew. Every single individual in the room was aware they had to listen to the quiet but confident agent and his aides who sat in the back. In fact, Mr. White was probably the only person Susan was willing to listen to as well—and everyone knew that, too. He didn't speak often, but when he did he was listened to. As was normal for Mr. White, he had spent the last few days in the way that a swashbuckling CIA agent should—doing deep financial research on his laptop.

Mr. White's thought process began and ended with the gym. The only way the terrorists had been able to escape the raid was because of the old construction hallway below Best Diner. But Hanafi and his crew would have needed to ensure that their escape route was clear. The gym's sub-basement was new construction. There were at least two locked and reinforced doors that led from the sub-basement to the rest of the building. However, none of the locks had been broken. They were all unlocked. It seemed as though Hanafi and his crew had simply walked through an open portal to freedom.

"I can understand the doors . . ." Mr. White talked out loud to Susan, who turned to listen.

"You're still thinking about the gym?" Susan prodded. "You read the maintenance guy's transcripts, right?"

The NYPD had interviewed the owner of the gym's maintenance man for eight hours. He checked out. He was just a dude with a job. He had reported that he didn't remember unlocking the doors to the utility room in the sub-basement, but he also didn't remember locking them—because they were always locked. It was possible, he'd explained, that he'd simply forgotten at some point. He didn't go into the sub-basement much in any event, sticking to the main supply room in the basement.

"That's why I said I can understand about the doors . . ."

Susan watched as Mr. White continued to click through folder after folder of dense financial files.

"But what I can't understand is the cameras," Mr. White continued. "New construction and a new owner, and a fully installed camera system. But they tell us their system had been down for about a month prior. What sort of establishment lets their system go down for a month? Does that ring true?"

"I think the owners were cleared. Fong and Moseley have been running through all of it," Susan replied.

"Right, right . . ." Mr. White continued to click on his laptop. "It got me thinking. Let's take a step back. On one hand, Hanafi may have just gotten lucky. It's certainly possible. On the other hand, maybe Hanafi knew this was his escape route, and he had some way of making sure the doors were open. Maybe someone at the gym, or the owners of the building, had a reason to help Hanafi. So for plausible deniability, they broke their security system nice and early—so that if and when we came along, they could say it was a months-long problem, not something that conspicuously happened that night."

"Possible but improbable . . ."

"We are so far past improbable," Mr. White said.

"Where's the lead?"

"I've been looking for it for about three days, Susan," Sheldon said. He finally broke his attention from the computer screen and turned to address her. "Is Hanafi married?"

Fong perked up from across the room. "No marriage records in any of the fifty states. Still trying to pull data from our foreign partners."

"I think Hanafi's married, which means I think we might have found our edge," Mr. White finally announced.

The whole room turned towards Mr. White, eager to understand.

"I sure ain't a real estate investor, but that building with the gym bothered me. Yeah, the doors. The cameras. But not just them. It's the whole goddamn hulking thing. It's so damn pretty, right? It's gorgeous. I am aware of the concept of gentrification that you city folk always like to complain about. But no other development has arrived on that street. Not like that. So with one building, the place goes from zero to hero? I'm not so sure. So that made me start digging deeper into the building itself. Who's the developer? Well, last night I paid a visit to the guy who built it. He's completely legitimate. Big builder in New York—a hundred employees and another thousand subcontractors. But he told me something interesting. He didn't originate this project. He was a hired gun. Another company, an LLC based in a corporate factory in Delaware, gives this developer a low-interest loan to buy the land and build the building. Simultaneously, a related LLC signs a contract saying they'll buy the finished building from the developer for a fixed price above the interest and equal to his profit margin. So, of course, we go after these

LLCs. Don't find a lot there either. Except they're both run by an attorney named Ronald Fitzpatrick out of Long Island. Here's where it gets really interesting. Fitzpatrick is either the trustee of trusts or the officer of corporations that own multiple buildings along that street." Mr. White paused for a moment and then continued, "Including Best Diner."

"Holy shit," Jake Rivett said. He'd just stepped into the room and listened to the end of Mr. White's story. "Should I go back in and ask Hanafi about Fitzpatrick?"

"No," replied Mr. White curtly.

"So one person owns all of those buildings?" Susan asked.

"Or one organization. One big pool of money."

"Where's Fitzpatrick? We're gonna go get him, right?" Jake said.

Mr. White whipped his laptop around and clicked on an application, which loaded up a live-feed video. Onscreen, the attorney Fitzpatrick sat surrounded by serious men in suits.

"FBI is talking to him right now. A bunch of Mack's guys. I can assure you they won't be nice."

"And what's he saying?" Susan asked. "How does this relate to Hanafi having a wife?"

"That's what's interesting." Mr. White glanced at Susan. "Lawyer is telling us jack shit. More he opens his mouth, the more he's buying himself time in the fed pen. I know this because while he lies to us, we've been pulling his bank accounts warrant by warrant. Still haven't figured out who actually owns all these buildings, but it isn't Fitzpatrick himself. Fitzpatrick says he's only dealt with foreign lawyers in Panama and denies knowing his ultimate client. He also denies knowing Hanafi personally. Meanwhile, Hanafi only communicated with a real estate management firm. But Fitzpatrick's lying through his teeth. There is a connection."

"What is it?" Susan asked.

"Fitzpatrick is married with three kids. For all intents and purposes, he seems happy. Good social media. No cheating on his texts or emails. And his phone doesn't have him straying past Long Island, and certainly never to the countryside of Pennsylvania."

"Pennsylvania?"

"Huh?" Jake interjected.

"The Hiller School."

"Say again?"

"The Hiller School. Fitzpatrick makes tuition payments to a high-end private college-prep school in the middle of Pennsylvania. It ain't cheap. He's paying over seventy thousand dollars a year for two kids of Pakistani descent. So either Fitzpatrick has some secret children he's storing in Pennsylvania . . ."

"Or Hanafi does." Jake finished Mr. White's statement.

"Exactly," Mr. White said. "I'm sending Moseley and Tony to Pennsylvania to take care of it."

"Warrants might be a little tough. Lot of supposition . . ." Susan said.

"I know," Mr. White said. "The agency has learned a lot over the years." Mr. White chuckled. "First we tried good—cigarettes and porn. Then we tried evil. You probably read all about that in the newspapers. But what we've come to realize is neither of those work. It's all too one-dimensional, too literal. Everyone knows those tactics now. Especially on US soil. You saw that firsthand, Rivett. Hanafi knows all of our limits."

"Yeah . . ." Jake trailed off.

"Don't get down," Mr. White said.

"What can you do different?"

"Tricks, Rivett. That's what we do. We play tricks," Mr. White said.

CHAPTER TWENTY-NINE

THE NEXT DAY WAS VERY Queens—hectic, dirty and frustrating. Sometimes Queens was also magical, but not at present. Jake had spent the whole morning chasing down leads. The leads themselves were like wild geese and the chasing had gone just as well. It was slightly frustrating, albeit nothing out of the ordinary. If he was being honest, Jake was still a bit upset that Mr. White and Susan hadn't allowed him to head down to Pennsylvania. That was a real lead—at least it seemed to be. Maybe Mr. White didn't trust him. Or maybe Susan had spoiled the well. Either way, it grated on Jake while he spent the day humping around the borough.

Jake's primary mission was to locate Omer Amin . . . *again*. Overnight, the security team at Twitter had quickly provided an IP address, which was tracked to Omer's cell phone. However, when Jake and a few detectives had arrived at the cell phone's location, they had found the device inside a trash can just blocks away from the Charcoal Stop.

Now the detectives were midway through an interview with Omer's family at their house in Astoria, and it was abundantly clear that none of them knew where Omer was. Jake was silently kicking himself inside. If he hadn't let Omer go, they might be further along. But at the same time, if he had stayed even a few more minutes with Omer, it's possible that Times Square would have gone much worse than it did. Adding to the conundrum, the Amin family was claiming that their son had been kidnapped by another one of their sons.

"And your cops . . . Know what they did while my business burned? Nothing!" Moradi Amin raised his voice as he complained to Jake about his destroyed business.

Moradi's dry-cleaning business was the last thing on Jake's mind. While the other detectives listened patiently and attempted to mollify Moradi, Jake spent his time carefully padding around the Amin family home and taking everything in.

"We get it, sir," Jake said. "But like we told you, that's not our department."

"It's my life," Moradi replied. "Aren't you detectives?"

"Terror, Mr. Amin. Terror. That's what I care about. So are you gonna answer our questions about Omer?"

"We have nothing to hide, nothing at all . . . I've answered everything!" Moradi exclaimed.

"So your other son, Murad . . . He and the doctor Maximilian Borin show up . . ."

"Sure. The one from your pictures . . ."

"How long were they in the house?"

"Murad came to look for Omer. He was here for about an hour beforehand and then not long after."

"Do you have any idea where they took Omer?"

"No." Moradi shook his head. "I told you. I mean, it was very traumatic. I don't remember absolutely everything . . ."

"So they could have said something about where they were going, but you might not remember?"

"I remember," Salma Amin said as she popped up, sitting next to her quiet mother.

"And?" Jake asked.

"They didn't say where they were going. No. But . . . there was one thing."

"What's that?"

"When the SUV showed up—the black one that they all got into . . . The doctor said something about a man in Dubai. But, like, the man was here. The man from Dubai was picking them up. Something like that . . ."

"The man from Dubai? Who's that?"

"No idea. They didn't say his name. That's all they said—'the man from Dubai.'"

Jake sighed. Another wild goose. And this one from Dubai.

▪

The winter sun had already begun to dip below the horizon as Jake headed south, away from Queens and towards Mona. It was only midafternoon, but he was done for the day. As usual, the case was bothering him. But he planned to do his best to disconnect. That's what he'd promised Mona and what she wanted—no, needed. And he understood that. He also had a band practice scheduled for that evening but was about one text away from cancelling it.

He hoped Mona would be in a good mood. The last two weeks had frayed both of their nerves, although he knew most of it was his own fault. Jake was excited about spending his entire life with Mona, but the irony of a terror attack occurring on the very night he'd proposed was not lost on him. It was truly a newsworthy international incident that manifested itself as a giant signpost about the issues that they would continue to face in their relationship. Jake wasn't a person who was used to drawing a line between work and life. The two would always be inextricably linked to one another. After all, his most successful cases of the past had required fanatical obsession. Criminals never slept, so why should he? And while Mona had met him on the job, she was probably still coming to terms with exactly how deep Jake's devotion lay. That's what happened when you were the only thing standing between good and bad.

Thankfully, when Jake arrived at the apartment, he found Mona in a downright chipper mood. Something was up. She sat on their couch next to her laptop, with a menagerie of printed materials strewn out across the coffee table ahead of her.

"What's all that?" Jake asked as he walked in. He kissed her.

"Sit down for a second."

Jake did as requested. On the coffee table, he noticed a number of wedding-invitation mock-ups, both printed and pulled from magazines.

"Wedding invites?"

"What do you think?" Mona beamed.

"What do you mean? I can't wait to get married."

"No—the invites. Which one is your favorite?"

Jake looked over the invites on the table. They all looked quite similar, as though they'd been pulled from the pages of a bridal magazine.

"They're . . . nice."

"White and pink, right? Or white and blue?"

"Whatever you want, darling."

"Okay!" Mona popped up. "I don't like any of them."

Jake couldn't help but grin. She knew him too well. He didn't want to rock the boat, but nothing she'd shown him was really that thrilling.

"I was thinking of black," Mona finally announced.

"Drama."

"You and me, right? I've been working on this for two weeks," Mona announced. She was a graphic designer who knew her way around Photoshop just as well as Jake navigated the stage. She pulled out a printed image from behind her back and held it up. The whole card was black, except for the dark-grey outline of their two faces staring at one another.

"That is . . . truly fucking next level, darling."

"Thank you," Mona beamed. "There is a problem, though." She flipped the invite to the other side. "Usually when people send out a wedding invite, there's a date."

"I know," Jake said. "I've been thinking about that. Do you want to wait another year?"

"Well, the venues . . ."

"I asked what you want."

"No. I don't want to wait."

"Then we won't," Jake announced.

"Really?"

"The very first day you want it is when we'll do it."

"What about in four weeks? New Year's Eve?"

"Done."

"Holy shit," Mona replied. "That was easy. And . . . I got a lot of work to do."

"Yeah, yeah. You probably do."

"Promise me one thing, Jake. No matter what's going on with the case, you'll be at your own wedding."

"I guarantee you I'll be there," Jake said. "And I want to say something else. I'm really sorry. I'm sorry about how I've been acting. I'm sorry about this case. I'm sorry about all of it. I can't promise you that I'm going to change overnight. It might be slow. But I will change. And I will do it for you."

Mona paused. "Thank you," she finally said.

"So we've got a date. How should we celebrate?"

"Don't you have band practice tonight?"

"Yeah. I decided I should blow it off. I mean, that won't be exactly unusual."

"No, no. You need to go."

"Why?"

"Those are some of your only friends in the world. And you love it. It's important that you do what you love. I'm pretty sure you're the guy who told me that."

"I know . . . But this is a special evening."

"I'm just excited to keep working." Mona grinned.

"For the person who complains about how much I work . . . Pot calling the kettle black over there."

"The nice thing about invitations is they print when you say print. Criminals don't provide the same feedback."

"Very true." Jake paused for a moment. "Well, I guess I gotta go hit the shower."

"Wait a minute. I know we're not married yet, but I don't care about a little sin if you don't . . ." Mona stood up in the living room and pranced past Jake with a mysterious look on her face.

"What?" Jake grinned.

"I think you know what . . ."

"Oh yeah? Wouldn't your grandma tell you that once you're out of the garden, there's no going back?"

"You and I haven't seen garden gates in a long, long time."

"Isn't that the truth. But I thought you wanted me to go to practice."

"A man can't multitask?"

"Never been too good at it. But I can try."

"Try hard," Mona said as she pulled a strap off her shoulder and headed down the hallway.

Jake hurried, as fast as he could, to follow her.

CHAPTER THIRTY

MAXIMILIAN BORIN SAT ON A small folding chair in the back of the room, watching his subject inside his machine and the late-afternoon sun behind him. The young man, Omer, was responding admirably to treatment. Borin had high hopes that the machine would once again prove him right, and this time it would be in front of his financier. Omer was Dr. Borin's most interesting case yet. In the past, the team had stuck with either predisposed or neutral subjects. Now Dr. Borin had a subject who was clearly and ardently disinclined towards the mission.

Yes, Dr. Borin wanted more time—especially with a subject like Omer. But the man from Dubai, his bodyguard Mr. Wasi, and Murad were all clearly stressed out. Dr. Borin knew they were making preparations to leave the country after the final strike. They would be taking him with them, because he was the golden goose. It wasn't the technology itself. It was him—Dr. Borin—who mattered the most. No one could run the machine except for him, at least not yet. And similarly, no one could build the machine except for him. In the back of his head, Dr. Borin knew this was why he was able to operate with such a high level of impunity. But he also knew that once he was out of America, he would need to begin to make progress towards his ultimate goal. He knew what he wanted in the long run: a research institution. He wanted to be in charge of an entire campus, crawling with scientists who would do his bidding. He would definitely leverage his command over the technology into this dream. Even if the institute had to be in some desert nation-state in the middle of nowhere, it would be his. And at his institute, no one would be able to tell him what to do—no administrators, no bosses, and especially not his mother Maxine.

Dr. Borin stood up and sauntered over to the computer. On the screen was a projected feed of Omer's brain activity, being dynamically read by the MRI machine. He checked a few status indicators. Everything was good. The subject was stable and calm—just as the doctor wanted. Dr. Borin looked out over the huge city through the massive windows. He'd miss New York, but not the luxury of the place. His future was filled with more luxury than he could ever imagine. He knew that was true. No, what he'd miss about New York were the experiences that money couldn't buy. He'd miss the hot dog stands, the wafting scents from the street vents, and the honking of taxicabs and cars while jaywalking. He'd miss the bagels and lox, the little wine bars, and the public libraries. And, yeah, he'd probably miss his mother too. He'd miss a lot, a very lot, but he wouldn't miss these things enough to not go. Scientific revolution required sacrifice.

After confirming that Omer was still doing well, Dr. Borin stepped out of the room. In the living room of the apartment, he saw the bomb. The kitchen had been turned into a workshop, and Murad and Mr. Wasi were putting the final touches on the device. It wasn't much to look at— basically a bunch of plastic bricks secured to a large chemical container. A few wires ran from an electronic starter unit to the explosives. Dr. Borin shuddered at the thought of what would happen if the men made a mistake while they finished the contraption. That's why he was there to supervise. Not because he cared about what Murad and the man from Dubai had in mind—*not at all.* Nope, he really didn't want to think about it. He just wanted the bomb to be done, because he wanted the thing covered up, carted out, and sent down the freight elevator.

The faster it was gone, the sooner they could leave, and the closer Dr. Borin would get to his research institution.

CHAPTER THIRTY-ONE

THE HILLER SCHOOL WAS TWO hundred years of stone masonry atop the rolling grass of old Pennsylvania cornfields, punctuated by a massive clock tower in the middle of the property. The school was about as far away as anyone would have imagined a terrorist would hide his family, which might be why it was perfect for Fatima Akon.

Mr. White and the joint task force had spent the last twenty-four hours researching Ms. Akon, but they hadn't deduced much actionable intelligence about her. She was a naturalized citizen, having come in via sponsorship from an aunt in the mid-2000s. It wasn't entirely clear if Akon was her birth name or a more recent change, but her immigration application was still being pulled out of cold storage somewhere in DC. She lived in a quiet upscale bedroom community. Everything about her was quite vanilla, down to the part-time job that she held at a local interior design firm in Swarthmore, Pennsylvania. The only strange statistic about Ms. Akon was that she had two children who both lived with her, but no husband in sight. In and of itself, this wasn't unusual. But the kids went to a tony school, they lived in a lovely home, and Fatima made barely any money at all. The financial contradiction was the only break in her facade—that, and the fact that Ms. Akon didn't seem to have any family or personal connections to suburban Pennsylvania.

Tony Villalon and Shep Moseley sat inside a white SUV parked in the school's parking lot. To assure the success of their operation, they hadn't disclosed much information to the school's headmaster. It was better that way—for both sides. The headmaster was a stone-cold liberal who was critical of many federal policies, but once he saw a signed letter from the FBI director and heard that the investigation revolved around the Bryant Park and Times Square bombings, he hadn't asked any more questions. For a place like the Hiller School, all publicity was definitely not good publicity. The administrator just wanted it over with, and quickly. So did Tony and Moseley. It didn't thrill them to begin this operation at a school, but their plan was very specific. It was vital that they encounter Ms. Akon not only with her children, but also out in public—as opposed to within the safe confines of her house. It wasn't that their plan was illegal, but it wasn't entirely legal, either.

The sun was just beginning to set and it wasn't even four yet. The pickups of kids involved in sports programs were beginning, and for the time being, Tony and Moseley had nothing to do.

"How long have you worked for Mr. White?" Tony asked.

"My whole life, man."

"College? The CIA does internships?"

"No, bro. I used to cut his grass."

"Huh?" Tony glanced at Shep for confirmation. Moseley wasn't joking.

"Yeah. In Gaithersburg. Where I grew up. Mr. White and his wife lived four houses down, and I started cutting his grass when I was thirteen. I was earning the entrepreneurship merit badge for Boy Scouts. Later on, he got our congressman to write a recommendation letter to

Georgetown for me. We stayed in touch."

"Wow. That's crazy," Tony replied. "So that's how you got into the CIA?"

"*If* I did work for CIA," Shep said as he shrugged, "it would be 'CIA.' Not *the* CIA."

"So you got in by cutting grass?"

"We pick people carefully," Shep said with a shrug. "When you know where a kid comes from, how they grew up, you pretty much know everything about them. The older you get, the more water under the bridge, and the harder it is to figure out . . ."

"Shit," Tony said. "I guess that means I can't apply to the CIA . . ."

"CIA, not *the* CIA."

"Has Mr. White always been the same as he is now?"

Shep chuckled. "Rad dude, isn't he?"

"He's like a nerd with a big swinging . . . you know what."

"All the power's up here." Shep tapped his head.

The two men paused to observe the school pickup procedure happening ahead. The parking lot afforded a perfect view of a large overhang that extended from the side of one of the school's buildings. The families of the the Hiller School most definitely kept multiple local German car dealerships in business. The vehicles passing through the pickup zone were a procession of large and expensive SUVs driven by mostly yummy mummys, with a sprinkling of cool dads as well. Each driver placed a sign with a big number in the windshield, and a faculty member with a microphone would announce the numbers—at which point, the student or students would come out.

"Not how my school pickup worked . . ." Shep remarked.

"What pickup?" Tony replied. "For us, it was more like, jail release—

Wait. That's her!"

Ahead of them, a smaller Jeep Cherokee drove into the pickup zone. Two kids—a boy and a younger girl—ran out and into the car.

"Yep," Shep confirmed. He had a bag of electronic equipment at his feet. Shep pulled out a DSLR camera with a massive magnifying lens. He squared the Jeep up and snapped a series of pictures, which immediately read out onto a tablet in front of them.

"Two thousand fourteen Jeep Cherokee, yeah?"

"Correct," Tony replied, glancing at a series of car specs on his phone. "Plate's right."

"Better to check something twice than be sorry once," Shep answered, putting the camera down. "That's something else Mr. White taught me."

"Smart guy."

"We'll see how smart his plan is . . ." Shep answered. "Ready to rock?"

"Literally," Tony said with a chuckle. His cell phone was transmitting background music to the car stereo via Bluetooth. He turned up the volume on the current song, and Mythics' newest screamo track blasted into the car. "Pursuit music," Tony announced.

"It's truly terrible," Shep said.

Reading Shep's opinion, Tony reached for his phone to turn the volume down. But Shep stopped him with a wave.

"Keep it going. Makes me feel alive."

"That's what Jake says," Tony said.

"Rivett likes this stuff?"

"This *is* Rivett."

"What are you talking about?"

"It's Mythics—Rivett's band. He's singing."

"Badass," Shep said.

Ms. Akon drove around the long circular driveway in front of the school. She passed by the exit to the parking lot. Tony carefully pulled their SUV out of its spot and ripped across the lot in pursuit.

▪

Tony and Moseley tracked Ms. Akon through the back roads of Swarthmore, PA. About a mile from the school, the two cars took a turn onto an old country lane. The local FBI office had been running surveillance on Ms. Akon for the last two days, so the agents knew that she took this route on her way back from school. It was perfect in many ways. First, it was secluded and rarely traversed. Second, the road was not lined with trees or forested wetlands as many of the other rural roads in the vicinity were. That was important because their plan relied heavily on technology that could be diminished by any form of signal interference. Tony kept a sixty-yard distance between their SUV and Ms. Akon's Cherokee, while Moseley worked to assemble another piece of equipment on his lap. The device looked like a tactical briefcase—bulky and protected by a thick metal Zero Halliburton shell. Once open, it resembled a very basic laptop, although the machine contained fewer keys and no mouse or trackball. On both sides of the briefcase were two large antennae, each the size of a portable umbrella. Moseley quickly extended the two antenna and began typing commands on the device.

"Two thousand fourteen . . . Rear-wheel drivetrain . . ." Shep muttered under his breath.

"This is some major conspiracy theory stuff right here," Tony announced.

"You're lucky you got the read-in, man. Don't blow it," Shep said. "Isn't even the beginning of our capabilities . . ."

"Ready? Only about two miles left . . ."

"Yep," Shep announced. He pressed a button on the device.

Tony and Moseley followed Ms. Akon's car for another half mile, and nothing happened.

Until . . .

A dark cloud of smoke began to waft from the front of the Cherokee. The Jeep slowed, and Tony slowed behind it, maintaining the same following distance. It was clear that something was wrong with the car's engine. Thick black smoke billowed from the engine compartment of the Cherokee. By this point, Ms. Akon had her blinker on and was pulling her car over to the right side of the road. Only seconds after she'd parked the Cherokee on the side of the road, flames began to lick around the edges of the car's hood.

Tony navigated their SUV to a stop just behind the Cherokee, watching as Ms. Akon jumped out of the driver's seat with a panicked look on her face. She stared at them for a moment before sprinting to the back door and helping her daughter and son out of the car. In the meantime, Moseley was running to the back of the Tahoe and yelling at Tony.

"Pop the trunk, dude!"

Tony did as he was told. Moseley reached for a giant fire extinguisher attached to the back wall of the SUV. Without delay, Moseley sprinted towards Ms. Akon and her burning car.

"I got a fire extinguisher, ma'am. Stay back!" Moseley aimed the extinguisher's plume at the car, but underneath the closed hood, the fire seemed undeterred. By that point, Tony had reached into Ms. Akon's car and managed to pop the front. When the hood rose, a giant cloud of smoke erupted, but Moseley was on it. He spent a good minute or two spraying every inch of the car's engine compartment with the fire extinguisher and was finally able to stop the flames. He stood back, an accomplished smile on his face.

"Thank you so much!" Ms. Akon said to Shep. She was still quivering in shock.

"Honestly, ma'am, it's my pleasure. I'm just happy I remembered my wife put that fire extinguisher in the back of the car there. Never thought it would be someone else on fire!"

Tony glanced over the engine compartment. "Looks like it was just the engine. You *might* be able to salvage it. Sure isn't drivable."

"You and your kids want a ride?" Shep asked. "We've got plenty of room in the Tahoe. Where are you headed? We're on our way back to Chadds Ford."

Ms. Akon looked over Shep and Tony. It was clear she was going to go it alone.

"I'm okay. We'll call an Uber or a tow truck."

Tony nodded towards Shep. "Shep here has a great tow-truck contact," he said.

"Oh, thank you so much. But I have Triple A. So I'll just give them a ring. You really think it's not totaled?"

"I'd say it has life in it yet. But I'm not a betting man—especially not when it comes to cars," Shep said. "Hey, kids, keep your mom safe, all right? No more blowin' up the car!"

And with that, Tony and Moseley got back into their Tahoe and drove away.

▪

Fatima Akon had been having a bad day and then her car blew up. Just her luck. Now she was stranded on the side of the road with her two kids, waiting for a tow truck to arrive. Thankfully, it wasn't too cold, and the children were occupied with homework while sitting on the grass against a long fence in the countryside. But Fatima was still a nervous wreck. It had been a rough week, and she had been looking forward to a relaxing Friday evening at home—tuning out the news and perhaps watching a movie. Now she was sure to be handed a multiple-thousand-dollar service bill or, more likely, have to buy a new car. Those guys who stopped and helped put out the fire said they thought it could be repaired. But what did they know? They looked like two accountants on their way to the bar after work—certainly not experts. All she could do at that point was pray.

Perhaps Fatima's prayers were being answered, because seconds after she closed her eyes, the tow truck showed up. She knew Triple A usually took about an hour. But it had been less than twenty minutes and here he was! Maybe her luck was finally turning around.

The tow-truck driver shook her hand and confirmed her name and address before starting to hook up the car. After a few minutes, the Cherokee had been hoisted onto the back of the tow truck and Fatima and her two kids were inside the truck's two-row cab, heading down the road.

"You want me to head to the Jeep dealership, right? Not the independent place?" the driver asked her.

"I think so, yeah . . ."

"You can probably get a lower price somewhere else," the driver informed her. "But I get it. When you want a job done right, can't beat dealer service."

Ahead of them, the tow truck slowed for a stop sign at the end of the rural road that Fatima and her kids had been driving on. When they stopped, Fatima gazed out the window and was surprised to see the white

Tahoe with the men that had helped them earlier. It was still there, parked on the side of the road. Outside the SUV stood the guy who'd extinguished the fire. She thought his name was Shep. He was waving at them.

"You know him?" the tow-truck driver asked.

"No, not really . . . You can go."

The driver didn't drive. Shep approached the passenger side of the tow truck. As he did, the tow-truck driver reached to his left and unlocked the doors. Shep jumped into the car, pushing Fatima into the middle between him and the driver.

"Hey, Ms. Akon," Shep said with his huge perma-grin plastered on his face.

"Can I help you?"

"It's a long ride to the dealership. Thought I should accompany you."

"Excuse me?" she asked, startled. She turned around and pointed to the door in the back seat of the cab. "Open the door, Saheeb," she said to her son.

Saheeb grabbed the handle, but the door wouldn't open.

"Child lock," Shep said.

Fatima looked back at Shep, who still had that stupid grin on his face.

"Ms. Akon, me and your driver here, Mr. Fong . . . We're not going to hurt you."

"That's the truth. Sorry to trick you back there," Fong confirmed.

"Now, don't start to worry or anything," Shep continued. "We're federal agents. Everything's completely by the book. We're simply going to escort you to the dealership."

"What are you talking about? This is totally illegal." Fatima pulled out her cell phone and attempted to dial 9-1-1.

"Having some reception issues?" Shep asked. "Yeah, it's probably going to be like that the entire trip."

"What do you want?"

"Absolutely nothing. Not from you. Like I said, we're escorting you. It's just that . . . it might be a really, really long ride. We might miss the dealership. We might go in circles. I don't know." Shep shrugged. "All of it would be by accident, of course . . ."

"Tell me what it is you want. Why are you here?"

"It's totally out of my hands," Shep said.

"Then who's in charge?"

"One guy's in charge. His name's Ali Hanafi. Know him? At the end of the day, Ali Hanafi is going to choose how long your trip lasts and where you go."

Fatima didn't respond. Instead, she became dead silent. She reached behind her seat and gripped her son's and daughter's hands and said nothing at all. The depth of what Shep was saying had finally having sunk in.

Shep played with the tow truck's radio controls. He hooked his phone up to the vehicle's speaker system and scrolled through song options.

"I just got this new album. It's not really relaxing. But to be completely honest with you, it's growing on me. I think I sort of . . . maybe just a little, little bit love it." Shep hit play on a Mythics album, and Jake Rivett's screaming voice soon entered the fray. Then Shep loaded the camera application on his phone and tapped the icon for selfie mode. He leaned in to Fatima and held up the phone in front of the two of them.

"But first, we need a selfie," Shep said.

Click.

CHAPTER THIRTY-TWO

THE RECORDING SPACES WERE ALWAYS different but always the same. Since Mythics didn't have a label contract, let alone an agent, finding a place to practice their craft was an art in and of itself. The responsibility almost always fell upon Schaub to organize. While Rivett may have been the soul of the band, Schaub was definitely the glue that kept it together. Without Jake, Mythics had no lead singer. But without Schaub, Mythics would never practice or play. Jake knew that. It was one of the reasons he'd decided to carve the time out for practice that evening. Also, Mona had practically demanded it. After Jake had arrived and figured out how to navigate the serpentine route up to the correct studio on the fourth floor of the facility, he found Schaub in a particularly good mood.

"Don't even need to throw into the pot today," Schaub said.

"Why?" Jake asked.

"Dude, remember I told you about that agent that's been reaching out to me? Get this—he paid for the space. All he said is he wants a first look at any of our new stuff. No commitments . . . but we *want* him to commit."

"Didn't you think that should be a band decision?"

"Are you kidding? No way. Someone else wants to pay, we're gonna let them," Schaub replied.

"Who is this guy?"

"No one's saying you should quit your day job, Rivett."

"How 'bout my night job . . ." Rivett muttered under his breath.

"What?"

"Nothing. Sorry. I don't—"

"Spit it out. You know you will eventually," their keyboardist, Sam, added.

"I think it's cool about the agent. I don't want to be the one who lets you guys down."

Schaub pointed to the other two members of the band, Janzen and Sam. "We meet you where you are, man. Wherever that is, that's where Mythics is. We get it. You wanna keep it as a hobby, it's a hobby. No one even says this guy will hand us a record contract. He's just a fan. And if one day you're ready . . . maybe a label will be ready, too."

"Thanks, Schaub." Rivett pulled his old friend in for a hug. It felt good to be understood. It was also rare. "Got alot on my mind right now. Hey, by the way, what are you guys doing for New Years?"

"Isn't that in, like, a few weeks?" Schaub asked.

"Yeah."

"Impossible to know. Way too far out," Schaub said.

"Well, you might want to write this down in Sharpie, 'cause you've got plans."

"What's that?"

"That's when your old boy is getting hitched," Rivett said.

"Unbelievable!" Janzen erupted.

"I'll clear my schedule," Schaub said with a grin. "That's sick, Rivett. Proud of you."

In the background, Janzen strummed chords on the electric guitar.

"I've been working on something, gents. Want to listen?" Janzen asked.

"Take it away," Schaub said. He nodded at the studio producer in the booth.

Janzen stood in the middle of the room and began to thrash the guitar as hard as he could. His hair flew in every direction as he hit the chords—if you could call them that. His new piece of music was deeply discordant and full of utter rage. It was also classic Mythics. The band was known for heavy doses of hard-rock screamo, with a thin slice of pop, and this song was no different. To the side, Schaub began drilling on the drum set in unison to Janzen's piece. It was music for men on construction sites, for workouts, and for maniacs in the mosh pit. It was awesome and wild and hard and absurd.

But Rivett wasn't feeling it—not that night. He held out his hand for Janzen to stop playing. When the music faded out, Jake spoke.

"I felt like we were onto something different with *Out of the Mist.*"

"Yeah, but screamo is who we are . . ." Janzen replied.

"I wasn't going to say it myself," Schaub said. "But Rivett's right on. I love headbanger stuff—don't get me wrong. But the agent only found us because of *Mist.*"

"So we're just gonna sell out?" Janzen asked.

"It's not about the agent," Jake said. "Think about it this way. Do you think Radiohead is selling out?"

"I think Mythics ain't Radiohead," Janzen replied. "But I'll do whatever . . ."

"So what are you thinking, Rivett?" Schaub asked.

"Go slow. Then double slow."

Schaub started beating out a midtempo beat on the drums. It still had an edge of hardcore to it but was much more melodic and tonal. Janzen followed with the electric guitar, and Sam echoed on the keys. Jake nodded his head slowly. The poppy beat continued for a few more minutes as the band waited for lyrics to materialize. Usually Schaub came up with the words and then Jake modified them for delivery, but no one was volunteering anything.

"What do you think, Jake?"

"I think the beat works. But it isn't what I want to play," Jake finally announced.

"Then what?"

"Slow it down even more. Sam, start with the keys. *Lento*."

Sam brought the rhythm down to a creep, the level of a slow ballad. Schaub followed up with possibly the slowest drum beat his hands had ever performed. The new song dripped with melancholy and romance. It was like the soundtrack to a candlelit dinner. And for Rivett, it was perfect. He began to sing.

"Steal my love . . . In the night . . . So far gone, but it feels right." Jake's words didn't flow from his head that evening. Instead, they came from his heart. It was only midway through the song when Jake realized what was happening. He was swinging at his very first love song. "Rock me never, but hold me tight . . ."

After a few minutes, Jake stopped singing. Clearly there was only one person he'd been thinking about while singing this song—*Mona*. He wondered what she would think. Perhaps she would be amused that Jake Rivett was writing a love song? He finally opened his eyes and glanced at the band. He wasn't sure what to expect. Maybe the guys would be disgusted. But instead, all three of them were ecstatic.

"Wow," Janzen finally exclaimed.

"That crushes," Schaub announced. "Never thought I would see the day where I would say that Mythics is gonna break out . . . on a ballad. That's a fuckin' hit, Rivett."

"What's it called?" Sam asked.

"Mona."

▪

Omer Amin wasn't accustomed to being driven by a chauffeur. But at the moment, he sat by himself in the back of a town car as Mr. Wasi drove him through Manhattan and into Brooklyn. Remarkably, the man from Dubai was sitting up front in the passenger seat. Omer enjoyed the role reversal. He deserved it. Omer had experienced an epiphany recently. Before, he had been living a life without purpose. Now he knew why he was here and what he had to do. He loved the simplicity of his new perspective. It demanded everything of him but felt like less work. And obviously, given his position in the car, he was now respected.

Omer knew his target. Although there were moments where he tried to distract himself from his mission, they were fleeting. He simply couldn't avoid what he was about to do. The mission was imprinted inside his brain. He knew that only the elimination of the target would cure him. For some reason, Omer didn't feel any fear. He had been told that he might, but maybe he was already numb. Maybe the doctor didn't know how effective the technology really was. Or maybe it was just him. Either way, Omer felt the opposite of scared. He felt more alive than he ever had. He felt so good that it confused him. But the confusion would be over soon. For that, he was thankful.

Omer watched through the window as the car moved into Brooklyn and passed block after block of small townhouses, detached duplexes, and apartment buildings. He was nearing the target's location. Omer knew there was a bigger game being played, but he didn't care. He wasn't concerned with what his brother or the doctor or Mr. Wasi or the man from Dubai or anyone else was up to. He didn't worry about the bomb. He didn't care about the machine. In the past, he might have obsessed about those things. He might have tried to stop them. But now all Omer cared about was his mission. After he completed his mission, he would be free. That much was guaranteed. And the promise of a subsequent return to normalcy was what drove him. It meant he could go back to school. He could return to his family. He could keep going to concerts. He could go back to being himself.

Eventually Omer recognized the target's building from a picture he'd been shown earlier. The town car slowed to a stop. They had arrived outside the target's apartment. Omer fingered the gun in his lap. He switched the safety off and pushed the weapon into his pocket. The man from Dubai turned around and gazed at Omer.

"You good?" He asked.

"Yes. I am."

"Inshallah."

"Sure."

"Sure?"

"God has nothing to do with my mission," Omer said as he reached for the door and cracked it open. He put one foot on the pavement outside and was about to step out when Mr. Wasi piped up.

"That worries me," he said.

"It shouldn't," replied Omer.

"One more time . . . Who's the target?" the man from Dubai asked.

"I know the target."

"Say it with me, one more time," the man from dubai said.

"I told you . . . I know."

"Say it," Mr. Wasi demanded.

"His name is Rivett," Omer intoned.

■

It was the best selfie Sheldon White had ever received. Mr. White stared at the photo of Shep with Fatima Akon and her two kids. The joint task force didn't have actual genetic proof that the children, or she, were related to Hanafi. Mr. White hadn't demanded a swab yet, because it would push him and his team further out onto an already very thin extrajudicial branch. But there was a reason that Mr. White was Mr. White. The man played poker every day of his life, except the house was international geopolitics and the chips were lives. He strode towards the interrogation room housing Hanafi and entered.

"Alim, how are you?" Mr. White asked Hanafi, who didn't seem to be taking his imprisonment too terribly. He had been provided with sufficient snacks, water, and even coffee and a blanket.

Hanafi didn't reply.

"No? Nothing?" Mr. White inquired.

"I want to see my lawyer."

"Absolutely . . . We are working on that right now. It was the phones in here. They're complicated. So many buttons to press, and we've got all sorts of new faces wandering around the halls, so everyone had to be trained. Then we had to find the public defender's number. Took a few tries. But they're making the calls right now, rest assured."

"Good," Hanafi answered.

"I'm really just the hospitality department . . . I want to make sure your blankets are warm enough and your tea has honey in it."

Hanafi couldn't help but chuckle. Mr. White was funny.

"So how you doin'? Everything good? Coffee taste fine? Brewed it myself. Need any cream?"

"Coffee's strong. Thanks," Hanafi said and then added, "I want my lawyer."

"Absolutely." Mr. White turned back towards the door to the interrogation room. With his hand on the door, he spoke again. "I'll need to make sure one of these idiots can make coffee just as good as I can, because I might not be back for awhile. I gotta go on a little road trip to Swarthmore—Pennsylvania. Ever been?"

Hanafi's eyes squinted slightly and almost imperceptibly. He remained silent.

"Heard it's beautiful down there. Some people might think it's remote, but the area's still trendy and not really the boonies. Like the perfect suburb or somethin'. I don't know. I'm still partial to DC, but that's 'cause I'm a touch southern boy myself."

"I've never been."

"Yeah? You never know. Just curious . . ." Mr. White began to open the door. "Oh my gosh! I'm so freaking silly."

Mr. White closed the door and paced back to the interrogation table. He leaned in until he was inches from Hanafi's face, and his entire complexion changed in an instant. "For a second there, I was almost okay with you lying to my face," Mr. White said. "But I'm really not." He swiped the coffee cup away from Hanafi and held it up in the air.

"I'm not lying to you, sir."

"You are. We picked up Fatima Akon and her two children this morning." Mr. White pulled his cell phone out of his pocket and brought up Shep's selfie of the family. He showed Hanafi. "See? There's Fatima and the kids. What do you think?"

"I told you . . . Lawyer," Hanafi answered.

"Right, right," Mr. White said. He became more and more animated. He stepped back from Hanafi. It was exciting, actually. Hanafi didn't realize, but he was the one being pitched to. Hanafi was the buyer. Mr. White was attempting to make the sale. And just like a master pitchman, Mr. White had to start small, go big, and end with the completely unavoidable hook.

"I am so intrigued about your relationship with Ms. Akon. It's sort of brilliant. Answers so many questions that I have—like why you don't have a family in Queens? Very strange for a conservative religious figure. But you can sort all that out for us later. That's just my personal question. There are more pressing issues. The main one, for you, is where we're going to drop your wife off. See, she had a little car trouble. And a few of my guys were kind enough to pick her up and offer her a ride to the mechanic. That ride has been going on for a while now. Maybe two hours. Maybe three. It's a long trip to the dealership sometimes. I mean . . . to a good one. I won't beat around the bush. I'll let you in on a little secret. They're not going to a mechanic. At least not until you and I are done talking. 'Cause my guys . . . They have another option. In Philadelphia there's a nice-looking office building that's operated by Immigration and Customs Enforcement. You know . . . ICE. *Ice cold ICE.* Now, what I'm going to do is take this coffee cup here and get a rapid DNA test on it. We'll compare that to the DNA from Ms. Akon's car—the kids, especially. We've already got your wife's immigration application pulled up. It was in the back of some warehouse in Virginia, but it's truly amazing how quickly the feds can get things when they really, really need them. Anyway, I digress. Turns out she already had at least one child when she applied, but you're not on her application as the father. So if you are related to Ms. Akon or her kids, and she didn't reference you on her application, you know what that means? That means ICE has a perjury case. Then, honestly, it's totally out of my hands. I don't know the ICE guys. Real low-rent operation, if you ask me. I feel like maybe they used to be lazy, but, holy shit, are they now on the fucking eight ball. I mean, they have turned deportation into a machine. And they go after the kids now, too—separate them from the parents. The whole nine yards. But like I said, I don't know them personally. No connections there. So once anyone goes into ICE, that's it. Game over. The only people that I know are the two guys that are driving around your wife and kids right now." Mr. White paused and took a few deep breaths. Hanafi was sweating heavily, his eyes completely focused on Mr. White. The sell was working. The hook was in. All he had to do was pull the string. "But, you know, I could also just have my men drop your family back at their house— simple as that. 'Goodbye! Thanks for the ride! See ya never!'"

"What do you want?"

"First, you'll tell me where Maximilian Borin and Murad Amin are right now. Then, you'll tell me everything else."

"And if I do, you'll drop them off?"

"I will," Mr. White promised. "Even at the mechanic, if that's what they want."

"How do I know you're telling the truth?"

"You'll know I'm telling the truth the second I know you're telling the truth," Mr. White answered.

Hanafi made his decision.

"I know exactly where Murad and the doctor are."

"Where's that?"

"They're at the man from Dubai's apartment."

▪

Rivett, Schaub, and Janzen loitered at the entrance to the recording studio. Loitering used to be their jam. Back in the old days at City College, way before Jake was a cop, they had mastered the art of chilling. In those times, Jake didn't have a care in the world except for showing up at his dishwashing job and making it to band practice—and sometimes school. Obviously, things were different now. More pressure. More responsibility. Even so, the recording session had been a cleansing experience for Jake. He was always reminded of his love for music when he made music. As usual, Mona had been right. It was worth it to go to practice. It wasn't that Jake didn't listen to Mona. He did. It was just that he didn't always follow her advice. But that would change. It already was. He'd just written a love song, for God's sake.

And just then, there was another small blessing: snow.

Jake stared out over the East Village street and allowed himself to take in the beauty. Of course, the case was still active. But for now, just for one moment, he allowed himself to breathe. Jake reached into his pocket and pulled out his phone. He dialed Mona, but the call rang through. She didn't answer.

"Alrighty, boys," Jake turned to Schaub and Janzen. "Next time . . ."

"When's that?" Schaub said. "Should we set something up? For next week?"

"Make it the one after," Rivett replied.

"Two weeks usually means two months."

"I know," Rivett said. "Not if I break the case."

"That's what I like to hear," Schaub replied.

"And, anyway, now I got Mona."

"The song or the girl?" Schaub asked.

"Both."

"In my professional opinion," Janzen added, "you sound like a man in the depths of a deep love addiction."

"You got me, kid," Jake answered. "Now I gotta get home . . ."

Jake felt his cell phone ringing in his pocket. He pulled it out.

"Mona?" *Nope.* Rivett glanced at the screen. He had answered too quickly. It was the office. "Mr. White. What's up?"

Jake listened intently to Mr. White on the other side.

"I'll meet you there," Jake replied. He hung up. "Dammit," he said to his bandmates but also to no one in particular.

"What's up?"

"My other girlfriend."

"No rest for the weary . . ." Schaub said. He patted Jake on the back as he climbed onto his motorcycle.

"YAYAYAAYAAAA!" Rivett let out his trademark scream, the same one that punctuated the end of most of Mythics songs. He started the Ducati and skidded out into the icy night.

■

While Rivett rode, he wondered what the joint task force was about to encounter. Mr. White had told him they had an address for the man from Dubai. It was a multi-million dollar apartment—very uptown, very high rent—right in the middle of the beating heart of Manhattan.

Jake also thought about Mona. He had called her twice in the last ten minutes, but she hadn't answered. She usually picked up. Probably because he didn't call enough. Even if she didn't answer, she'd always call back. Maybe she was asleep. He didn't know. What he did know was that evil had a home address, and he was gonna knock down its door.

CHAPTER THIRTY-THREE

EVIL *WAS* CALLING—ON JAKE and Mona's front door.

At first Mona thought she was dreaming, because she had been. Soon the echoing noise couldn't be muted and Mona woke up in their bedroom with a start. She could hear something slamming against the front door of the apartment. Without pause, Mona jumped out of bed and reached for the massive Maglite flashlight Jake insisted they keep next to their dresser. She strode out of the bedroom and past the bathroom and kitchen, looking for the noise. The banging had stopped. She paused to listen but heard nothing. Maybe it was Jake?

"Jake?" Mona asked.

No response. Mona reached for a light switch to illuminate the small entrance hall. She flicked the light on.

Baammmm!

Before Mona's eyes could acclimate, a gun shot rang out—then a second. Mona dove to the side. The shooter seemed to be aiming at the lock, but one of the bullets made its way through the doorjamb. She could feel a burning sensation in her leg. Mona glanced down and knew she had been shot. She pulled herself up just as she caught a brief glimpse of a young man—he looked to not even be eighteen years old—opening the door and scrambling towards her. Mona raced back to the kitchen. She could hear the footsteps of the intruder chasing her. She grabbed a long knife from the knife block and pushed her body as close as she could to the refrigerator, which partly blocked the entrance to the kitchen. She waited for the man.

"Where's Jake Rivett?" she heard him yell from the living room.

Mona didn't dare say a word. She watched as a shadow paced past the kitchen. The man headed down the hallway to the bedroom and bathroom in the back. He hadn't realized where she was. She felt her pocket for her cell phone. *Damn it.* She'd left it on the nightstand.

She began to listen as the man rustled through their bedroom. The guy seemed to be murmuring to himself. He certainly wasn't a random burglar. He was very clearly looking for Jake. Mona deduced that whoever he was, he wasn't very experienced. Why hadn't he come after her first? He looked and acted like an amateur. Maybe she could take advantage of that. She continued to listen, using her ears as sonar to figure out where he was. The man began to walk back down the hallway. This time his pace was slower, more deliberate. The second she saw his foot pass the kitchen threshold, she knew it was time to act. She lunged.

The knife sliced through the air. She aimed her weapon directly for his lower abdomen area. Jake had taught her a few basics. Go for the stomach and push all the way through. Don't simply aim for the target— extend towards the wall behind the target. She hit the intruder directly as intended. He screamed out in pain, a massive plume of blood pouring from his wound. The blood caused Mona to recoil the tiniest bit. The man spun away from her and into the living room.

Mona pursued him, but this time the man was ready. He rotated towards her, pulling the trigger on his gun and shooting three times.

Mona ducked and dove behind a couch. She avoided the shots, but her knife flew out of her hands, spinning across the room and out of reach.

The man took the opportunity to jump on top of Mona. He straddled her on the floor, his blood gushing all over the two of them. He was holding his gun directly in her face.

"You're not the target. I need the target. Who are you?"

"Who's the target?" Mona asked. She was slapping at the man's forearms in an attempt to deflect his gun, but he held strong. His finger tensed around the trigger.

"Everyone knows that. His name is Rivett—Jake Rivett. Where's Jake Rivett?" the man screamed.

"I—I can find Jake Rivett for you. Get off me . . . I'll call him . . . I'll have him meet us here."

For a second, the man seemed to take Mona's suggestion seriously.

But she didn't care. All she was doing was watching the barrel of the gun inches from her face. When the barrel moved two inches to her right, Mona made her move. She'd lost the knife, but she felt the Maglite under her back. She fingered the flashlight with her left hand and rotated her core with as much velocity and force to the right as she could. Mona smashed the dense flashlight against the man's head. Her attacker fell off her and crouched on all fours. He was completely stunned. His gun lay next to him. Mona kicked it away, and the man didn't try to stop her. He shook his head. Mona held the Maglite with two hands way up in the air, like an axe, and brought it down on the guy again.

Improbably, he kept moving. He was crawling back towards the gun at the center of the room. Mona collapsed on top of the man, scrambling to pull his hand away from the firearm. The man was a mere two feet from the gun. She snaked one arm into a half-nelson position around his neck, slowly and excruciatingly pulling him away from the weapon. Soon, Mona was able to get her second hand, holding the flashlight, around his neck, and she got her attacker into a full-nelson submission hold—aided by the Maglite.

"Stop . . . Stop . . ." Mona pleaded. The man slowly stopped struggling. Eventually, she realized his strength was fading. He was still losing blood from the stomach wound. All she had to do was hold on a little bit longer and she would get out of this. That's all. *Just hold on.*

Mona continued to hold her attacker in a full nelson. After another minute, the man stopped moving. Mona breathed a sigh of relief, but she continued to hold him. She wanted to make sure he was fully unconscious before she made her escape.

After another minute, Mona let go. The man fell to the ground limp —perhaps dead. She pushed off of him and sat on the floor in shock. Finally she stood.

That's when she heard the noise. It was the sound of a gun cocking.

Mona twisted around.

Another man—with a rough face, wearing all black—stood in the living room. His gun was trained on Mona.

He pulled the trigger.

CHAPTER THIRTY-FOUR

WHILE JAKE RIPPED THROUGH THE city, his mind was spinning. He missed Mona. Where was she? Using his Bluetooth headset, Jake called her a third time.

Ring. Ring. Ring.

Her phone rang through to voicemail. Jake glanced at the time. It was late, but not so late. He wasn't sure why this was bothering him. It never had before. Usually he was the one who was impossible to find. But something was nagging him.

Jake knew Mr. White, Susan, and the rest of the joint task force were expecting him at the building by Central Park—*ASAP*. But the raid was going to happen whether he was there or not. SWAT wasn't going to wait. He was just needed to mop everything up afterwards.

And Mona, well . . . She wasn't that far away.

Jake tilted his body to the side and spun the Ducati into a screaming hundred-and-eighty-degree turn over the yellow lines and across the street. A car behind Jake screeched and slid to a stop in the snow to avoid crashing into him. The driver slammed his horn, but Jake didn't even look back.

Jake and the Ducati raced towards the Brooklyn Bridge, away from the assignment but towards Mona.

CHAPTER THIRTY-FIVE

MR. WASI HUGGED THE SHADOWS as he slipped out the front door of Jake and Mona's apartment. He padded across the street, his footsteps making slushy impressions in the snow. Mr. Wasi opened the driver's side door of the black town car. The interior light illuminated the man from Dubai, now sitting in the back. Mr. Wasi nodded at his boss.

"Murad? And the doctor?" Mr. Wasi asked.

"No time . . ."

The town car raced down the street and disappeared into the snowy night.

-

CHAPTER THIRTY-SIX

THE MONSTER THAT WAS NYPD SWAT stalked the pristine hallway. The team members were fierce as beasts but light as butterflies. Usually SWAT would go through more preparation for an operation of this magnitude. In this case, there wasn't any time. Susan Herlihy and Mr. White had made that very clear, but in actuality, none of the operators needed more motivation. In fact, they had never been as inspired for a raid as they were for this one. This raid was for Captain Markle. It was for Pete Mack. It was for their team members in Times Square. It was for all the people of New York.

The SWAT team—twelve operators to start and another twenty-four backing them up—stole down the hallway of the target's luxury condo residence just south of Central Park. When they reached the door, three operators took up defensive positions to the sides. A fourth crouched in front of the threshold and pulled out a tablet-sized portable device. The machine was a heat-signature scanner, which could tell if any humans were in the immediate vicinity beyond the door. The device could even ascertain the depth of any heat-emitting objects. But no heat signatures showed up on the scanner. The SWAT operator gave a thumbs-down sign and stepped away.

A fifth and sixth member of the team appeared behind the door, each holding a separate battering ram. The building manager hadn't been able to produce a key to the apartment in time, so alternative entry was required. Normal procedure called for one ram—but two was ultra. The lead operator glanced at the rammers. One was left handed and the other right handed. Each of them was utterly stacked. They were the strongest two men in the squad. The rammers stood on their respective sides of the door in the ready position. Each had a shoulder rotated backwards, torqued up, and ready to accelerate their dense steel beams into the door. The second the lead gave the sign, the rammers ignited.

Bam. Bam. Bam. Bam. Bam.

In a perfect staccato rhythm, the men aimed their battering rams for a semicircular area three inches above the door handle and directly below the lock. One ram impacted after the other, never pausing and never slowing. It took no longer than nine seconds before the lock began to implode, a quarter-inch steel splinter appearing between the locking mechanism and the frame. Another operator joined in, leveraging a crowbar against the door. After another four seconds, the door creaked open.

The SWAT team blasted in the room like greyhounds released to the track. They charged into the apartment's living room and fanned out into all of the bedrooms.

There was nothing—*no one.*

The apartment was completely empty. The place looked as clean, orderly, and downright boring as a hotel room. A secondary search of every closet, cabinet, and potential hiding place verified the SWAT team's conclusion.

Their targets had escaped.

▪

Mr. White passed by the SWAT operators standing sentinel and entered the apartment with Tony by his side. He spent a few minutes observing the interior of the apartment, gazing at the expensive artwork on the walls and sculptures standing in the living room. He stood by the enormous floor-to-ceiling windows that overlooked Manhattan and stared upon the northern view. The city, and the massive park, was starting to be dusted with a light blanket of snow. It was beautiful but eerie.

"What do you think, sir?" Tony asked.

"Terrorists don't have apartments like this."

"I know. Who are these people?"

"Not sure—not entirely," Mr. White said, shaking his head. "The accountants will have their hands full for a long time before we can be a hundred."

"You have an idea?"

"I do." Mr. White nodded. "Just wanted to see it with my own eyes. Whole agency has been working for years to find these people, and now we might have. Course, the guy is probably halfway across the globe by now. But at least I got some of his paintings."

"Who?"

"Oh . . ." Mr. White turned back to Tony. "I don't know his name. He's a jihad banker—takes money from people all over the world who want to fund terror but don't know how to and don't want their hands dirty. Then he finds middlemen like Hanafi to do his bidding. Every time a Hanafi goes to jail, there's another one to take his place. But there's only one man from Dubai."

"Shit," Tony said.

Mr. White put his arm around Tony's shoulders.

"No, no, Tony . . . This is good. But the man from Dubai isn't our biggest problem right now."

"The bomb."

"The bomb."

Tony looked down at his phone. "Building security just texted. They pulled surveillance footage from their garage. The doctor and Murad Amin load up an old van with a bunch of electronics. Then what looks like the bomb was loaded into a box truck down there. The doctor leaves first, in the van. Then the truck, with Murad driving, exits the garage about forty-five minutes ago." Tony paused. "But we don't know where he's going. Hanafi gave you nothing?"

Mr. White shook his head.

"We got spotters everywhere. I mean, the whole city is crawling with blue," Tony said.

"No one will find him," Mr. White said. "The man from Dubai is too smart. Even if Hanafi gives us something, they had to know he was compromised. That's why they got out of here so fast. Must have changed their whole plan."

"Then what do we do?" Tony asked Mr. White.

"Hell if I know, Tony," Mr. White said. He looked around. "Where's Rivett?"

CHAPTER THIRTY-SEVEN

THE WILLIAMSBURG STREET ECHOED WITH the rocking engine noise of Jake's Ducati. Rivett ripped directly over the curb in front of his apartment and parked on the sidewalk. When Jake's eyes caught the front door's broken lock, panic ensued. He ricocheted off the bike and into the apartment.

·

Jake tore down the hallway screaming Mona's name. The first thing he saw was the blood and the crumpled body of a man on the ground in the living room.

And then he saw her.

Mona lay on the couch in the center of the living room. Blood spilled from two gunshot wounds in her chest. Jake ran to Mona and cradled her in his arms. The devastation was utter. He began to scream and cry at the same time, while checking for her vitals. She was still alive. She was trying to say something, opening her mouth and closing it. Jake put his ears as close as he could.

"I . . . love . . ." she murmured.

"I know, I know . . . Don't talk, darling," he replied.

Jake pulled out his cell phone and dialed 9-1-1, identifying himself as law enforcement. He began CPR.

"Stay with me, Mona. Stay . . ." he begged between breaths.

She couldn't stay with him. She stopped responding as he pumped her chest and tried to force oxygen into her lungs. He kept pumping. He kept giving breaths. But she kept growing colder.

It wasn't working and Jake knew it. Mona was leaving and she wasn't coming back.

She was gone.

He knew that meant he was gone, too.

▪

Jake could barely feel the phone buzzing in his hand. Two paramedics attempted to console him while police officers streamed into the apartment. No one was sure of the correct protocol. No one knew how to approach Rivett. The cops normally would have taken over control of the crime scene, but Rivett was technically their superior.

His cell phone. It was ringing. He stared down at Mona's lifeless body covered by a plastic sheet and then back at the phone again. It was Tony. Jake picked up.

"Mona's dead," Jake said.

There was a long pause. "*What?*"

"These fuckers . . . They came here, killed her . . . It was that kid. *ShyScreamo*... uh, Omer. He's here. Also dead."

"Where are you? At your apartment? I'm coming over right now. Are paramedics there?"

"Okay," Jake replied. "Everyone's here."

"Stay put, Jake. Do not move. I'm coming," Tony answered.

"Tony . . ." Rivett said. "What happened with the raid?"

"Doesn't matter . . ."

"Tell me."

"Empty. They got a bomb in the back of a white box truck somewhere in the city," Tony said.

"Right now?"

"Yes," Tony answered.

"Where are they going?"

"We don't know."

"Goddamn it."

"It's not your problem," Tony said. "I'm coming. I promise. I'll be there soon."

Jake was completely numb. He mindlessly watched the flurry of activity around him, from Mona to the cops assembled around Omer's gun to the paramedics sitting nearby. Finally, Jake looked down at Omer. No one had tended to the kid at all. He was their last priority. But Jake stared. Omer had a huge gash in his stomach. Maybe Mona had done that. He hoped so. The kid's stomach and arms were drenched in blood. It had spilled out all around him, and his hands had wiped it around . . .

Omer's hands. Jake blinked and stared at Omer's hands again. He realized Omer had drawn a message in his own blood on the floor.

Jake jumped off the couch.

He stood above Omer and looked down at the wood floor.

"You still there, Tony?" Jake asked, pulling his phone back to his ear.

"I'm not hanging up until I see you, Jake."

"I know the target," Jake announced. He turned towards the apartment's window. "I'm looking right at it." Framed through the apartment's large bay window, Jake stared at the Brooklyn Bridge.

And below Jake, Omer Amin had written two words in blood on the floorboards:

Brooklyn Bridge.

▪

Rivett was no longer just a detective. He was fury incarnate.

The Ducati spit a plume of ice behind Jake as he ripped towards the Brooklyn Bridge. He was only a mile away from it, and on a motorcycle he would be able to get there quicker than anyone in a car. As Jake ripped past the Eastern District courthouse and Whitman Park, he noticed that traffic was already backed up. He navigated between jammed cars and began to traverse the iconic bridge that connected Brooklyn to Manhattan.

After another minute, Jake realized there were no cars on the opposite side of the bridge. No vehicles were emerging from Manhattan at all. Not good. Jake proceeded for another hundred yards until he saw a large white box truck stopped on the eastbound side of the bridge. The truck was parked diagonally, blocking all the lanes of eastbound traffic. Although the sides of the Brooklyn Bridge were encased in steel latticework, Jake could make out Murad Amin in the driver's seat of the truck.

Jake slowed his bike and maneuvered from the center lane to the inside margin. An angry motorist honked at him when he stopped his bike and hopped off. Jake jumped a barrier onto a utility walkway that connected the two sides of the bridge. The interior passageways of the bridge were not intended for public use. Suspended over a hundred feet over the water below, the panels were rickety with loose joints and rusted metal. Jake gingerly worked his way across the walkway and onto the eastbound side of the bridge.

Murad ran directly towards Jake, having simultaneously eyed the same passageway. But when he noticed Jake emerging from underneath the bridge, he turned heel and sprinted back past the front of his truck. Jake watched Murad head down the open road ahead of him. He was seemingly attempting to sprint down the full length of the bridge to freedom. Jake raged out of the utility passageway and pursued Murad at top speed. It didn't take long for Jake to reach him. He tackled Murad from behind, the two men rolling onto the snowy pavement. Jake held on to Murad, ripping both the side of Murad's face as well as his own forearm against the wet concrete. Murad scrambled, pushing up with both legs in an attempt to buck Jake. While they scraped and scratched for control, Jake thought one thing.

Why hadn't the bomb gone off yet?

"Where's the trigger?" Jake screamed at Murad as they wrestled. Murad was finally able to jerk Jake off his shoulders. Jake flew into the air and landed flat on his back. He watched as Murad pushed off the ground and prepared to take off. Jake used all his energy to sweep his legs around and trip Murad just before he stood. Murad careened back onto the pavement, and Jake clawed on top of him, sitting on Murad's stomach. He finally had time to pull his sidearm from a holster. He trained his weapon on Murad.

"Why isn't it going off?" Jake screamed again.

Murad didn't answer. He was too busy fighting.

"I'm calling the police!" Jake heard someone yell from behind him. Jake's head rotated around. Behind him, some of the drivers whose cars were stuck on the bridge had gotten out of their vehicles and were approaching Murad and Jake on foot. In addition, a large group of onlookers stared down at Jake from the elevated passenger walkway above, which ran the entire length of the bridge.

"Get back! There's a bomb!" Jake screamed.

The bystanders weren't sure what to do, frozen for a moment.

"I'm a police officer! Get back!" Jake screamed again.

Murad took the opportunity to slam Jake's gun from his hand with all his strength. The gun skittered across the side of the bridge, fell between two cables, and then dropped off the side of the bridge. Jake drove his elbow into Murad's neck, but Murad jolted to the side just in time. Murad rolled quickly away from Jake and stood.

Murad began stumbling, this time towards the outside edge of the bridge. While he did, he reached into his pocket and pulled out a cell phone. Jake raced towards him. He watched as Murad attempted to type into his phone while running. Murad tapped diligently on the phone for a few more seconds before stopping. It was almost as if he was trying to catch his breath. But then he looked up and smiled at Jake, who was rapidly shortening the distance between the two of them.

"It's done!" Murad yelled.

Jake shortened the distance between them to ten feet. Finally, he stood in front of Murad in a ready position.

"Coward. You weren't even going to go down with the truck," Rivett screamed. "Stop it! Stop the bomb!"

"Why?" Murad said quietly. A strange calm seemed to come over him. "What'll you do? Kill me? Not a problem . . ."

"How long's the timer?" Jake yelled.

Murad only shrugged in response. He held out his phone in front of Jake, tempting him to act. "This is what you want?"

"How long's the fucking timer?" Jake screamed again, looking over his shoulder at the white box truck that had yet to ignite.

With a flourish, Murad tossed the phone over the edge of the Brooklyn Bridge.

"Not long. I don't know. I didn't design it," Murad said. "Seconds . . . A minute, maybe . . . It's done for." Murad smiled with evil intent at Jake. He didn't seem inclined to keep running or fighting. "Thank you, Detective Rivett."

"For what?"

"You inspired me to be better. You're wrong. I'm not a coward. Would a coward do this?" Murad began to slowly walk back towards the truck. Jake followed him. Once Murad was about ten feet from the truck, he sat down cross-legged on the pavement of the Brooklyn Bridge. He closed his eyes and began to pray.

Jake sprinted towards the box truck.

When he reached the truck, he passed by the bystanders from the cars that were backed up.

"Run the other way! Run!" Jake screamed. He pulled himself into the truck's cab. Jake could see the timer assembly leading into the back of the truck. He wasn't an explosives expert—far from it. Defusing the bomb was impossible. There was only one option.

Luckily, Murad had left the keys to the truck in the ignition. Rivett slammed the accelerator and jolted the truck forward. He sped ahead on the bridge, aiming directly at Murad. As the truck raced towards Murad, Jake saw the terrorist stumble to get up. Murad had heard the truck approaching, and he tried to sidestep it. But Jake made sure to twist the wheel at the last moment and collide the truck's grille directly into Murad. The truck smashed into him, crunching his body underneath it before progressing forward. Jake rumbled over Murad and kept going, watching his lifeless body roll to a stop on the pavement in the side view mirror.

A minute had definitely passed, but the truck had not exploded . . . *yet*.

Jake wasn't sure where he was going, exactly, but he knew he was going to get the truck away from as many innocent people as possible. He jacked the accelerator and sped up, roaring down the empty eastbound side of the Brooklyn Bridge. A few hundred yards from the bridge terminus, Jake saw a police cruiser coming his way with lights flashing and sirens ringing. The car was headed his direction, against traffic. It was followed by an utter horde of police vehicles. There were cruisers, unmarked SUVs, and a number of patrol cars from the nearby courthouse gunning for him. He hadn't counted on them. The police slowed to form a barricade ahead, and Rivett barreled towards it at about ninety miles per hour.

Then the first bullets hit the windshield.

Crack. Crack. Crack. The glass splintered in front of Jake.

The cops didn't know who was driving. Jake ducked down as low as he could, but he didn't slow. Instead, he drilled the accelerator. The snow was picking up. The icy condensation had turned into large fluffy snowflakes, which danced through the air as they fell. Jake guided the truck through the winter wonderland, backlit by the police barricade ahead.

When the first cruiser was just fifty feet away, Jake finally reached the point on the Brooklyn Bridge where the steel latticework on each side disappeared. All that separated the bridge from whatever was below was a three-foot-high rail.

Jake ripped the truck's steering wheel to the right and into the rail. The truck collided with the rail at one hundred miles per hour, and the guardrail did almost everything it was supposed to. The truck gnashed through almost all of the barrier, but the steel still held. The truck had momentum, however, causing its back wheels to fishtail and slide towards the edge. Jake held on for dear life as the truck pivoted. The back side of it impacted again with the guardrail, and this time there was enough leverage for the truck to flip completely over the barrier. Jake felt his body go weightless for a moment while the truck flew over the side of the Brooklyn Bridge.

Jake realized that this portion of the bridge—where the guardrail began—was not positioned over the water. Instead, the truck fell about twenty-five feet through the air and landed on a massive concrete bulwark that was built against the edge of the East River. As the truck landed, Jake felt his head smash into the side of the cab's door. The truck rolled over two times before all movement stopped.

Jake was dazed but not unconscious. With all that was left in his body, he reached for the broken window of the truck. He pulled himself painstakingly out of the cab. He attempted to stand up but couldn't put enough weight on his legs.

All of a sudden, Jake heard a shrieking noise emitting from inside the truck. He looked back and caught a small flash of light in his peripheral vision.

The truck exploded in a supernova of chemical explosive and metal, splintering everything within a two-hundred-foot radius with lethal energy.

Jake didn't even have time to roll into the river. Instead, he was blasted. He flew in the air over the concrete bulwark and careened into the East River.

The bridge shuddered at its foundation, but the truck had rolled just far enough to not critically damage the bridge's infrastructure.

Within seconds, Jake Rivett was underwater.

The police watched from the bridge above as Jake began to sink.

At first, he was motionless.

But then . . . Jake's arms began to sweep horizontally.

He started to rise through the water.

He broke above the surface, and he breathed a huge breath of oxygen.

CHAPTER THIRTY-EIGHT

ONE WEEK LATER

Mona's funeral was an outpouring of love, but Jake couldn't feel anything. He hadn't yet entered the grief stage. No, instead, with every passing moment he felt more and more anger. Everything around him was foreboding. The priest speaking was the thunder, Adriana and her daughters' crying the lightning, and hundreds of Jake's police comrades the grey-blue clouds. It was clear a storm was coming. The storm was Jake Rivett.

He tried his best to keep it together. He did this by staying tunnel-vision focused on the love of his life—Mona. Visions of her kept running through his head. Good memories. She was always smiling—more than he. She was always happy—a contrast to him. She was always smart—and teaching him. The images kept Jake from completely falling apart in public. He knew he would spend plenty of time in the future on the floor, crying his eyes out. But he wasn't there yet. The adrenaline hadn't fully worn off. Instead, it was growing.

He had no interest in niceties. He hated the formalities flung his way.

If he had more perspective, he might have noticed the piles of flowers gracing every surface of the church. He would have seen the entire senior leadership of the NYPD, including Susan Herlihy in her finest blacks, sitting across from him. He could have noticed his band standing solemnly in the back row. He would have felt Adriana's hand gripping his own for dear life. He might even have stopped to realize that his mother and his father were sitting a row behind him. He would have listened to the wonderful anecdotes the bishop, Mona's priest since childhood, was telling about Mona. He may even have noticed that Mr. White's eyes were glued to Jake the entire funeral and never veered away.

In some ways, he did register all of those things. But mostly he didn't. Because none of it was happening with him. It was happening around him, despite him, to him. He was the least willing participant in a cavern of unwilling participants.

In that moment, Jake Rivett permanently changed. He was no longer a fiancé and he knew he could no longer be a cop. He dreaded what was next, but it was the only path for him.

CHAPTER THIRTY-NINE

TONY VILLALON'S SPARE BEDROOM HAD become Jake's sanctuary for the past week and a half, which included Christmas. Jake wasn't officially on leave—not yet. And Susan wasn't pushing, but Jake knew he would eventually have to go on disability or get back to work. For now, she was letting it ride and allowing him to do whatever he wanted. That was often the best strategy with Jake. Meanwhile, Tony and his partner had always been there for Jake, and this time was no different. Their spare bedroom had been designed with delightful prints on the bedspread and trendy interior decorating. After a few days of Jake inhabiting it, however, the room had turned into a disaster zone. It was messy, but the mess had meaning. Jake Rivett had his purpose, and it was very simple:

Find Einstein.

Jake had pulled down the mirror over the desk and replaced it with a corkboard. Pinned to the board was an elaborate chronological schematic of Dr. Borin's entire life. Jake's board included a timeline of the doctor's important relationships, jobs, and addresses. And more. Paychecks. Photographs. Research reports. It was all there. After a few days, the schematic had grown beyond the confines of the corkboard itself. It was spreading like a spider's web and creeping along the wallpaper. Luckily for Tony, Jake had the forethought to use tape instead of pins after his research had exited the corkboard. But anyone who opened the door might deduce that Rivett was becoming just as crazy as the mad scientist he was chasing.

Jake and the rest of the joint task force had successfully smashed up the Brooklyn terror cell based in Best Diner, and the risk of another attack was virtually zero with Hanafi in jail. That result was certainly a success. But after everything, Dr. Borin was still on the loose with his machine. From what Jake knew about him, it was almost unbelievable that Dr. Borin was the one member of the cell who had gotten away. It was also poetic. Nothing seemed to stop Dr. Borin. He was like quicksand. The more Jake researched him, the more he understood that Dr. Borin had no allegiances at all.

Jake's morning task was to watch every single video that Katinka Johanssen had ever posted online. It was weird to watch videos of a dead person, and it might have bothered Jake if he wasn't already wallowing deep down in a pit of darkness. In that sense, the videos actually became a slight outlet to distract him from thinking about Mona. The unfortunate problem was that Katinka's videos weren't revealing any new information. They'd already been examined with a fine-toothed comb by multiple forensic specialists. Anything related to her research or work with Dr. Borin had been transcribed, filed, and analyzed. But that didn't matter to Jake. He was conducting his own investigation now—from scratch. Katinka's most recent videos had all been directed at Dr. Borin personally, but her account had started years earlier. Back then, her posts had been both fewer and farther between, as well as quite random when it came to content. These were the ones Jake was watching.

On the screen, Katinka was waxing eloquent about her friends in the undergraduate program at Penn State: "I decided I'd stay for summer school, because my friend Liz had a spare bedroom in her apartment and I could keep the job in the cafeteria and . . ."

In the middle of her diatribe, the door cracked open. It was Tony.

"How you doing?"

"Fine," Rivett replied.

"Susan called."

"Did you kiss the ring?"

"She said she's been trying your cell all week . . ."

"Don't know where it is." Rivett pointed to a foot-high pile of papers and folders on the desk. "Somewhere under there."

"There aren't very many cops who refuse to answer the chief of police's phone call."

"Doesn't she have bigger and better things to do than worry about me?"

"She just can't quit you, I guess. Told me you're on her mind. Then there's the thing with Axel Bossonov that we're doing. She wanted to know if you're in."

"I'm not in."

"I know."

"How was she? All warm and fuzzy, I'm sure . . ."

"She's about to put in paperwork for mental-health leave—for you."

"No," Jake replied.

"Well . . . You better get on the phone and tell her that. Otherwise, you know Susan. She doesn't ask for permission."

"If I go on leave, am I gonna come back from it?" Jake asked.

"That's for you to answer, buddy."

Jake didn't reply.

"Listen, we're going to go to the bay for the fireworks tomorrow night. Want to come?"

"I got a lot of work," Jake replied.

"Come along with us. Consider it your rent payment," Tony said.

"Wait a minute . . ."

In the background, Katinka's video had continued to play. Jake rotated back to his computer and rewound the footage by thirty seconds. He hit play again. Katinka spoke:

"But she's working at this doctor's lab, so I think I might get some part-time hours there, too. It's, like, seventeen dollars an hour, which is great. Guy seems nice. Liz said that he did a barbecue retreat at his lake house in Mattituck for all the researchers last weekend and he wasn't even sleazy about it . . ."

"You hear that?" Jake asked Tony. He rewound the video again.

"If you don't call Susan back, they'll cut your logins . . ." Tony deflected.

"Tony, did you know Dr. Borin had a lake house? Maybe his mother? Cause there's nothing showing that Max owns one . . ."

"No, I don't think so."

Jake popped out of his chair, suddenly filled with more energy than Tony had witnessed in weeks. He began scrounging around for a backpack. Tony interrupted only when Jake pulled a personal gun from a small case and tossed it into the pack.

"Jake . . ."

"Yeah?"

"I know you're not going to listen to me if I tell you what to do. So I won't. But I just want to remind you that grief and depression are not things to be ashamed of."

"I don't have mental-health problems, Tony."

"Think before you act. Please."

"Action requires thinking."

"I don't want you to do something that changes your life forever."

"Are you kidding me, Tony?"

"Huh?"

"That already happened, man. Mona's gone. I'm not worried about my life anymore." Jake pushed past Tony and headed for the door. He turned back one more time. "Love you, Tony," Jake said.

"You too," Tony replied.

▪

Shep Moseley did a double take when Jake Rivett arrived at the joint task force's office in One Police Plaza. No one had seen Rivett since the funeral, and the office itself was quiet now—nothing like the days before the terror cell was busted. Moseley himself had actually been packing up, because this was his last day in the city. He'd already checked out of his hotel and was about to drive back down to Maryland to join his family for the first time in a month—for New Year's Eve fireworks.

"Hey, Rivett. Whatcha doin'?" Shep asked.

"Maxine Borin . . . Where are her files?"

"The doctor's mom?"

"Yeah."

"Over there." Shep pointed to a filing cabinet.

Jake stepped up to the locked cabinet and typed in a PIN code.

When the lock popped open, Shep exhaled. "Wasn't sure if you even still had access up here. Didn't want to have to do some ninja moves on you. They're cutting mine tomorrow."

"How come?"

"Last day, bro."

"Maybe mine too—if I can find his fucking vacation house."

"Vacation house?" Shep questioned.

"I know the Borins have some sort of lake house. In Mattituck. But nothing's on Max's tax returns," Jake said. He continued to scan through Ms. Borin's paperwork. "And it's not on hers, either. How's that possible? No capital gains sales. And if they own it, they gotta pay property taxes somehow . . ."

"I dunno. I mean, I can get into those records, too . . . Need some help?" Shep answered.

"The husband. Borin's father. Deceased. Can you look up his old returns?"

"Maybe," Shep replied. "But why? You're still hunting down the doctor? I wouldn't worry about him. He's not dangerous. We already sicced the US Marshals on him."

"They didn't get him yet."

"Hold up." Shep started pulling up old tax records through an access point from his agency into the IRS. "Sure, I found the old man's records. I'll print them out for you . . ."

Jake practically sprinted over to the printer, scanning through each tax return as it rolled out. He didn't have to look long. The elder Borins had filed married-but-separate returns, and listed on Dr. Borin's father's return was a property-tax deduction for a house different from their primary home.

"One Forest Park Lane," Jake said. "Where's that?"

After a few taps on the computer, Shep answered, "Mattituck—Long Island."

"Bingo," Rivett answered dryly. He folded up the paper with the address and pushed it into his pocket. Then he turned, his shoulders slouched, and headed for the door.

"What's up? You going out there?" Shep asked Rivett, who didn't reply. "Listen. I'm supposed to drive about six hours down to Maryland tonight. But if you need backup, I'm there for you. I'll do that shit for you. I don't like fireworks. I like the real thing."

"Thanks, Shep," Jake replied. "But I'm just going home."

"After all that? You're going home?"

"Damn right," Rivett replied. He stepped out of the office.

It wasn't thirty seconds before the door opened and Mr. White walked into the joint task force office.

"You just missed Rivett," Shep said.

"Rivett?" Mr. White asked.

"Guy's tuned up."

"Drunk?"

"No. Mad as shit, and he's gonna go kill the doctor."

"Tell me everything," Mr. White commanded.

"He came in here talking about a lake house he was convinced Dr. Borin owns. Turns out he might be right. Family had a vacation house up in Mattituck. Not sure if the marshals know about it," Shep said.

"Shep," Mr. White said.

"Yeah, boss?"

"I don't think we're making it back to Chevy Chase tonight," Mr. White said.

CHAPTER FORTY

NEW YEAR'S EVE

The Southold region of Long Island, on the north fork, still maintained a woodsy ambiance without the pomp and circumstance of the Hamptons to the south. Jake rode his motorcycle past a mix of new developments, old shacks, small farm communities, and bustling wineries as he headed towards the far northeastern edge of Long Island—a massive contrast to the Gotham from which he had just departed. As Jake rode, his burdens finally began to lift—just a little. It wasn't full relief, of course. He had no idea when that would come, if ever. But at least he felt slightly better.

His entire life had been dedicated to getting to New York. From the moment he'd discovered punk music back in his hometown of Albany, as a way of getting away from the rants and tirades of his father, he had prepared for the city. New York, Gotham, the heavy steel and the dark alleys—all of it had been his driving force. But Jake knew change was afoot. He was going to leave the city permanently. He had no idea exactly what the future would entail. Who knows . . . Given what he was about to do, it might involve a lot of time in a jail cell. But Jake did know he wasn't going back to New York.

He was sure that Maximilian Borin would be at the lake house at One Forest Park Lane. Even though he'd spent his entire career as a detective double-checking and verifying, there was nothing that Jake was more sure about. Dr. Borin would be there.

▪

When Jake arrived at the house's long driveway, he slowed and jumped off his bike. He rolled the Ducati about twenty feet into the woods and began to walk the rest of the way. He avoided the driveway and carefully tracked through the wet forest surrounding the cabin.

Eventually, Jake emerged beside a small lake. He could see Dr. Borin's lake house across the water. Still camouflaged by his surroundings, he strafed around the lake until he was just twenty or thirty feet from the house. Borin didn't make it hard for Jake. Within a few minutes, Jake spotted him through an open window, pacing around the living room of the lake house. Jake pulled out his gun and strode towards the front door. He assumed it would be open, and it was.

▪

"Hello, Max," Rivett said. He stepped into Dr. Borin's living room.

Dr. Borin turned. He stared at Jake.

"Not very security conscious, are we?" Jake remarked.

"Jake Rivett. Omer failed . . ."

"You failed."

"I knew someone would find me. It was inevitable," Borin replied.

"That's why you left your door unlocked?"

Dr. Borin shrugged. "I wasn't running. Nowhere to go. Had work to do."

"Your machine?"

Jake nodded at the parts to Dr. Borin's machine. The electronics filled the entire living room. This lake house was no longer a vacation home. It had become, in fact, the doctor's final laboratory. Dr. Borin had dragged all the furniture in the living room to the edges, leaving the center of the room open. In that area, he had used four-by-fours to construct the frame that held his MRI device up in the air. Underneath the MRI, Dr. Borin had duct taped a cheap plastic chair to the tile floor. The whole contraption lacked refinement, but in some ways, that made it look all the more menacing.

"I wondered what it looked like," Jake said. "Your terror machine."

"It's so much more than that," Dr. Borin said. "I needed to make sure it was perfect."

"Why?" Jake shook his head.

"Because it must be ready."

"For what?"

"For you, Detective Rivett."

Jake took a step back. The doctor's response unnerved him slightly. He trained his gun on Dr. Borin.

"For your people—your scientists. Once there's a proof of concept, it's out there. Proof can never be cancelled. Even if they decide to destroy the machine, the feds will always know it existed. There will be reports. If you think for one second that the government won't study my work intently, you don't know how the world works. And one day they'll have a need for something like this. They'll go back to my records, my schematics, my designs . . . I don't care about being caught. Going to jail . . . doesn't bother me at all. Because it's what I added to the world that matters the most. And no one will be able to take that away from me."

"You killed a hundred innocent people, Max."

"I didn't condone what Hanafi was doing."

"Well, you might be right about your machine," Jake replied, "but you're definitely wrong about one thing . . ."

"What's that?"

"You aren't going to jail." Jake pointed at the machine with his gun. "Turn it on."

"Excuse me?"

"Turn it on."

▪

A few hours later, the sun had set over Mattituck and the lake. Rivett stood in the kitchen of the lake house and observed Maximilian Borin. Dr. Borin was handcuffed and tied onto the seat of his own creation. Jake had found enough duct tape and rope inside the garage to do the job properly. The MRI device was positioned over Borin's head, and it was running. Borin sat placidly inside his machine, repeating phrases as requested.

"I want to go swimming," Dr. Borin said.

"Say it with me, three times," the machine's digital voice commanded.

"I want to go swimming. I want to go swimming. I want to go swimming."

As Jake listened to Dr. Borin drone on, the words eventually faded away like a grandfather clock's chimes—present but invisible. Jake gazed outside. It was chilly, and there was some snow on the ground, but the weather wasn't unbearable. The winter had been forgiving, and the lake wasn't even frozen over yet. After making sure Dr. Borin was still fastened securely, Jake stepped out of the kitchen and sat down on a lounge chair on the front porch.

The last yellow and orange hues disappeared from the sky just as the first explosions ignited.

Bang. Bang. Bang.

At first Jake flinched. Then he relaxed. *Duh.* It was New Year's Eve. The fireworks were small, erupting in random locations high in the night sky. They weren't being launched above the lake, and they weren't for Jake. Most likely, they were coming from the ocean-side beaches and piers a few miles away, designed for fun-filled gatherings of family, friends, and loved ones.

Jake allowed himself to enjoy the incandescent show just for a moment, until finally the grief began to hit. The sadness blasted into him like the fireworks above. All of a sudden, Mona was all he could think about. This wasn't supposed to be what New Year's Eve looked like. New Year's Eve was their wedding. It was too much to handle, even for Jake Rivett. The fireworks above began to crescendo, but he stopped watching. He leaned forward on the chair and put his head in his hands.

And then Jake Rivett wept.

CHAPTER FORTY-ONE

AS USUAL, PETROV DROVE AND Roschin talked.

"Anyone else feel like what we're about to do is a little bit wrong?" Roschin asked.

Petrov grunted in affirmation.

"Shut up, Roschin," Axel Bossonov said from the back seat of the truck.

"Why you tellin' me to shut up? I'm talkin' bout *ethical-ness*."

"We need to be on our A-game," Axel replied.

"When I talk, it gets me amped up."

Slap. Axel Bossonov smacked the left side of Roschin's face. "When I tell you to shut up, you shut the fuck up. And don't even think about bringing up the concept of ethics. Not today," Axel said.

Needless to say, Roschin shut up.

The sun rose on a new year while the three men drove east from Brooklyn towards a warehouse district in Long Island. While perhaps slightly hungover, not even Roschin had hit the bottle hard the night before. Today's mission was too important. The three men were at an utterly pivotal moment in their lives and careers. The exchange needed to go perfectly.

▪

The warehouse was nothing to look at. They never were. Down a street that looked like an alley, with all manner of industrial real estate on each side, this was an area of the city that was designed to be cheap and functional. That's all. Each business had a small sign, or maybe just a number, and anywhere from one to a dozen large roll-up cargo doors for trucks to on and off-load. These warehouses were resting places. Goods were not made there, nor did they end up there. The garages were simply distribution points for the entire US economy. Everything went through these spaces—including highly explosive chemicals.

When the door rolled up in front of Axel Bossonov and the brothers Petrov and Roschin, a skinny man greeted them with a huge smile on his face.

"It's nothing less than an honor to meet you, Mr. Bossonov," the skinny man said. "The Belarusians say very good things . . ."

"Joey, right?"

"You got me."

"Sure do." Axel chuckled and checked his watch. "Where are the containers?"

"Oh? Thought you knew. They're at the other location . . ."

"That wasn't what we discussed."

"What's it matter?"

"I'm here now. We have a truck. We're ready to take delivery like you promised," Axel said.

"And you will, you will . . ." Joey replied. "After you come to our second location."

"No," Axel replied. "Deal's off."

"That's funny," Joey said. "Me and Tiko were taking bets on you.

What you've ordered . . . That ain't in high demand. Fact is only been ordered one other time this year. And that client . . . Well, let's just say that client was a serious problem. But at least they were real. So I told Tiko, if you weren't Axel Bossonov, I wouldn't have even taken your call. But you are. Big man of Bensonhurst. So then I told Tiko exactly how we'd know if you were for real. If you were real, Axel, you'd be okay with driving to the other location."

"Screw you," Axel replied. "No one's gonna talk to you again after they hear 'bout this."

"How are they gonna hear about it when you're dead?" Joey asked. Behind him, a bodyguard named Tiko and two other henchmen stepped out of a side office. They all held guns trained on the Bossonovs.

"Fine." Axel pulled the keys to their truck from his pocket and flung them at the skinny man. "If it matters that much to you, you drive. I don't care. We need the stuff. Let's go get it."

"C'mon," Joey commanded Tiko and his henchmen. They lowered their guns. The group stepped out of the warehouse and warily looked around.

Just a dead street, just as it had been before.

"Where are they?" Joey asked.

"Who?" Axel replied.

"The cops."

Axel began to laugh. It was a big and deep guffaw that emerged from his lower belly. "I hate cops, Joey."

"All right, let's get in your truck. Tiko, one of the brothers goes with you."

The men loaded into the Bossonovs' truck, as well as their own SUV. The two vehicles started up and drove away from the warehouse.

▪

Inside the truck, about a half mile from the warehouse, Joey began to calm down.

"You weren't bullshitting me, were you?"

"Are you going to get me what I need, or does the street gotta hear how unreliable you are?" Axel asked.

"Joey don't let anyone down. Sorry about all that. It was just a test."

"So where are we going?"

Joey sent a text on his cell phone and then commanded Petrov to turn the truck around.

"Back to the warehouse."

"Same warehouse?"

"Yep."

"You've got to be shittin' me."

▪

A few minutes later, the two vehicles arrived back at Joey's warehouse. The skinny man jumped out and rolled open the garage door. Both crews walked into the warehouse for the second time. Sitting in the back were two large refrigerator boxes. They'd been there the entire time. Joey strolled up to one of them, grasped the cardboard in his hand, and pulled it vertically off the ground. The boxes were not holding fridges. In actuality, they were simply covering two large slightly opaque containers of a green-hued liquid.

"Tada," Joey said. "Synthesized peroxysulfuric acid with tetrahedral geometry."

"You know what all that means?" Axel asked Joey.

"Nah." Joey pointed to a small label on the canister. "That's just what we order from the Chinese."

Axel barely glanced at the containers before turning to his nephews. "Load it up," he commanded.

Petrov, Roschin, and Tiko began to wheel the containers towards the truck using a small forklift. When they reached the back of the truck, Petrov grabbed the lift remote and pressed a button. The liftgate began to rotate downwards. Suddenly, as the liftgate of the truck reached ninety degrees . . .

Sirens erupted.

The back of the truck sprung open, and before Joey could reach for his gun, a phalanx of hyperaggressive SWAT operators pounced on him.

"On the ground! Hands up! You are under arrest!" A full-on SWAT team poured out from the back of the Bossonovs' truck, while multiple police SUVs converged on the warehouse.

▪

Joey and his men lay on the ground in handcuffs. Police officers stood around them—while the Russians milled about freely with nothing to do. After the crime scene was fully secured, Tony Villalon strode over to Axel.

"That's a wrap, right?" Axel asked Tony.

"Yeah, you're all done," Tony confirmed.

"I'm not going to get any more calls from the DA either, ya?"

"Little trust goes a long way. It won't be in writing, but you should be happy. You're the luckiest man in Brooklyn."

"I'll take that as a compliment—and an assurance," Axel replied.

"Don't worry . . ." Tony said.

"What?"

"Maybe your past is wiped clean, but I'll keep on hunting you," Tony said.

"I'd expect nothing less. And you don't worry, either, detective."

"Why?"

"'Cause I'll keep running," Axel said.

The two men chuckled, but they didn't shake hands.

CHAPTER FORTY-TWO

THE MORNING WAS BITTER COLD. Jake had found an old axe in a shed beside Borin's lake house and had spent about twenty minutes cutting logs to prepare enough firewood for the rest of the day. Once he was back inside, he carefully placed the logs in the fireplace. After a few minutes, flames lapped up the sides of the wood, and soon the fire was roaring. Jake turned back to the center of the room. Dr. Borin was still strapped into the machine. He'd spent the entire night hooked up. Jake reached for the handcuffs around Borin's hands and unclasped them. He began to untie the doctor and then lifted the MRI machine off his head. The man said nothing. His eyes were open but glazed over.

"Still there, doctor?" Jake asked.

"Yes," the doctor mumbled.

"Do you want to lay down for a while?"

"I do."

Jake arranged some pillows on a couch in the back of the room. He nodded to the couch, and the extremely groggy and compliant doctor stumbled his way towards the furniture and collapsed upon it. Within seconds, Dr. Borin was asleep.

After he was sure the doctor was out, Jake set upon the machine.

Using a wrench, a hammer, a pair of pliers, and a screwdriver, Jake carefully disassembled the technology. He chose to leave the plastic pieces of the MRI chassis and all of the wood to the side in a pile. It was the circuitry he was interested in. Whenever Jake found a circuit board or wiring system, he broke it down to small components. He threw each piece into the fireplace. The room quickly began to smell with a pungent chemical odor, but Jake kept going. He took each of the professor's three computers and pried the cases off them. The circuit boards were thrown directly into the fire, but Jake went further with the hard drives. He drilled holes through each of the computer hard drives with a wide bit. After the hard drives and the machine itself had been physically destroyed, Jake took his time while he searched the entire cabin for any and all physical documents. The doctor had lugged a few file boxes' worth of paper material—his life's work, apparently—to the cabin. Jake made sure it burned. Then he turned to the rest of the cabin, incinerating every single bill, piece of mail, document, receipt, or photograph he could find. By the end of the process, the cabin had a thick cloud of dark smoke inside. But Dr. Borin was still asleep.

Jake grabbed him roughly. It took a few slaps to the face before Dr. Borin's eyes slowly opened.

"What?" Borin asked, squinting through the haze.

"How do you feel?"

"I . . ."

"Max, focus. What do you want to do?" Jake asked.

Suddenly, Borin's eyes jolted wide open.

"I want to go swimming," Borin said.

▪

The two men stood on a dock outside Dr. Borin's lake house.

"Get in," Jake said, nodding to a small rowboat floating in the water next to the dock.

"No," said Borin.

"But you want to go swimming, don't you?"

"I . . ."

"Say it with me," Jake commanded.

"I want to go swimming."

"Then get on the boat."

"But I can't swim," Dr. Borin said.

"But you want to go swimming, right?"

"I do," he said. He stepped onto the rowboat as instructed, gripping the sides of the craft with clenched fingers. Jake followed. Jake rotated the rowboat's oars and slowly rowed the two of them towards the center of the small lake.

"You made a lot of mistakes, doctor."

"I can see that now . . ."

"Why not before?"

"I'm not a normie." Borin shrugged. "You wouldn't understand. I don't fit in with the rest of the world. I become addicted to my goals. I have blinders on. Whatever I'm thinking about becomes the only thing that matters. Unfortunately, I guess it's all for nothing. But you only learn that at the end."

A long silence ensued.

"I understand—more than you know," Jake finally said.

"Good," replied the doctor. He stared at the ice-cold lake. "My mother always wanted me to learn to swim. Didn't have the patience . . ."

"You should be happy about one thing, doctor."

"What?"

"You're the proof of concept."

"I know. I thought about that." The doctor smiled.

"Right before you go down . . . you'll know. You did it. You succeeded."

"It's time?"

Jake nodded. "Jump in."

"I don't know . . ."

"Yes, you do."

"I . . ."

"Say it with me," Jake suggested.

"I want to go swimming," Dr. Borin said.

Dr. Maximilian Borin stood up in the rowboat. He crouched for a second before launching himself over the side of the boat. He hit the lake with a large splash, but once he was submerged, his arms and legs didn't move. He didn't bother trying to tread water or paddle or even splash his hands. Dr. Borin didn't do anything to save himself at all. Within seconds, his mouth had fallen below the surface of the water, and all that remained was the top of his head, surrounded by a ring of bubbles.

A minute after that, all the bubbles were gone.

CHAPTER FORTY-THREE

JAKE RIVETT'S MOTORCYCLE KICKED DIRTY snow as it shredded the road leading out of One Forest Park Lane, but the camouflaged men in the woods did not move. One of them kept his binoculars pinned to the lake, while the other continued to shoot high-resolution photographs on a camera with a zoom lens. The spot where Dr. Borin had gone under turned to a quiet ripple. After another five minutes, his lifeless body floated to the surface at the center of the lake. His face was still submerged with his back to the sky. Only once the lake was still as glass did the two men move. They slowly and methodically packed their gear into cases. After that was complete, they scanned their surroundings for any sign of their presence. Once they were sure they had left no trace, they slowly walked through the forest and away from the lake house.

CHAPTER FORTY-FOUR

WHAT RIVETT HAD DONE TO the doctor didn't make him happy, but it didn't worry him. There was the law, and then there was Rivett. He wasn't scared; he was liberated. He ripped down the country roads, leaving the agricultural pastures and farmlands of northeast Long Island and watching the behemoth of New York begin to peek back over the edge of the horizon. The city was an hour or two away, but he wasn't going back there. He might pass through, sure. But for the first time in his life, New York City had no pull. Neither did his job. The technical fact that he might now be a fugitive only weighed on him ever so slightly. There was something else out there for Jake, something much bigger than being a detective. He just hadn't put his finger on what it was yet. He'd know it when he saw it.

But first, he heard it.

Over the steady roar of his motorcycle engine, Jake began to make out the torrential clamor of a much louder engine. He whipped his head back briefly and saw a Black Hawk helicopter in the sky. The helicopter zoomed past Jake until it was about a mile or two ahead and then abruptly began to descend to the ground. Jake realized that the Black Hawk had an objective—he was the objective.

The helicopter set down upon the country road ahead of Jake. Another car, on the opposite side of the helicopter, was forced to slow and stop. The car began honking wildly before turning around and driving away. Jake slowed down as he approached. The helicopter's rotors were still whipping through the air when a man pushed the cabin door open and ran out from underneath the vortex of wind. It was Sheldon White.

"We need to talk," Mr. White screamed.

"Is that an order?" Jake yelled back.

"Not like the one you gave Max Borin . . . Jump in."

Mr. White's comment hung between the two men as Jake pondered.

"What about my bike?"

Mr. White shrugged. "Do you still need it?"

Fair point. Jake rolled his Ducati to the side of the road. Then he took a deep breath and followed Mr. White. The two men ran towards the helicopter. They jumped onto the landing skids and entered the cabin, closing the door behind them. The Black Hawk took off.

▪

"Am I under arrest?" was Jake's first question.

"I'm escorting you. Not to jail," Mr. White replied.

"Where?"

"The way I look at it . . . to more like freedom."

"What?"

"Where were you goin'? Just now."

"I don't know," Jake answered truthfully.

"Why?"

"Because I got them all, so I'm done."

"That's where you're wrong, Rivett—very wrong. Hanafi's locked up and the rest of them are dead. You got the doctor. But what's that gonna do? I'll tell you. Absolutely nothing. They're just a cell—just a little branch on a big tree. Me . . ." Mr. White pointed to himself. "I don't like branches. I don't even care about cutting down trees. I'm trying to burn forests and then salt the fields, root by root."

"That's all you do—metaphors," Jake shot back.

"I'm going to find and kill the man from Dubai. How's that for a metaphor?"

"Who is he?" Jake asked.

"The real power center. He's the jihad banker. Funds plots all around the world. He and his family have been doing it for years. You want to stop them?"

"What are you offering? A job? I'm gonna be a CIA agent? Contractor? What?"

"I can never get you Mona back, Jake. But what I'm offering you is the chance to save a thousand more Monas across the globe. I told you a long time ago what I do. I kill bad guys. The world ain't black and white, but I am. I think you are, too. I'm offering you the chance to be a good guy. What do you say?"

Jake stared out the window of the helicopter.

▪

The Black Hawk landed on a small airstrip in New Jersey. As Jake and Mr. White jumped out, Jake saw a gleaming Gulfstream jet idling on the tarmac. Shep Moseley ran down the stairs of the Gulfstream, wearing festive patterned shorts, a billowy white linen shirt, and a wide-brimmed safari hat.

"Nice outfit," Mr. White said.

"'Be prepared.' It's the Boy Scout motto. It's a hundred and ten where we're going, and heck if I ain't going to dress for who I want to be," Shep replied.

Mr. White turned back to Jake, who was decked out in black leather from head to toe.

"So who do you want to be, Rivett?"

"A good guy," Jake replied.

Mr. White nodded with approval, and Jake Rivett boarded the jet.

THE END

DEAR *RIVETTER:*

1) Reviews are the lifeblood of an independent author. I would be grateful if you would post your review on <u>Amazon</u>, <u>Goodreads</u>, or any preferred site.

2) Stay up-to-date by signing up for my mailing list: **<u>DenisonHatch.com/signup/</u>**

Most importantly**, thank you for reading** Jake Rivett!

ABOUT THE AUTHOR

Denison Hatch is the creator of Rivett. Denison is a writer in Los Angeles. His original screenplay, Vanish Man, is set up at Lionsgate. He is presently working on a standalone science fiction adventure, as well as the fourth Rivett novel.

For more information:
DenisonHatch.com
Facebook.com/DenisonHatchAuthor
Twitter.com/DenisonHatch

The Rivett Thrillers:
FLASH CRASH
NEVER GO ALONE
TERROR MACHINE

Sign up for new book announcements:
DenisonHatch.com/signup/